PSYCOP
partners

Wonderful to
meet you in
person, Cait!

Jordan Castillo
Price

An anthology of the first and second
PsyCop books: Among the Living
and Criss Cross

Jordan Castillo Price

JCP BOOKS

Second edition published in the United States in 2012 by
JCP Books LLC
www.jcpbooks.com

ISBN: 978-1-935540-37-3

PSYCOP STORIES

www.PsyCop.com

Beautiful • Mysterious • Bizarre
fiction by Jordan Castillo Price
Don't Miss the Next Story ~ Sign up for Jordan's
Free Monthly Newsletter Today!
www.psycop.com/newsletter

AMONG THE LIVING

Once upon a time if you told doctors you heard voices,
they'd diagnose you as schizophrenic, put you on heavy drugs, and lock you away
in a cozy state institution to keep you from hurting yourself or others.

Nowadays they test you first to see if you're psychic.

Maurice was a sixty-two year old black man who had a lot more gray in his hair at his retirement party than he'd had when I first met him. We'd never been close in a way that some partners at the Fifth Precinct are. We didn't hit sports bars after our shift for a shot and a beer. We didn't watch the game at each others' houses. We didn't invite each other to family functions—not that I have any family to speak of.

Maybe it was the race difference. Or the age difference. But despite the fact that we didn't connect on any sort of deep, soul-searching level, I was gonna miss working with the guy.

I stood behind the kitchen island and watched through the glass doors that led to the deck as Maurice ambled by. He laughed as he tried to balance a Coors Light, a styrofoam tray of bratwurst and a small stack of CDs. He looked genuinely happy. I supposed he was ready to retire—not like those guys you hear about that are forced out, along with all of their years of honed experience, in favor of some young buck who'll work for half the salary.

Maurice set the CDs in a sloppy, listing pile next to a tinny boom box and drained his beer in one pull. I wondered if being retired would entice him into a long slide down the neck of a bottle, but then I felt a little guilty for even thinking it. Because Maurice never, ever made comments about my Auracel—whether I had taken any, or was out, or was rebounding after a weekend of "accidentally" doubling or tripling my dosage. Nothing.

Maybe that was the actual reason I was gonna miss him so much.

I turned away from the deck and made my way back down the hall, and tried to remember where the bathroom was. I veered accidentally into the rec room and a bunch of black kids, mostly teenagers, all fell silent. I nodded at them and wondered if I'd managed to look friendly or if I just came off as some creepy, white asshole, then headed toward the basement where I remembered there was a half bath off Maurice's seldom-used woodshop.

"That's him, Victor Bayne," one of the kids whispered, so loud that it was audible to my physical ears. Not that my sixth sense would've picked it up, given that I was pretty far into a nice Auracel haze, and besides, I wasn't particularly clairaudient. "He was my dad's partner on the Spook Squad."

I quelled the urge to go back into the rec room and tell Maurice's kid that his dad would probably shit a brick if he heard that expression in his home. But that'd lead to a long-winded discussion of civil rights, yadda yadda yadda. Plus I'd be absolutely certain to come off as a creepy, white asshole then, in case there was any doubt at all.

I groped around the cellar wall at the top of the stairs for several long moments for a light until I realized the lights downstairs were already on. I made a mental note to rib Maurice about the availability of light bulbs greater than 40 watts come Monday. Except Maurice wasn't gonna be there on Monday. Damn.

My eyes adjusted and I took the cellar steps two by two. I imagined what Maurice's kid was probably saying about me to his cousins and friends. It was pretty plain that I was the psychic half of the Maurice/Victor team, since Maurice was about as psychic as a brick wall, and damn proud of it.

A pair of opposites forms a Paranormal Investigation Unit. The Psychs—psychic cops—do the psychic stuff, just like you'd expect. And the Stiffs—look, I didn't name 'em—are oblivious to any psychic interference a sixth-sensory gifted criminal might throw out there. It was rough at first getting used to riding around with a guy who put out about as many vibes as a day-old ham sandwich. But I got used to it, and eventually I grew to see the practicality of pairing us with each other.

Halfway down the steps I reached into my jeans pocket and found a tab of Auracel among the old gum wrappers and lint. I felt around some more, but only managed to locate the one. I'd brought three with me. Had I taken two earlier? I only remembered taking one in the car. Oh, and there was the one I took when Sergeant Warwick came in. The irony. Popping pills within spitting distance of someone capable of cutting off my precious supply.

I swallowed the Auracel, grabbed hold of the bathroom door and barely caught myself from slamming face first into Detective Jacob Marks, the golden child of the Twelfth Precinct Sex Crimes Unit.

He was a big, dark-eyed, dark-haired hunk of a guy with a neatly clipped goatee and short hair that looked like he had it trimmed every single week. He'd always looked beefy to me from afar, standing in the background, tall and proud, as his sergeant praised his work on high profile cases during press releases while the cameras flashed and the video rolled. But up close it was obvious that he was as wide as two of me put together, and it was all solid muscle.

I think I excused myself and staggered back a step or two. The Auracel I'd taken on the stairs was stuck to the roof of my mouth and I swallowed hard, worried that its innocuous gelatin coating would dissolve and give me a big jolt of something bitter and nasty. The Auracel didn't budge.

"So," Marks said, deftly swerving his bulging pecs around my shoulder as he maneuvered past me. I stood there gaping and trying not to choke. "Lost your Stiff."

A comment about the crassness of calling Maurice a Stiff stuck somewhere around the last Auracel, as I realized that Marks not only knew who I was and what I did, but that he seemed to be flirting with me. Detective Marks—queer? Who knew? And besides, he was a Stiff, too.

Or maybe he was just a jerk and the flirting notion was merely something that my mind constructed from the high it'd gleaned from two Auracels and a few fumes.

I shrugged and raised my eyebrow. Nothing like being noncommittal. Especially when I only had access to five senses, and even those were pretty fuzzy around the edges.

Marks leaned back against Maurice's workbench and crossed his arms over his chest. That pose made him triple my diameter, and his tight black T-shirt was stretched so taut over his biceps that it probably wanted to surrender. "New partner lined up yet?"

I wondered if "partner" was also supposed to be flirtatious, as in "sexual partner." But even my Auracel-addled mind figured that'd be a pretty far stretch. I had nowhere to lean, so I stuffed my hands in my jeans pockets and hunched a little, as kids who are taller than their classmates tend to do. Marks was as tall as I was. I like that in a man. "It's all hush-hush," I said, belatedly thankful that I didn't make a tongue twister out of those last couple of words. "I think they had like a hundred applicants."

Marks cocked his head to one side, considering me. The bitterness of Auracel spread over the back of my tongue and I swallowed convulsively—smooth move. "Probably more like a thousand," Marks said, "but they screen ninety percent of them out before the interviews start."

A thousand people wanted to be the Stiff half of a Paranormal Investigation Unit—homicide, no less? I imagined I'd be flattered, if I weren't choking.

I stifled a cough and dry-swallowed three, four more times. My eyelashes felt damp.

And Jacob Marks had pushed off from the workbench and pressed right up against me. "What's in your mouth?" he said, and his voice was a sexy, low purr. He pulled my face up against his, pried my mouth open with his and skimmed his tongue across the inside of my upper lip. "Auracel? Isn't that the strongest anti-psyactive they make?"

How would he know what Auracel tastes like? I probably would've asked him myself, except I wasn't quite fit for speaking. Or even breathing, for that matter. I squeezed my hand up between us and managed to push back from Marks before I hurled all over him. The bathroom sink was only a yard away, and I turned both taps on, scooped up tepid water with both hands, and struggled to dislodge the pill from my soft palate.

Finally, the foul thing tore free and made its way down my throat. It felt like it'd left behind a chemical burn on the roof of my mouth and the back of my tongue. I cupped a few more handfuls of water from the tap, drank them, and then splashed one on my face for good measure.

I stared down at the sink as the water dripped from my hairline. Cripes. Jacob Marks kissed me, sorta, and I was too busy choking on a pill to get into it. I assumed I'd just blown a perfectly good shot at some hot, nearly-anonymous sex when I heard Marks' voice again coming from the doorway. Apparently I hadn't succeeded in scaring him off. His reflection met my eye in the medicine cabinet mirror.

"One in every five hundred people is certifiably psychic, and they're all clamoring for something to shut their talent off. What kind of sense does that make?" he asked. There was a friendly lilt to his tone of voice, but the look in his eye made his words feel like more of a challenge.

Well, didn't he know his facts and figures? I ran my hand up through my half-wet hair. The mirror reflected it back at me. It stood up in a crazy, black thatch. I needed a haircut.

I flipped open the door to see if maybe there was some Listerine in there to wash away the taste of the Auracel, but found nothing but a bottle of Jergen's lotion and a few yellowed aspirin left over from the Reagan Era.

"You're a PsyCop." I turned to face Marks. "Why don't you ask your partner?"

"Carolyn's all natural," he said. And I wondered if they were fucking each other, though I guessed it was really none of my business.

I think his prying would normally have pissed me off. But I'm not normally three Auracel to the wind, so I played along. "Good for Carolyn," I said. "Do dead people like to talk with Carolyn? All day, all night? Describe how they died? In excruciating detail?"

"Carolyn can tell if people are lying."

"A human polygraph," I said, and I supposed it was clever. You didn't need someone's consent to use your psychic ability, not if you had a federal license. But you did need a court order to hook someone up to a lie detector. "No wonder you collar so many perverts."

Marks broke into a smile that was almost more of a leer, and I realized he was probably a lot more fun than I'd ever imagined he'd be. "It helps," he said. "But Carolyn's only a level two, and criminals can be incredibly evasive." He pushed the bathroom door shut with his foot and locked it behind us. The tiny doorknob twist lock seemed pathetically inadequate, considering that any cop upstairs could kick the door in without even breaking a sweat, but maybe the sanctity of the bathroom would protect us from discovery.

Marks eased up to me and then stopped, that infuriating—yet sexy—grin plastered on his face, framed by his impossibly neat goatee. I wondered what he wanted. More witty repartee? The third Auracel was kicking in and I hardly had two brain cells to rub together, so I closed the distance between us, slipped my arms around his neck and initiated a kiss of my own.

His tongue tasted beery, but pleasantly so, like he'd just had a drink or two at the party. I wished I could drink, but while alcohol loosens me up just like anyone else, it also amps up the voices. I don't drink.

He got a hand around my waist and slipped the other around the back of my jeans, kneading my ass hard, showing me his strength. I grazed his lower lip with my teeth and he grunted a little into my mouth, ground his fly against mine.

Marks backed me into the towel rack, which settled right beneath my shoulder blades, and started kissing me hard, rubbing up against me while his sweet tongue swept over my bitter one.

I was the one to fumble with buttons and zippers, to expose our stiff cocks to the ambient light of my ex-partner's bathroom. Marks seemed pleased enough to let our experience take him where it would and to have me call the shots. But then again, Marks could probably pick people up whenever he was horny. I had to jump on any chance that presented itself to me and hope I was on Auracel—or at least able to get my hands on some. I really hate threesomes when one of the participants is dead.

Marks had a thick, fat cock, rock hard and ruddy. Mine had a certain delicacy and grace beside his as he took them both in his hands and pumped them, hard, even strokes, while I cupped his jaw between my palms and languidly tongued his mouth.

He knows, I thought, and though his grip was harder than I might have liked, my body still responded to it, thighs clenching and warmth building at the base of my spine. He knows who I am. And he knows what I do. And he's willing to jack me off anyway.

I trailed my fingertips over his scalp, through his closely-shorn hair, and he groaned into my mouth, his hands moving faster on us. My breath hissed in and I caressed the tips of his ears and the curve of his jaw with a feathery touch. I sucked on his tongue.

He pulled back to watch himself as he came, his jiz rolling down over his knuckles as he clenched his cock hard, and I suddenly liked his face a whole lot better. Open like that, and vulnerable. Not the handsome, self-assured detective who always got his man, but just a guy jacking off with me. His mouth was so pretty—a little swollen now, from kissing me. I imagined it closing around the head of my cock, taking me into its soft, wet warmth, and then my hips gave a twitch and I was coming. It was a pretty energetic spurt, given the amount of drugs in my system, and the first rope of come managed to paint itself down the front of Marks' T-shirt and across the leg of his black jeans.

I sniggered a little as I shot again, more weakly though, just over his bare forearm, and again. Marks stared at me, our sticky cocks loose in his grip, and then he broke into a big grin, too. My vision was going all starry around the edges and I was glad of the towel rack behind me, and the big cop in front of me. I still had my arms draped over his shoulders, and couldn't think of any good reason to let go.

Someone banged on the door. "Bayne? You in there?"

I pressed my forehead into Marks' shoulder and exhaled carefully. I could've ignored it, if it was anyone else but Sergeant Warwick. But that voice, in that tone, would need to be answered. "Yeah, Sarge."

Marks gave my cock a slow, teasing stroke. It gave up a final bead of semen.

"I need you at the station. Now."

On a Sunday? When we were all at a party, some of us drunk, some of us pill-buffered, and some of us getting lucky? Whatever it was, it wouldn't be pretty. "Okay," I said. I considered dropping something into the toilet to make it sound like I was taking a big dump, but then I'd either have to fish the object back out or leave it in there to screw up Maurice's plumbing. Instead, I tugged at the toilet paper roll and tried to make it rattle. "I'll be out in a minute."

We both listened to Warwick's footsteps as he headed back upstairs. Marks' face had shifted back into cop-mode, his shrewd, dark eyes scanning the empty air in front of him as he analyzed whatever theories he was assembling inside his head. "Something big just went down." He pulled a yard of toilet paper from the roll and wiped my jiz off his leg.

2

Sergeant Warwick was a square, middle-aged man with a thick neck. His graying blond hair was thinning on top, but at least he had the decency not to subject us all to a bad comb-over. He sat behind his clunky metal desk, rolling a pen between his thumb and forefinger like he did every time something really pissed him off. "Bayne, this is your new partner, Lisa Gutierrez. She's worked homicide four years now, in Las Vegas and Albuquerque. Gutierrez, Victor Bayne."

Lisa Gutierrez looked as Latina as she sounded, her long, dark hair pulled back from her fresh-scrubbed, no-makeup face so hard it almost made my head hurt to look at it. She was young, mid-twenties, and my guess was that she'd been a uniformed cop in her previous job. She must have done something extraordinarily special to land her current assignment—a job that a thousand other people lost out on, at least according to Marks.

I tried to look really focused as I shook her hand, but maybe I was just kinda making my pale blue eyes bug out at her instead. Three frigging Auracels, three, not even counting the one I'd had the night before, and the whole world seemed like it was made out of cotton candy with some interesting sprinkles thrown in for shits and grins. I'd come right over from the party and I hoped to God I didn't smell like sex. I thought our encounter was brief and furtive enough that I probably didn't. I considered taking up smoking to cover any inappropriate smells I might someday harbor. I didn't necessarily have to inhale if I didn't want to.

"Are you medicated?" Warwick said. Because it's so professional to accuse someone of being high right as you introduce them to their new partner. It's some kind of newfangled team-building exercise, all the rage in L.A.

"I was at my partner's retirement party," I snapped, deciding I would have to admit to one Auracel, but not three. They couldn't prove I'd taken three without a really expensive and time-consuming drug test. "What do you think, I wanted that idiot who hung herself in his garage to follow me around the whole afternoon? That's my idea of a great party, lemme tell you."

Warwick twirled the pen harder while his jaw worked. "Detective Bayne is authorized, when he's off duty, for the use of Auracel..." he started to explain.

"An anti-psyactive," said Gutierrez. "I know what it is. Now tell me what's so unusual about this case that you'd call Bayne in instead of assigning it to the team on call."

Warwick blinked, and then pulled out a manila folder, opened it, scanned the contents and began gathering his thoughts. I stuck my hand in my pocket in order to stop myself from giving Gutierrez a high-five, since she seemed so clipped and professional that she'd probably leave me waving in the wind. But damn, I liked her.

———

I was happy to let Gutierrez drive since I was legally impaired, although a breathalyzer wouldn't have been able to pick up on it. She was just in from Albuquerque and didn't have a car yet, so we took mine. She had to move the seat up three whole clicks.

"That was…um…cool," I said as I got into the car, wondering if I could possibly sound any more retarded. "The way you got Warwick off my case."

She glanced at me. "Your pupils are totally dilated. You should put on some sunglasses before you damage your retinas."

Maybe she was genuinely concerned, or maybe she wasn't so lax on the whole drug thing after all. She had that deadpan delivery that was kind of hard to read. I rummaged around my glove compartment and found an old pair of shades crusted with mysterious dust. How did things get dusty while they were shut inside a glovebox? I also saw half a tab of Auracel cradled inside the hinge. I took a pen and flicked it out to stop it from being crushed when I closed the door, and then moved my registration over to cover it up. Gutierrez' eyes were on the tiny GPS navigation screen. Also dusty, I noted.

"It'd be faster if you turned up Clark," I said.

Gutierrez ignored my directions, preferring instead to trust the Magellan. She'd turned the audio down, but still glanced at the map occasionally.

"Were you a PsyCop at your last job?" I asked.

A little smile played on her lips, and she was actually kinda cute in that moment, like a kid sister. "They don't even have 'em in New Mexico." She pronounced Mexico with an "X" in the middle, like I would. I wondered if the "Me-HEE-co" pronunciation was reserved for the country.

We passed Clark again, a diagonal street that defied the grid of the rest of the city, and I sighed. "Then how'd you land this job? Not that I'm complaining, but I heard the competition was pretty…fierce." I wondered if she thought I was crass enough to say "stiff."

Gutierrez shrugged and turned on Lawrence. Her jacket didn't quite fit her in the shoulders. She was petite and a little stocky, would probably need something tailored. I wondered how I knew that, given that I owned only two sportcoats and my sloppy dress shirts were about twenty years out of style. I figured it was the Auracel thinking for me. And then I realized I was still in jeans, a big no-no given the department's dress code. That's what they got for calling me away from a party on the opposite side of the city from my apartment.

"My track record's good," she said. "Beyond good. And besides," she gave me a sly look. "I count as two minorities: a woman and a Hispanic. Your boss's got his quotas to fill, just like everybody."

I stared through my dusty plastic lenses at a string of Indian grocers and sari shops and noted that I could kind of see over one lens but not the other. Therefore, the shades were probably crooked as well as dusty. Charming. "Our boss." I tried to straighten out the glasses and failed.

The Magellan beeped as Gutierrez missed a turn onto Artesian and then readjusted itself to plot her a new course to the scene. I figured she must've been sightseeing and just passed it by.

"The Auracel," she said, taking the next right, "it works for you?"

"It makes the dead people shut up," I told her. And, by golly, the high was just an added bonus. I didn't tell her that. Oh, and it only muffled the ambient dead people. If I really, really wanted to, I could try real hard, pick one out and make him spill his guts. But I didn't mention that, either. A guy's gotta have some boundaries.

She nodded and pulled up behind a pair of squad cars. I glanced down Artesian and saw a pair of orange-striped sawhorses blocking the area and a surly resident getting nasty with the uniformed officers for not letting him park in front of his apartment building. Good thing Gutierrez missed that turn or we would've still been struggling to get around that moron to flash our badges and get onto the scene.

Even though it wasn't my regular shift, I knew the men on duty, and thankfully they weren't weird around Psychs. I introduced Gutierrez and let the officer in charge walk us through the scene.

"The victim was found by his downstairs neighbor. Says she pounded on the ceiling with her broom handle so long that she put a hole through the plaster trying to get him to turn his music down. Came up to tell him to his face and found him...well, you can see for yourself."

"The door was unlocked," Gutierrez said, more than asked, and the officer nodded. She stopped at the door to slip on a pair of latex gloves and plastic booties. I looked at my jeans as I slipped the booties on over my holey Converse All-Stars and wondered if I'd gotten any jiz on them in Maurice's bathroom. I didn't bother with gloves since I didn't plan on touching anything.

Gutierrez paused in the victim's vestibule and then stepped aside to let me enter. She stared straight ahead of her into a living room where a couple of techs were setting down numbered cards around a sofa-bed and snapping photos. I came in behind her and nearly had to scoop my jaw up off the floor.

The victim was splayed buck naked on his red velvet bedspread like a piece of fucking performance art. Shards of mirror surrounded him, at first making it appear that a disco ball had taken vengeance on an unsuspecting naked guy. But on closer inspection, it was obvious that every piece had been painstakingly placed around the body so that, from the proper angle, the whole thing became a glittering, psychedelic swirl.

It might've even been fun to look at, given my current state of medication, if it weren't for the hot dead guy in the middle of it all. Not a mark on him, but obviously quite dead.

Gutierrez was already getting briefed. The victim was one Anthony Blakewood, twenty-seven, Caucasian, single, worked downtown in the Loop at a brokerage firm, no known enemies.

"Sexual penetration?" Gutierrez asked the Medical Examiner's tech, a thin girl with a blond ponytail who was still snapping photos.

"We haven't flipped the body yet, but it's a good possibility. The Coroner will have the final word on that."

I fixed my gaze on a completely irrelevant nail hole on the wall and pretended they weren't talking about anything gay. I always figure I'm going to get some kind of telltale look on my face and tip somebody off about my own "lifestyle." As far as I knew, the only one besides Hotshot Marks who might've guessed about me was Maurice, and Maurice just didn't talk about those kinds of things, period. That was that.

I then noticed that Blakewood had a little collection of miniature furniture with Scotty dogs painted on it, arranged on a semicircular shelf in the corner. Yeah. He was queer.

I wondered what I had in my apartment that would incriminate me to a casual observer. Not much, surprisingly. I tended not to hold onto stuff, because stuff usually held vibes, and vibes are a pain in the ass.

I almost ran my fingers through my hair again, but stopped myself just in time to keep from contaminating the crime scene by shedding. I jammed my hands into my pockets instead. The tech said that judging by the open container of lube nearby she'd just spotted, the victim had likely been penetrated, though the Coroner would have to verify that. A psycho murderer who lubed. How considerate.

3

I stared up at my featureless white ceiling as I waited for the Seconal I'd taken to kick in. I'd loaned my car to Gutierrez with the stipulation that she wake me no earlier than noon. The victim hadn't spoken to me while I was at the apartment, and I'd taken three Auracels I needed to sleep off.

And while three was a pretty high dose for me, it wasn't like I'd never imbibed that many before. (Actually, my record is seven, but at that point you can't walk anymore and you tend to start vomiting.) Even after three Auracels, I should've been able to talk to Blakewood. Yeah, that's right. Even with my sixth sense trapped under all those meds, if I tried really hard, I should've been able to hear him. And I hadn't—not even a peep. So I was beginning to get concerned.

Anthony Blakewood, collector of Scotty dog miniatures, reamed out and discarded among several thousand other glittery bits. I wondered if he kind of dug it, being snuffed out in his prime and displayed so lovingly…or at least exactingly. I might have asked him as much, if I'd been able to find his ghost.

I dreamt of shards of silvered glass, seven years' bad luck and who's the fairest one of all. I woke with a post-Auracel sandpaper tongue and a piercing pain behind my right eye. I considered downing a handful of aspirin, but knew I'd only be asking for heartburn after lunch if I did.

I was at work on my second pot of coffee when Gutierrez called on the intercom. I buzzed her up from the lobby.

"Coffee?" I asked her as she stared over my shoulder and into my three-room apartment.

She hesitated for just a second, and then came in and took one of the two barstools by the kitchen counter. "Sure."

I looked around, not seeing the place anew, exactly, but reminding myself how stark it looks to a anyone who's never been there. "I'm kind of a minimalist."

Gutierrez' shoulders relaxed a little at my admission. "Is everything in here white?"

I handed her a white coffee mug and then pointed out the cream. She shook her head and sipped it black.

"White matches white," I said, and fiddled with my own cup, which had chilled and grown a skin on its surface. "I guess it seems easiest."

"I talked to the Coroner," she told me as I dumped my congealed coffee down the drain. "Our perp's even sicker than we thought."

You have absolutely no idea what I was thinking, I said to myself. But I didn't know her well enough to tease her like that. And besides, I didn't need anyone trying to read between the lines about anything I had to say on this particular case. With the gay and all. "Yeah?"

"The Coroner found pieces of mirror stuck under the victim's eyelids. But they'd been placed there so carefully they hadn't even scratched him."

I tried to imagine why I hadn't noticed that my victim had something angular beneath his closed eyelids, but since I was pretty much looking everywhere *but* at him, I wasn't very surprised. "I was so busy trying to talk to him…" I said, thinking that it wasn't altogether untruthful. I had tried.

"On Auracel?" Gutierrez asked. She drained her cup and came over to put it in the sink. "Why even bother?"

"I dunno." I pulled a black sportcoat off the peg on the back of my kitchen door. "I had to do something."

"We'll go try again now. You, uh…. You have better reception at the scene or at the morgue?"

Reception. I liked the way she was trying to be so casual about it. "His spirit's probably at the apartment," I said. "Accidents, suicides and murders tend to be sticky."

"Okay, we'll start there." She offered me the keys, but I waved them toward her. She'd get to know the city that much quicker if she was the one who drove. And there was that lancing pain behind my eye to consider.

Traditionally, the younger partner was the one to do the driving anyway. Maurice let me slide on that responsibility when I told him that on bad days I tended to get visuals of accident victims, and that on certain intersections they got pretty numerous. They didn't look quite as solid as real pedestrians, but when you're doing forty-five on a residential street you don't necessarily have tons of time to study them. Maurice had said it explained a lot of the swerving I did. I'd let him think that. It seemed less incriminating than admitting that the Auracel didn't help my driving any, either.

At the scene I donned the plastic booties, and this time, the gloves, too. It irked me that the night before I'd been in the same room as a homicide victim and he hadn't said a word. But I was fairly clean now, having taken my last Auracel about twenty hours prior. I was ready to hear Blakewood's side of the story.

A couple of guys from the lab were combing through the apartment with their powders and brushes and ultraviolet wands. One of them muttered "Spook Squad" in a voice so low I almost didn't catch it, and the other one straightened his tie and looked nervous.

"Just tell me where we won't be in your way," I said. I was actually only paying them partial attention, because I was sure that any minute I'd be bowled over by Blakewood's spirit.

"Can you work from the kitchen?" the tech who'd called us Spook Squad asked. "We're done processing the kitchen."

I figured he wanted to get rid of us so they could gossip, and I almost suggested that Gutierrez and I go have a sandwich and come back later, when it occurred to me that a dead queer might very well be hanging out near the fridge. I jerked my head toward the kitchen doorway and Gutierrez followed me. Undoubtedly she'd been given a job description the size of the phone book, but I thought I could summarize for her in a few sentences.

"So here's how it works," I told her. "You record all the factual stuff, plus whatever impressions I give you. Then you record your impressions about my impressions." I peeked into the kitchen, but didn't see Blakewood in there. I was glad. I really didn't want a visual on those mirror eyes. "You score points for being as skeptical as humanly possible."

"So I'm supposed to shoot you down," she said.

I stepped into the kitchen and opened the fridge. Chinese takeout, Diet 7-Up and fat-free yogurt. "If my impressions are right, the facts'll back them up and you won't be able to debunk me."

"That's bullshit," she muttered. "We're partners. We've gotta watch each other's backs, not tear each other down."

"Hey." I gave her a smile over my shoulder. "Don't take it so personally. I never do." I liked hearing her swear. It left me free to do the same.

I walked into the kitchen and waited for that telltale sensation, like a drop in temperature that only I could feel, before the voices started. Except the kitchen was toasty, and the only sound in it was the motor on the refrigerator.

"Blakewood," I whispered, but the kitchen felt as flat and spiritless as…mine. "What's his first name?" I asked Gutierrez.

She flipped open her pad. "Anthony."

"Anthony," I said, figuring that maybe he'd died so horribly that he couldn't leave the side of his sofa bed. "Tony," I called softly. "You here?"

I planted my hands on my hips and looked around. Nothing.

Gutierrez stared at me with her pen poised over the tablet. She was a lefty.

"Forget it," I said, easing past her into the small foyer. "There's nothing here."

I stood there while Gutierrez scratched what sounded like lots and lots of notes onto her pad. I didn't see the victim, didn't hear him. I wondered if it was possible that he died of natural causes and was just set up pretty by some kind of necrophiliac. Sure, that would be weird. But I've seen plenty of weird in my time.

"What now?" Gutierrez asked.

I crept closer to the archway that opened into the main room where we'd found him. "Anthony," I said, quiet, just barely moving my lips, but the tech who thought I was creepy blanched and started tugging at the collar of his shirt.

I listened hard, but didn't hear anything but the sound of Gutierrez' pen. "You're not picking anything up," she murmured, "are you?"

I shook my head just a tiny bit and we backed up into the vestibule. "We can come back when those guys are through," she offered. "Maybe they're blocking it."

I looked at a set of keys hanging beside the door. There was an embossed Scotty on the key fob. "Believe me, it'd take a lot more than a couple of guys with powderpuffs to block a fresh murder victim."

Gutierrez scratched out some more notes. "Okay, then. What if he didn't die here?"

I considered her theory. No one had mentioned any evidence of the body being relocated, but given what I wasn't hearing, it made sense. Her brow furrowed, as if she'd found a hole in her own logic, but I thought we should explore the idea more conclusively before we shot it down.

"What if," I said thoughtfully.

4

My cell phone rang, displaying the number for the Coroner's office. "The crime scene was definitely the victim's apartment."

Unfortunately, Gutierrez and I had come to the same conclusion, given that a neighbor had sworn he saw Tony walking back home that night with some new boyfriend he didn't recognize and, predictably, couldn't describe—except to say he was very handsome.

I sat in the passenger seat of my car and picked the brim of a styrofoam coffee cup into a dozen small, ragged pieces. I hesitated before letting them fall to the floor, and then I realized that it was my own damn car and I could do what I wanted. Styrofoam fluttered to the carpet around my shoes.

"That ever happen to you?" Gutierrez asked. "A dead guy that won't talk?"

"Never." I said it quietly, through clenched teeth, to keep myself from yelling at her. What did she know? It was her first time on the Spook Squad…er, PsyCop Unit.

She flipped open her notepad, rested it against the steering wheel and scanned it. "There's gotta be a reason, then. Something unique to this case. We just need to figure out what it is."

My cell phone rang. I pulled it from my coat pocket and flipped it open. "Bayne."

"Gutierrez with you?" Warwick asked.

I refrained from asking him where the fuck else he thought my partner would be in the midst of an investigation. "Yeah."

"Get back to the station. Both of you." He hung up on me before I could try to figure out if he knew that the victim was giving me the silent treatment. What if one of the techs had overheard me talking to Gutierrez and had called him to tell him that I was a waste of taxpayer dollars? No, that was stupid. They had no idea how easy talking to dead victims usually was for me. They didn't know the silence was freaking me out.

If Gutierrez had any smarmy platitudes to offer on the way back to the squad house, she kept them to herself. The GPS unit beeped every now and then and styrofoam squeaked under my heels, but at least my performance anxiety wasn't exacerbated by a bunch of meaningless comforting phrases.

We went straight to Warwick's office. He motioned for me to shut the door behind us. "Interesting report came through from Albuquerque today," he said.

Albuquerque? Gutierrez was from Albuquerque. I thought that was a pretty odd coincidence until I realized the whole face-to-face could very well be about her, and not me.

"Test results," he said, spreading the pages of a gray, degraded fax in front of us. "Did you know that your scores were identical on every psy-test you took, Lisa? Different tests, different days, and on each and every one you hit the exact score of random probability. To the percent?"

"Correct me if I'm wrong," I said, "but isn't that a good thing for a Stiff?"

"Stiffs vary," Warwick said, and I noted that a red flush had broken out across his formidable neck. "Usually between six and thirteen percent. This," he said, gesturing at the fax, "this is not random."

Gutierrez had ability? That probably explained what I'd seen in her right away that set me at ease. Normally I'd be happy to hear it, if she were my dry cleaner or my bridge partner. But certifiable psychics weren't allowed on the force without spending half a year training at Camp Hell. Otherwise known as Heliotrope Station, to those who've never done time there.

"You're off the case," Warwick said. "In fact, you're off active duty until I can figure out what to do with you."

Gutierrez' face was a bland mask as she handed over her badge and gun. She hadn't said anything to defend herself. And she hadn't denied her ability, either. She turned and walked out without a word.

"Where are you with this case?" Warwick said to me. His voice seemed normal, but his color was way too high.

"We, um." I missed Gutierrez already. "The victim." I shrugged. "It's a tough one."

"I'll assign a pair of uniformed cops to back you up. Broaden your contact area and see what you can find."

Great. I'd have a pair of superstitious flatfoots following me around as I went from the cemetery to the victim's childhood home to anywhere else he liked to hang out while he'd been alive. I wondered if he had a favorite bar and, if so, the chances of eluding my babysitters and getting lucky. Ideally with Detective Marks, who'd just so happen to be there. Not that he hung out in gay bars or anything. At least, that's what I assumed, though I didn't hang out in gay bars either, so I didn't actually know for sure.

Warwick turned back to his notes and picked up the phone. I was dismissed. He'd call me when he had someone lined up. I could go to my desk and start trying to make sense in writing of what was going on, but writing had never been my strong point. Even Maurice, with his two-fingered, misspelled typing, was Shakespeare next to me.

I went out to my car with the intention of grabbing a very late lunch when I saw there was someone sitting in my drivers' seat. Since Gutierrez still had my keys, I realized that was a good thing.

"Wow," I said as I got in. "That was...." The fact that she'd been crying stopped me dead in my tracks. I can't stand it when girls cry.

"It's not fair," she said. "I earned this job."

I tried to recall a time in my life where I would've gotten as worked up as she was over a job, and failed. But that's just me. And then I had to remind myself that she'd needed to beat out a thousand other applicants to get it, and I could empathize at least a little.

"For what it's worth, I like working with you."

She gave me a sidelong glance. Her eyes, nose and lips were all red and puffy.

"What if I want to be a Stiff?" she said. "I make a better Stiff than a psychic. I'm a good cop. Really good."

"You got pretty far without being found out," I said. "Give yourself some credit for that." I realized that was a pretty stupid thing to say, since now that she'd been discovered, her career with the force was likely over.

She just hunched and looked down, getting tears on my steering wheel.

"Maybe they'd pay to retrain you. Your abilities might be bigger than you know."

"You saying I should try for Camp Hell?"

Oh. I wouldn't have wanted to be a woman there. It was hard enough being myself there.

"Look," I said, desperately trying to change the subject. "We shouldn't be sitting here like this in front of the station. Let's go to Dairy Queen. I'll buy you a milkshake."

"That's okay," she said. "You're gonna get called back in any time now. I'll just go home and try to figure out what I'm doing next." She pulled away from the curb into the lazy, midday traffic.

"Too bad I'm not precognizant," I said. "I'd try to give you some advice."

She smiled at that just a little, her eyes fixed on the road. "Your dead people got any ideas for me?"

I looked out over Montrose. "There's this fat Korean guy, hit by a bus, who's always hanging around the intersection at Damen. But I dunno that you want to follow his advice."

Gutierrez had picked a place in an old brick hotel less than a mile from the station. It'd been converted into studio apartments thirty years prior. The old lettering had been taken down long ago, but they'd left behind pale impressions on the brick that still read "Parker Inn."

My phone rang just as we got out of the car. She tossed me the keys over the hood and I had to juggle a little to grab them while I tried to flip my phone open. "Bayne."

"Get back to the station."

"Okay…?"

"There's been another murder."

5

The vinyl miniblinds on Warwirck's door were tilted open and I could see him at his desk with his fingers steepled in front of his face as I approached. I opened his door and staggered back to avoid plowing into Jacob Marks, who'd been lurking to one side of the doorframe. I noted belatedly that his partner, Carolyn, sat on the other side of Warwick's desk with her hands folded on her lap. She was a neat, small blonde and her skirt suit fit a lot better than Gutierrez'.

"Got a call from the Police Commissioner," said Warwick, "and it seems we're gonna try something a little different." He said the word "different" like some people say "colored," or "alternative lifestyle."

"Detective Marks," Jacob said, sticking out his hand to shake mine. I took his hand in a daze and let him jerk my arm up and down. It was smart of him to pretend he didn't know me, I realized. And I supposed I looked blank enough to pull off his little act. "This is my partner, Carolyn Brinkman." Carolyn nodded. I stammered my name, wondering if she would notice that, technically, Jacob was lying to her. But maybe he wasn't. After all, her name was Carolyn Brinkman.

Warwick piped up. "Now I know that all of your training—years of training—says that a Psych and a Stiff are like salt and pepper, yin and yang, or whatever metaphysical bullshit you want to call it."

Ham and eggs, my brain said. Ernie and Bert. Shit and shinola. My brain could just go on and on for days. Apparently, it was panicking. Not enough to miss the fact that Marks looked like some kind of Italian supermodel in his suit. But enough to spew out random words that I had to struggle to keep from saying aloud.

"But the Commissioner don't give a damn what all your gurus and your mental masters say about the PsyCop pairbond. See, he don't work with PsyCops, not directly. He's old school. And if it were up to him, crimes would get solved with sweat and brains and elbow grease and luck."

"And maybe a few hundred thousand dollars' worth of the latest crime database technology," Marks added smoothly.

Warwick made a little barking sound, and I realized that it was a laugh.

I'd never made him laugh.

"But the Commissioner says we gotta do something," said Warwick, "and unless it puts one of my men at risk, we do it."

I looked at Carolyn with her hands folded on her knee, and at Marks, who may or may not have had a secret smile playing over his expression.

"He wants us to team up?" I asked. I'd almost used the analogy of a three-way, but considering that I'd had a literal petting session with Marks, I thought better of it.

"Exactly."

Marks pulled a leatherbound notepad from his inside pocket and flipped it open. "The case does straddle both of our jurisdictions."

"The second victim…?" I asked.

"Anal penetration and mirrors," said Warwick. "Happened two nights prior to Blakewood, according the techs. You'll need to work out some kind of game plan to work the scene without stepping on each others' toes."

"Shouldn't be a problem," said Marks. "Carolyn and I would interview the victims ourselves, but our victims are usually alive. Seems natural for Detective Bayne to assume that duty. We'll handle the witnesses."

Warwick scribbled an address on a sticky note and handed it to me. The homicide was indeed on the border of the Twelfth and Fifth Precincts. It was as if the perp had specifically chosen the very method and location that would bring Marks and me back together in a sea of fumbling awkwardness.

"I'll meet you there," I said quickly, and snatched the note from Warwick's hand. I'd rather fly solo than ride along with Marks in the back seat of his car like a third wheel while prim little Carolyn sat up front and continually adjusted the air conditioning.

I arrived to see Marks parallel parking his Crown Victoria with stunning accuracy in a space adjacent to the scene. I found a spot a block away in front of a hydrant, slapped my police permit atop my dashboard and started jogging toward the duplex.

And since when did I ever walk any more quickly than was absolutely necessary? I slowed my pace as I felt the prickle of sweat in my armpits.

Marks was talking to the uniformed officers on the scene. Carolyn turned to face me. "Sergeant Warwick wasn't very clear about what happened to your new partner."

My initial impulse was to make something up about Gutierrez, help her save a little face. And then I remembered that I was talking to the human polygraph. "Turns out she has some ability."

"That's too bad. It would be better to keep our numbers even." She tugged her impeccable suit jacket down, though it hadn't needed straightening. "Next thing you know they'll be giving Psychs double duty, trying to spread us over two or three NPs." I hadn't heard that old term for Stiffs—NPs, or Non-Psychics—in ages. I guess it was more respectful, but still. I had to quell a smirk.

"But our ratio's tipped the other way," I pointed out. "Two Psychs to a Stiff."

"The brass won't look at it that way," she said. "Wait and see."

The thought of being told to do more work didn't worry me much. Overtime was fine by me. And when I felt overwhelmed, I'd just stand around and zone out, and everyone would assume I was talking to dead people. I think Maurice'd had his own way of doing the same thing. Sometimes I found pages and pages from his notepads covered in loop-de-loops.

Marks turned toward us and gave a little come-hither nod. I let Carolyn go first with the intention of tagging along behind the two of them, but Marks hung back so that he and I were side by side. "Sink or swim," he said.

"Desperate times call for desperate measures," I said, trading a maxim for a maxim.

Marks stopped in front of the victim's outer door and faced me. "Do you need anything from me in there that I should know about? With Carolyn," he said, gesturing toward her, "I'm the muscle. The people we're interviewing don't get inside her personal space unless she wants them to. But you?" He shrugged, and his crisp suit rode up and down on his broad shoulders. "I don't know what you need."

I needed Maurice, was what I needed. I struggled to articulate what, exactly, he'd done for me. He was solid. He didn't judge me. He believed me.

Maybe that was really it. He believed that when I mumbled to myself, someone replied, and that when I stared really hard, there was something there, even if he couldn't see it himself.

"General backup is fine," I said.

Marks gave me a withering look. I wasn't trying to be cagey. It just came out that way.

Ryan Carson was a junior architect at a high-priced firm that dealt with gigantic corporate clients. His duplex was probably worth a cool half-mil, and the interior looked like a great big Ikea display. Queer.

I snapped on the plastic booties and edged into the master bedroom, mouth-breathing against the smell. The closet had once had mirrored doors, but what remained of them was scattered around the room. I squinted and saw that the shards were set in more of a burst pattern than a swirl this time around, as if the killer couldn't stand to repeat himself exactly.

Ryan Carson was splayed in the middle, arms and legs outstretched like he was in the midst of winning some Olympic event, naked and triumphant, though starting to bloat in the middle. His eyelids looked wrong. Covering bits of mirror, I guessed.

But where was Ryan Carson's spirit? I looked around the room and saw nothing but a pair of techs, one snapping photographs and the other taking notes. "Ryan?" I said, quiet, but the techs heard. I'd worked scenes with each of them dozens of times before, but there was still that little pause while they seemed to steel themselves against my presence.

And to make matters worse, Ryan wasn't talking.

I usually got visuals on murders. The spirits were just so pissed off, they couldn't wait to tattle on whoever'd done it. Cases where the victim knew the perp were practically open and shut. But there was no visual on Ryan. Or anything else, for that matter. Just a cold dead body on a bed surrounded by mirror fragments.

I headed to Ryan's kitchen just in case he was hanging out there. On the way, I passed Carolyn and Marks. Carolyn was grilling a witness in a quiet and professional manner, while Marks loomed behind her, looking very big and threatening while he took notes. I had to give it to them, they certainly did have their method down pat.

The kitchen, a landscape of black enamel and stainless steel, was empty.

I cycled through the various rooms, edging around the perimeter and doing my best to fly under everyone else's radars. The Auracel was ancient history by then, and I should have picked up Ryan about as easily as I could order a pizza. So where was he?

I strained so hard in the living room that I actually got a visual on a dead goldfish. He just floated there above the mantle, looking translucent and bored. If Ryan's spirit was around, it wasn't in the living room.

The duplex had an attic—not the finished kind where there's a guest room and a spot for out-of-season clothes, but the creepy kind where you've got to pull a set of folding stairs out of the ceiling to get up there. I'd had no luck anywhere else, so I decided to see if maybe Ryan was haunting the attic.

The feeling up there was calm, though through the vents I could hear people on the street chattering, and the squeak of investigators' feet treading up and down between the first and second floors drifted up through the trap door. Ryan had a lot of stuff up there, but it was all boxed and labeled. Christmas decorations, camping gear, a bunch of old board games.

I reached out to him with my mind, trying to composite the dead body on the bed with the snapshots stuck to the fridge and come up with a semblance of how the victim had really looked. "Don't you want us to get this sonofabitch?" I asked aloud. "C'mon, Ryan. Throw me a bone."

I listened, and I reached. Nothing. I walked farther in, crouching beneath the slope of the roofline and squinting to make out the blocky architect's writing on the boxes: College. Badminton set. Mom's House. As my gloved fingers brushed against the final crate, I thought I heard the distant sound of a woman crying. But it was gone so quickly I couldn't have said for sure.

We reconvened back at the Twelfth Precinct, since Carolyn and Marks were the only two with tangible work to show for our afternoon of digging. Neither of them seemed to think it was unusual that I hadn't gotten a hit from the crime scene. And I don't think either of them would've hesitated to question me if they had. They were both similar shades of blunt, though Carolyn tended to be so soft-spoken she almost came off as polite.

"So the guy from the newsstand saw Ryan the architect come home with a Chinese guy," said Marks, "and the cab driver swears the second man was Pakistani. Is that what I'm hearing?"

Carolyn's gaze went wide, like she was watching a movie screen inside her head. "They were positive, Jacob. Absolutely certain."

"But given the timeframe," said Marks, "about twelve thirty p.m., they had to be talking about the same guy."

I broke in. "Maybe he was just, uh…tanned." I felt like an idiot the second I opened my mouth, but Carolyn's answer took the sting off.

"I thought of that," she said. "But when I was reading the witnesses, it wasn't a skin tone they'd noticed. From the guy at the newsstand, I kept getting images of his cousin back home. And the cab driver thought the subject looked exactly like some Eastern movie star."

"Then something else is going on," Marks suggested. "The perp's got talent and he's doing something to obscure his identity."

"We don't have enough to go on to work that theory," Carolyn said.

"Not yet," said Marks. "We'll have to dig up some more witnesses."

He looked at me. I wondered if he wanted me to find some dead people at the scenes, other than the victims, to canvas. How could I tell him that they'd both been total paranormal voids—except for the goldfish?

I hoped he could make do with a little show of support. "It's worth looking into," I said.

Carolyn flipped through Marks' notes and made ticks by a couple of his observations. "It's all we've got," she said, "so we might as well try."

We hit the street again and broadened our net. Anthony Blakewood, the Scotty collector, had likely picked up his date at a gay nightclub on Belmont that wouldn't open for another four hours. We did trace Ryan Carson's path back to a coffee house on Clark, though.

I was parking-challenged yet again and found Carolyn and Marks already there, questioning a barista. The girl was college-aged and chunky, and intent on battering a piece of chewing gum into submission with her molars. Carolyn made little squiggles and ticks on Marks' notepad while they talked.

"I'm sure you see hundreds of people every day," Marks was saying, "but just think back to last night and see if this man is familiar."

I flashed my badge and mumbled my name as I fell into place beside Carolyn. The employee gave me the briefest once-over and then focused on Marks' photo of Ryan.

"Oh, I dunno. Working in Boystown, they all start looking the same. Especially these quiet, plain ones."

I don't know that I would have called Ryan plain. He'd had a nice build and a sincere, open look about him. But maybe she meant plain compared to the kids with pierced eyebrows, noses and lips talking computer games over their lattes.

"Three nights ago," Carolyn prompted. "Maybe he lingered a while."

The barista began to shake her head, but then went still. "Oh yeah. The chai. That's right." She pointed toward the window. "He was sitting up there with a Powerbook and he had a croissant special, no meat."

"Them fucking fags. Maybe they'd get straightened out if they ate a little meat like regular people."

I swung around but there was no one visible behind me. The gargly, decayed quality of the voice clicked in my head and I felt my mind shift to a different kind of listening. I recalled the idea I'd had earlier about interviewing a dead witness. Whatever I learned wouldn't be admissible in court since technically it would be hearsay, but I was open to anything that'd help narrow down our search.

I reached over Marks' shoulder for the photo of Ryan and tried to pretend that I didn't notice the barista looking at me funny. "Could I, um...? Thanks."

I turned away from Marks and held the photo in front of my chest. "Did you see this man Friday night?" I spoke so softly that your average NP would think I was talking to myself.

"That one? Yeah. He comes in here two, three times a week and has a *chai*."

"Mmm hm. And was he with anybody?"

Gooseflesh rose on my arms as whomever I was speaking to grew excited. "How could I forget? Some faggot wearing a Halloween costume in June."

"Oh," I said, disappointed. "Like a drag queen? A transvestite?"

"You know I had a clean bill of health not three months before I kicked the bucket? Then they cracked me open. Massive coronary, they said. Arteries seventy-eight percent blocked. It's them HMOs that's the problem, ya know. Turn people around like short order cooks."

"What was she dressed as? The female impersonator."

"Are you stupid? When'd I say there was a Cher with a pecker in here, huh? That's nothing new. Them faggots do that all year 'round. I'm talking a real costume."

I imagined a mascot gone astray—maybe someone dressed as a hot dog. "Describe it," I said. I'd raised my voice a little, but Marks and Carolyn had shifted their bodies to block anyone from disturbing me. Their postures were casual, but their timing was fantastic.

"Scary," said the disembodied voice. "I dunno. Lots of black, like a big cape with a hood."

"What was he, a white guy? Hispanic? Young, old?"

"I…I dunno." The voice wavered and grew softer. "I couldn't see his face."

"How to you know it was a man?"

"I dunno. I just do."

A shiver coursed through me and my relative temperature returned to normal. I guess the dead blowhard couldn't stand being asked a question that he couldn't answer with obnoxious certainty.

I turned back to Marks and Carolyn, who were both staring at me, anticipation glittering in their eyes.

"The man who ordered the chai," I asked quietly. "Was he with somebody in a cloak?"

The barista burst out laughing. "What, like Dracula?"

I felt my cheeks color. "Maybe something *like* a cloak. A rain poncho. A long duster."

"I think I'd remember someone in a cloak," she snickered, then turned her attention back to Jacob Marks.

I made a mental note to reintroduce myself to the bar scene. Even if I'd had a drink or two in me, the music was so loud that I probably wouldn't be bothered by disembodied sob stories. Unfortunately, no live person at the bar knew Anthony Blakewood well enough to have any idea who he'd gone home with. Any dead bar-hoppers were drowned out by the music, and no one even cruised me. So the trip to the GloryWhole was a total bust.

I split off from Carolyn and Marks around 11:30 and swung by a 7-11 for something to eat. I reached for an avocado wrap, but then I remembered what the dead creep at the coffee house had said about queers and vegetarians, and opted for a roast beef instead. Halfway back to the counter I turned around and exchanged the beef for the avocado again. And I did my best to ignore the mostly-transparent guy with the afro jacking off in the corner, and the voice coming from aisle three that kept repeating, "But he loves me. I can't leave him."

I ate as I drove home, wondering how it was that I was queer enough to pick out an avocado wrap, but not queer enough to get cruised at a gay bar. It could've been my badge that they were avoiding, sure. But I think the idea of laying a cop gets a lot of guys off. And besides, plenty of 'em were drooling over Marks, not that I blame them. I took a bite of the wrap and mayonnaise squirted out the end and dribbled down my lapel. I steered with my knee while I tried to wipe it off, but only succeeded in getting mayo all over my hand. Maybe it was my wardrobe that was the problem. Not that I had any intention of doing anything about it in the near future, since I think shopping's about as much fun as going to the dentist.

I finished the wrap before I got home and spent an extra minute trying to get mayo off my sportcoat. I gave up when it became obvious that all I'd accomplished was embedding rolled-up fragments of cheap paper napkin all over myself. I realized that I'd dropped my other coat off at the dry cleaner's about four months prior. And I wondered if they would give the thing to me without the pickup slip, or if they'd foisted it off on Goodwill by now.

To top things off, the ghost of Jackie the Loudmouthed Prostitute had ranged up from her normal turf about two blocks south to tell me, yet again, about the john who'd shanked her. If I'd known about Jackie, I might have picked a different apartment. But she hadn't made her first nocturnal appearance until I'd completed my week long stake-out and written a check for the security deposit. Sometimes I thought about moving, but I reminded myself that she only harassed me a couple of times a month. The spirits around my old place had managed to waylay me every single week.

"So I said, 'You got a place, baby?' And he said, 'Come on over here, sugar, no one can see us back in this here alley.'"

Though they were infrequent, her tirades tended to get on my very last nerve. "Go find someone who gives a shit," I said, pushing open the gate to my walkway.

"Are you disrespecting me?" I felt a small chill, like Jackie might be gearing up for a temper tantrum, but it was weak enough that I was able to blow it off. "You hear me, white boy? I said, are you disrespecting me?"

There's a technique Camp Hell taught people like me—spirit mediums, to use the technical term—for when we were done talking. We're supposed to surround the entity with a bubble of light, white on the inside to draw them toward the light, and blue on the outside, to protect us from any potential malevolence. I thought real hard about putting one of those bubbles around Jackie. I formed it in my mind and I pushed until my ears popped, imagining my power coursing out to surround her and get her the fuck away from me.

But that was apparently all in my head.

"No one talks to Jackie that way," her voice continued. "You know what I'm sayin'? White boy—do you know what I'm sayin'?"

"Talk to the hand," I said, and waved her off as I went into my vestibule. She'd never yet followed me into the building. I think it might've been too far away from the spot where she'd died. At least, I hoped it was.

About a foot of free newspapers and sales fliers were piled up on the floor. They'd drifted back against the security door, preventing it from shutting completely. One of these days I was going to fling all that crap out onto the lawn. But not while I was covered in mayonnaise and had a pissed off hooker ghost railing at me from the courtyard.

I stuck my mail key into the bank of mailboxes on the wall, wiggled it to get it to that precise depth where it would turn, and opened my mailbox. Sales fliers slipped out and I let them join the rest of the paper on the floor. I studied what was left. A phone bill. A free sample of shampoo and conditioner all in one.

The outer door swung open, startling me, and I half-turned as a bulky figure pressed me into the open mailbox. "You know how hot you look when you talk to yourself in coffee shops?" Marks said. The cellophane-wrapped plastic packet of shampoo crinkled between us while he leaned in for a kiss. The after-work stubble around his goatee scraped my cheek, and he tasted like cinnamon gum.

I pulled back from the kiss, though, wanting to make sure that I had things straight. "You're not pissed off that you got stuck with me for this case?"

Marks tilted his head. His features were harsh in the yellow buglight. "I've got two Psychs on my team. Why should I be pissed?" He leaned forward again and his lips were softer on mine, gently caressing my mouth and parting my lips for a slow, tender sweep of his tongue. My knees went all rubbery.

Evidently, he wasn't worried about us getting caught fraternizing—and if he wasn't concerned, then I sure wasn't gonna make a stink. I'd always thought that rules were just for people who tended to get caught.

"Look," I said when he let me come up for air. I was just about to tell him that I could hear Jackie screaming about her no-good pimp and it was a total buzzkill, but I decided it would be better to take the paranormal things slowly since my talents were probably much freakier than Carolyn's. "Let's go upstairs."

We sprinted up to the third floor like we hadn't just spent ten hours combing for witnesses. I had my key in my hand, poised at lock-level, when I rounded the top of my stairs and saw that some long-haired woman was slumped against my front door. I was fairly sure she was alive, too.

The girl sniffled. Marks stopped behind me on the second stair to the top. I stared at her and tried to place her, and then recognized the oxford-blue blouse that had once been hidden by an ill-fitting suitcoat. "Gutierrez?" I said.

She peered at me through the zig-zag waves of her unbraided hair.

I tried to act like it wasn't all that unusual to find someone sprawled at my front door. "Marks, this is my partner, Lisa Gutierrez."

Marks stepped up beside me and peered down at her. Gutierrez made no move to stand. She seemed kind of distant. I wondered if she'd been drinking. Or maybe if she'd slit her wrists and I just couldn't see the puddle of blood due the lousy hall lighting.

She squinted at me and then nodded, as if she'd only just placed me. "Good, you're here. Ask me a question."

"Huh?"

"Just ask me," she said. She seemed to have a Spanish accent that I hadn't noticed before. "Something with a yes or no answer."

I shook my head. "What, trivia?"

"Anything," she said, drawing the word long and pronouncing the end like "theeng."

"Am I married?" Marks asked.

Gutierrez swung her head around to peer at him. Her brow furrowed. I waited for steam to come out of her ears. "I don' know. Ask something else."

Marks glanced at me and raised his eyebrow. I shrugged. "Am I Jewish?" he said.

Gutierrez thought hard, and then nodded with a satisfied smile. "I don' know."

Marks pulled a pen light out of his suitcoat, crouched down in front of Gutierrez and shined the beam in her face. "She's the one with the gift they just discovered, right?"

I nodded.

Gutierrez just sat there while Marks looked her over. "You give her any of your Auracel?"

"What, are you crazy? That's way too strong for someone without any tolerance." And then I took in her wooziness and her general ennui and I had to wonder. Where would she get ahold of something so tightly controlled—something for which I just happened to have a prescription? And then I remembered. The pill in my glove box.

Good thing it was only a halfsie or we'd probably be on our way to the emergency room.

I reached over Gutierrez' head to unlock my front door with the goal of getting Gutierrez inside and getting rid of Marks. "I can...uh...take it from here," I said.

Marks looked at me like I was nuts. "What, you just remembered you're not single or something? I thought you invited me up two minutes ago." He'd started helping Gutierrez to her feet as if caring for a massively stoned partner was all in a day's work.

"I hadn't planned on...." I gestured toward Lisa.

Marks managed to support Gutierrez with one arm and reach over me to push open my front door with the other. "But you know what to do, right? There's some kind of hangover cure for anti-psyactives, isn't there?"

"No," I said, mostly to myself. "Not really."

I hurried inside before them to flip on the light and made sure there wasn't a kitchen stool in the middle of the floor waiting for someone to trip over it. Marks looked around as he pulled Lisa inside. "Postmodern Institutional. Nice."

I bristled at the "institutional" remark, and did my best not to have a Camp Hell flashback. I supposed Marks thought he was being witty. Just because he was turning out to be a Psych groupie didn't mean that a psychic had ever told him a Heliotrope story. Most of us did our best to forget them.

"Put her on the futon," I said, figuring I could just buy another plain canvas cover if Lisa ended up puking on it. Marks steered her into the living room. I ran the tap until the water was as cold as it was going to get and then looked in the freezer for some ice. Both ice cube trays were empty. I wondered why I'd just left them there like that.

"Vic," Lisa said as she saw me come through the living room door. "You gotta do something for me." Marks sat beside her on the couch, relaxed, but keeping an eye on her.

I handed her the glass of water and some slopped onto her knee. "I'll try."

She leaned forward and more water dribbled onto the hardwood floor. "Tell my Papa I'm a good cop."

"I'm sure he thinks so," I said. "Parents are always proud when their kids make the force."

She shook her head, but the remainder of the water stayed in the glass. "Crackhead shot him down when I was seventeen. He don't know."

"He was a cop?" Marks asked.

Lisa nodded. "Twenty-three years."

I closed my eyes and tried to figure out how to sound genuine without being too truthful. Because chances were that Gutierrez' father was walking around in an outdated uniform complaining about the sonofabitch who'd shot him and reliving it down to the last freaking detail. Murders just are that way.

"They didn't have PsyCops then," Lisa said. "Not out west." She stared at me through her hair and it disturbed me, seeing her like that, her control stripped away by the drug. "He thought I wouldn't be nothing better than a fortune teller like my *abuelita*."

Marks was listening intently. He'd followed me home to have a good time, and he was getting it—just not in the form he'd expected. "What's your talent, Lisa?"

She clutched the water glass hard and turned her face toward him. "My sister and me call it *sí-no*."

"Sí-no."

"The yes-no game. We played it all the time. Will it rain tomorrow? Yes. Is Mama making chicken tonight? No. Will I like my new teacher? Yes."

"Limited precog," I said.

"Maybe not so limited," said Marks. "I'll bet she can work some pretty big questions into the *sí-no*."

"And her psych tests," I said. "That's how she managed to come out completely average. She knew that anything consistently above or below would have filtered her into the positive or negative psychic tiers, so she got half the questions right, half wrong, on purpose. Maybe you're right. Maybe her gift is incredibly accurate."

Marks eyed her greedily. "Can you imagine what she'd do with some training?"

I closed my eyes and remembered the night at Camp Hell when the doctors in surgical masks blew my synapses wide with a powerful psyactive. They'd left me strapped to a gurney for three days until I stopped twitching. "Training's a very personal thing," I said, doing my best to keep my voice even.

"My Papa'd want me to be a real cop."

I supposed I could've taken offense at the implication that I wasn't one, but maybe I secretly agreed with her. "Don't worry about that now," I said. "Get some sleep." I stood up to scrounge a blanket off my own bed while Marks managed to open out the futon with Lisa still on it.

Once we'd gotten her settled, Marks headed toward my bedroom. I followed him and paused in the doorway, watching him loosen his tie. "I don't think you should stay," I whispered.

"Why not?"

I glanced back toward the living room. "I'm not, um. Y'know."

"What?"

I crossed my arms and sighed, and hated that he was going to make me say it. "Out."

He smirked. "Not to anyone? You don't strike me as a virgin."

"Don't be stupid. You're a cop, too."

Marks eased over to me a hell of a lot more gracefully than someone his size had the right to. "I don't show up at the squad house in a pink tutu, no. But my family? My friends? My partner? I'm not gonna waste my time and energy playing games with them."

I looked back at Lisa, wondering if she was asleep or just zoning out with her eyes shut. "I only met her a couple of days ago," I said in my own lame defense. That was my excuse for not telling my partner. Family and friends? That was simple. I didn't have any.

Marks pulled a business card from the breast pocket of his suitcoat and tucked it down the collar of my shirt. He pressed his lips against my ear and spoke softly, his voice a low buzz. "Call me on my cell if you need anything." His tongue traced the outline of my ear and then darted inside to draw a long shiver out of me. "Anything."

I stared at the kitchen doorway long after Marks was gone.

8

I swabbed the shower out before Lisa woke up. Just because my whole apartment's white doesn't mean I'm a clean freak or anything, and I'd started noticing dust bunnies, clumps of hair, and fingerprints that would send a woman running for the Formula 409.

"I think my eyeball is gonna fall out."

I turned to find Lisa leaning against the doorframe of the tiny bathroom, picking a tangle out of her hair.

"Yeah. I get that, too." I turned on the hot tap and ran water into the tub. "A shower and a couple of aspirin will help. A little."

Lisa stared down at her nails. "I feel like I should ask you if I did anything stupid last night, except I actually remember it all."

I sat on the edge of the clawfoot tub and played with the white vinyl shower curtain that hung from an oval track suspended from the ceiling. I noticed some mildew on the bottom and tried to hide it in one of the folds.

"Who was that other detective? He your new partner?"

"Temporarily. He works for another precinct and he's already got a partner."

"That's too bad. He seemed like a good cop."

I found a black T-shirt in my closet that I'd accidentally bought a size too large and never worn, and tossed it into the bathroom while averting my eyes. Then I brewed some double-strong coffee and wondered if Lisa would have the stomach for chicken pot pies for breakfast. Probably not. We'd need to eat out.

Lisa emerged from the steamy bathroom with the end of a tight braid pinched between her fingers. My T-shirt was stretched taut on her, making her seem chestier than she'd looked in a suit. "Got a rubber band?"

"Um…door knob."

Lisa found a band and wrapped it around the end of her braid.

"How's your power today?" I asked her.

"I dunno." She sat on the second stool and took the cup of black coffee I handed her. "I think it's coming back. Answers pop into my mind when I ask questions, but I don't feel so sure of them."

"It comes back gradually," I said. "We're people. You can't turn us on and off like TV sets."

Lisa sipped her coffee and winced. "You really gotta clean out your coffee pot."

"Put some cream in there, you won't notice it so much." Lisa attempted to gag some coffee down while I slid a couple of aspirin her way. "If you want, I can take you somewhere with decent coffee."

Lisa peered at me suspiciously.

"Where the second murder victim just happened to be hanging out the night of his death," I added.

Lisa's eyes went wide. "You can't do that, Vic. You'll get in trouble bringing me in on the case while I'm suspended."

"But we're just going out for a little coffee," I protested.

Lisa looked into her cup. "The second crime scene—all covered with mirrors like the first one?"

I nodded.

"Those poor boys," she said, getting up to dump her coffee into the sink. That seemed like an odd thing to say, considering that they were probably about her age, but I didn't remark on it.

A kid with a pierced eyebrow was working the counter and I was relieved that I didn't have to deal with the gum-chewing girl who'd seen me talking with the dead guy. I got a latte and a chocolate chip bagel while Lisa just ordered a black coffee, extra tall. "Let's sit over here," I said, carrying our coffees to a table while balancing my bagel in the crook of my arm. I gestured toward a table in front with a tilt of my head. "That's where the second victim supposedly had chai with Darth Vader."

"And a dead witness told you this," said Lisa. She peeled off the lid and blew on her coffee. "Dead guys ever lie?"

"Why don't I ask you, Miss *sí-no*. Do dead guys ever lie?"

Lisa grinned. "Yes."

"And they get their stories all mixed up, too," I told her. "They're just as thick as the living. Sometimes worse, since they get stuck in these crazy ruts and keep repeating themselves."

She wrinkled her nose. "You hear any dead people talking now?"

I shifted my focus but the room felt quiet. "Not now. But this is a new building. The older ones almost always have someone hanging around. It's worse at night."

"No wonder you take Auracel. Once I took that pill and the *sí-no* was gone, I felt kinda lonely. I couldn't figure out why you'd want to get rid of your power—unless it stopped you from doing your job. But I guess it's pretty different from mine."

"And how could you ever think that a talent like *sí-no* would stop you from doing yours? You put yourself in some hot water by applying to be a PsyCop. If you'd just stayed in the regular force, you'd probably make detective with the first opening. What were you thinking?"

Lisa slouched against the back of her chair. "The *sí-no* told me to. I saw the job posted in the breakroom, with about a hundred others. PsyCops, they're still pretty novel in New Mexico. 'Should I apply for that job?' I asked myself. *Sí.*"

The *sí-no* told me to. The courts would have a field day with that explanation.

My cell phone rang—Marks. "Carolyn and I are at the Twelfth putting our notes together, and it looks like at least three more witnesses who saw the suspect would identify him differently."

"Hold on," I said. I hit the mute button on my phone and turned to Lisa. "Did the same person murder both Blakewood and Carson?"

"Yes."

"And is he doing something to disguise his appearance?"

"No."

I un-muted my phone. "Something's definitely up with the killer," I said, "but I'll be damned if I know what it is."

"I think it warrants some serious discussion over dinner tonight. Say eight o'clock? Cottonwood Lounge."

I stared hard at my phone. The restaurant was fancy enough that I could hardly mistake the invitation for anything but a date. And it was nowhere near either of our precincts. Marks was persistent, I'd give him that. "Um…okay. Sure."

"See you then," he purred, and the noise of his line cut off.

I realized Lisa was staring at me. "Ask me," she said.

"Huh?"

"You want to ask me a *sí-no*. I can tell."

I drummed my fingers on the faux-marble tabletop. "Is Marks…" I started, and then wondered how to phrase my question. The incriminating part seemed to be out of the bag with just that single word—his name. "Is he just some kind of player, messing with my head?"

"No." Lisa blushed a little and turned her attention toward the remainder of her coffee. I wondered if what I'd just done counted as "coming out" to my partner. Lisa was no dummy, so I suspected that was a "yes."

—❧—

I dropped Lisa off at her apartment and went back to my desk at the Fifth, figuring I'd hunt-and-peck my way through what little I had to report while I counted down the minutes until eight p.m.

I'd been there a couple of hours when my phone buzzed and Betty the receptionist's voice came through. "Detective Bayne?"

"Yeah?"

"Sergeant Warwick wants to see you."

Betty'd been at the station for something like forty years. She was the main reason they still used the same phone system they'd installed in the early eighties. But I gave her credit. She could take the most mundane sentence and, with the addition of a well-placed but subtle inflection, let you know exactly what was going on.

In this case, the way she lingered over the word "see" implied that I was in some kind of deep shit.

Warwick knew about me and Marks. That was all I could figure. I could see it now, a great big scandal. Two members of the already-controversial Paranormal Investigation Unit fired in a shocking gay sex scandal—details at eleven.

Warwick stood up and loomed over his desk as I came in. I closed the door behind me so fewer desk cops could hear me getting reamed. "You want to tell me what you were doing meeting with Gutierrez earlier today?" he demanded.

A small, giddy part of me wanted to tell him that I was fucking her. But then I thought of Marks, strong enough to tell his inner circle who he actually was, and I thought better of it. Besides, how could I do that to Lisa's reputation?

"We were discussing anti-psyactives," I told him, figuring that even Carolyn the lie detector wouldn't be able to find anything wrong with that explanation.

Warwick frowned, sure that I wasn't being truthful, but unable to discount what I'd said without challenging me. "You are not to discuss the case with her," he warned me. "She's suspended. And if I find out you're leaking evidence to her, that's where your ass is gonna be, too."

"Yes, sir." I suspect that legally he couldn't tell me not to see her on my own time. But it seemed that he thought if he glared at me hard enough, I would infer it.

Warwick picked up his phone and told Betty to get his wife on the line—his way of dismissing me without giving me the courtesy of saying it aloud. Maybe most NPs really think that every Psych is a mind reader, but Warwick was taking it that one extra step just to be an ass.

9

I hoped that buying a new jacket at SaverPlus Department Store wouldn't mark me as a complete and utter loser for the rest of my life, but I'd ended up working until 6:45 and needed to get something fast. An ancient salesman who smelled like cigars kept yammering on about how I needed a 39 long, an unusual size, but he thought he might have it in navy. I grabbed a 40 regular in black and headed for the cashier while he was still rummaging around.

I pulled the tags off in the car while I cursed at the GPS for taking me through the most congested six-way intersection in the city. I popped open my glove box and searched for a comb each time the traffic lurched to a fitful stop. Not that I'd ever actually put a comb in there. But it seemed like it'd be a likely place to keep one.

When I got to the Cottonwood Lounge, I found Marks sitting at the tastefully set table, sipping a glass of dark red wine like he didn't even notice I was fifteen minutes late. "I, um…traffic was lousy."

He shook his head from side to side like I'd said something funny. "Wine?"

"Wine? Um, no." I pointed to my head. "Doesn't agree with me."

"Really?"

I sensed that he wanted me to give him some kind of Psych story to gnaw on, but I just wasn't up for it. "Warwick laid into me for having contact with Gutierrez."

I thought he would ask me how Warwick knew, but instead he just shrugged and drained his glass. "And you're so worried about what Warwick thinks."

"He is my boss."

"How many years?"

I counted back, just to be sure. "Twelve."

"You were in one of the original three PsyCop units when the whole thing was hardly more than a crazy experiment. Your hit rate was the only thing that kept the program alive, especially after that witchhunt exposé on the psychic gambling ring that Channel 2 aired. You think he doesn't remember that?"

I sipped my ice water and thought back. Those things had all happened. But I didn't recall anyone ever acting like they were anything special.

Marks leaned forward and his casual demeanor fell away. Intensity blazed in his dark eyes, and he grasped my forearm from across the table. "We're gonna nail this bastard. Me and you. Carolyn and Lisa. And then see what kind of respect you command."

I considered Marks. It was easy enough for him to be confident. This case was like any other to him: get evidence, put evidence together, solve case. But me? My evidence collection was on the fritz and it was really starting to piss me off.

Over dinner I managed to get marinara sauce on my new blazer, though it left less of a telltale mark than the mayonnaise had on my old one. But at least I found Marks to be pretty good company—a lot easier to talk to than other men I'd attempted to date. There'd been the record store clerk who got squeamish when he found out I carried a gun. And the hairdresser who couldn't stop making wisecracks about my handcuffs. But Marks just commented on the food and gave me sultry looks between every bite he took. I could handle that.

I followed him back to his place, a small second-floor condo on the lake. It looked more lived-in than the architect's duplex, but just about as expensive. A phantom cat sat on his radiator, tail lashing back and forth, but other than that we were alone.

"It's good," I said, happy to get out of that new sportcoat. I threw it over the arm of his burgundy leather couch. "No one here but us."

Marks grinned as if he'd been waiting for me to say something spooky all night. He loosened his tie like he was doing a striptease, then pulled it off and let it fall in a silk heap on top of my jacket. I was relieved that he wasn't compulsively neat. "C'mere," he said. He put his arm around me, led me to a floor-to-ceiling window and pulled open a set of vertical blinds.

The lake spread out before us, tiny lights flashing here or there where a boat floated at anchor, and the yellow grids of high rise windows glowing in my peripheral vision. I'm not usually one to go out of my way to see the sights, but the view from Marks' window was pretty nice. "Wow."

His hands slipped around my middle as I said it, and my breath hitched as he pulled my shirt from my waistband. I felt his palms glide over my bare stomach and I shivered as he fit himself to the curve of my back, his breath warm on my neck.

I tried to turn around and face him, but he had me spread up against the plate glass window and there was no way I'd be able to move unless he let me. He pressed into me harder, grazing the nape of my neck with his teeth as his hands slid higher. His fingers closed over my nipples and he took them gently, just rolling them, rolling, rolling, as his teeth combed my neck and the bulge of his cock rubbed against the back of my pants.

I reached back over my shoulder with one hand to see if I could touch him, stroke him, anywhere. But I was splayed like a bug on the glass and couldn't do anything but writhe while Marks' hands played over my chest and his mouth seared tingling trails over my neck. Eventually I stopped trying and just pressed my cheek into the window, my breath fogging the lake skyline until it took on the spectral look of the dead world that dogged my existence.

Marks teased my nipples until they were stiff and then squeezed them harder—just a little—until I groaned aloud and pushed my ass back against him. He pressed his teeth into me and held me there by my neck while his hands slid downward and made short work of my fly. My slacks pooled around my ankles and my cock stood out in my boxer briefs, the tip butting against the cool glass through the thin fabric.

Once my pants were off, Marks' hands slid up my sides, along my ribs. They crossed themselves over my chest as he pressed himself into my back from chin to thigh. "Just stay there," he said, his voice low and rough. "I want to get you off."

Had he actually said that? Had anyone ever said that to me before? Ever? Another of my breaths bloomed against the window as Marks dropped to his knees behind me and took the waistband of my underwear between his teeth. My damp fingertips squeaked at the glass, searching for something to grasp, while Marks' goatee whispered across the skin of my bare ass as he tugged my underwear down. The briefs got caught over my hard-on, which was now sticking up at an angle, and he nibbled around the plane of my hip and the bony crest of my pelvis as he worked at undressing me. My cock snapped free and the glass was colder than I thought it would be, though maybe the smear of precome I was painting there was giving me a chill.

His head dipped low as he wedged it under my butt and pressed his lips against my inner thigh, trailing his hot tongue in slow swashes that inched higher and higher. My legs trembled as I stepped out of the underwear and spread my feet, the length of my cock now forced vertically between my belly and the glass that was no longer cold; the heat of my body had warmed it.

Marks' warm, damp breath enveloped the back of my balls as he sighed, and then his tongue was there, teasing at them as they shifted inside my scrotum, which wrinkled at the touch of his mouth. He kissed them and laved them and bathed them with his tongue, and all the while I jammed my cock against his window, squeaking it up, then down, and wishing there was something warm or wet or fleshy against it instead of a pane of hard, smooth glass.

"Please," I mumbled against the window while his tongue traced the divot between my balls.

"Please what?" he said, his mustache tickling me right below the asshole while his hot breath had me squirming.

Damn him for making me say it. "Suck me," I said, and it hardly even sounded like my own voice saying something so porno. He reached a hand around the front of me just enough to press my stiff cock downward and aim it between my thighs, toward his mouth. He led with his chin and could hardly reach me, but my whole body bucked against the glass when he dragged his lower lip over my cockhead, swirled at it with his tongue, and teased my slit between long, leisurely sucks of the tip.

"Please, oh God. Please do it deep."

He slid his hot mouth from me and then flipped me around, one strong hand keeping me from tripping over the wad of clothing at my feet. "That's right," he said, caressing the side of my cock with his cheek. "I want to look up into your face while you come."

And then my awkwardness increased exponentially as I realized Jacob Marks was gonna stare at me while my cock sank into his throat. He was gorgeous—simply beautiful. The most handsome man I'd ever been with, that I ever even dreamed I'd be with. And yet it was easier to spread myself wide open and half naked on that damn window than it was to look into his eyes.

I closed my eyes and concentrated on the rhythm he set, on the exquisite suction he maintained and the way he opened his throat every few strokes to take me all the way in. But then I heard a murmur of distant laughter—maybe just some tourists on the lake, but maybe not—and I opened my eyes again to keep myself with Marks, anchored in the present, among the living.

I grabbed his short hair, struggling to find something to hold on to, and he grasped me by the hips and sucked hard. My whole body tensed, poised on a painful brink, and then everything crashed open, my hips bucking as Marks rode out my orgasm. His fingers sank deep into my hipbones with a force that'd leave bruises.

Marks pulled off slowly and gave my wet, red cockhead a lingering lick while I stared down at him, dazed. He looked up at me for a long moment, and then kissed it again. And licked it. I pulled back from him, quelling the need to giggle at the sensitivity. "Stop it, Marks. You're killing me."

He sat back on his heels, still fully clothed, and licked his lips. "Why don't you call me Jacob?" he suggested.

10

Marks—Jacob, I mean—snores a little. I think I was relieved to learn it. If he was absolutely perfect, I'd have to be suspicious.

I woke around six, and while it would've been nice to get a few more hours in, I was surprised to have slept as soundly as I had. I hadn't spent a night in another man's bed since…I thought back. Maybe eight years earlier. That college professor who was always high—on weed, not Auracel. That was back before they even made Auracel and I'd needed to take Neurozamine with a Benadryl chaser to shut out the voices.

Eight years. I felt old. Jacob mumbled a little, as if my stirring had bothered him, and then rolled onto his back and settled into the long, slow breaths of deep sleep.

I stared at his gorgeous profile and told myself, yet again, that I was actually sleeping with him and that he'd been the one to initiate it. Maybe I'd just been poised for a little good luck. It was about time.

I'd showered and made a pot of coffee by the time Jacob shuffled out of his bedroom in nothing but a pair of blue paisley boxers. "It's seven o'clock," he said, squinting. "Are you crazy?"

"They did treat me for schizophrenia for a couple of years before they figured out I was talking to real dead people," I replied. I'd meant it as a joke, but it'd come out kind of edgy.

Jacob looked me in the eye for a long moment before he sighed and poured himself a cup of coffee. "Well, you're not a kid in an institution anymore," he said. He took a sip of the coffee and winced, then scooped a few spoonfuls of sugar into it. "You're a cop. You can speed. You can carry a gun. You can tell other people what to do and they'd damn well better do it."

Maybe in his world. He was a big, strapping guy with a deep voice and a piercing gaze that could nail you to the wall. I just talked to dead people.

But Jacob didn't see me that way. Psychs were like shiny new toys to him, endlessly fascinating and inspiring. If he felt cheated that he only had access to five senses, he didn't let it slow him down much. And why should it if he could demand the services of two federally licensed Psychs and a suspended cop with the elusive gift of *sí-no*?

"Someone told Warwick I was talking to Gutierrez," I reminded him as he speed-dialed Carolyn.

"And?"

"And he said he'd suspend me if...."

"Carolyn? Hey. Let's get together at my place today for some brainstorming. No, you don't have to bring anything. Mmm hm. Yeah, I do have some ideas, but it'll be easier to just show you when you get here. Right. Bye bye."

I got Lisa's number from the Fifth Precinct and convinced her to take a cab over to Jacob's. She insisted that there wasn't much she could do without her gun and badge, but I reminded her that she'd been at the Blakewood scene and seen the victim with her own eyes. We'd just bat some ideas around, I told her. I hung up and looked at Jacob. He had that grin on. Okay, and maybe I was also a little curious about how far *si-no* could actually be taken.

The girls arrived at Jacob's around noon and we convened around a table full of salty Chinese take-out. "So you've played the *si-no* game most of your life," Carolyn said, "but haven't had any formal training."

Lisa nodded. I think Carolyn intimidated her. Heck, Carolyn intimidated me a little.

"We'll need to be careful how we phrase our reports," Carolyn said. "You're not officially part of this investigation at this time." She looked at me. "Unless you think you can convince Sergeant Warwick...?"

"Not a chance. I thought he was gonna have an aneurysm."

"Fine. Then we'll just need to be aware that anything Lisa says is unofficial. Nothing appears in the report. If her talents lead us to the murderer, fine. But we'll have to scrape together some kind of evidence that could've plausibly led us there besides the *si-no* game. Got it?"

"Carolyn can't simply lie," Jacob winked at her. "The downside to her talent."

Carolyn ignored him and consulted her notepad. "Let's establish some boundaries first." She fired off a series of questions about current events and other factual things to establish a baseline.

"Does Lawrence Avenue run North-South?"

"No."

"Do I have an aunt named Mabel?"

"Yes."

"Has Jacob ever owned a dog?"

"No."

Carolyn looked to Jacob, and he nodded. "Poor baby," she said, the corner of her mouth twitching. He smiled. Carolyn turned her attention back to Lisa. "Am

I happy?"

Lisa stared.

"Well?"

"I—I dunno."

"Too broad," Carolyn said, scribbling notes. "Do I like my job?"

"Y-yes."

"You just let me unnerve you—don't worry about it. Not everything can be answered yes or no. Sometimes it's both. Sometimes it's neither. And sometimes the question is just too vague."

It occurred to me that Carolyn would make a good Psych Coach. She was just so nonchalant about it all, and yet you could see she had all eight cylinders firing. Plus, she knew if you were lying. Okay, maybe that part was a little bit scary.

"All right. Let's look at the case. You understand you are here in an unofficial capacity."

"Yes."

"Good. Let's focus on the killer. Is the killer male?"

"Yes."

I thought about the anal penetration and blushed. Lisa knew I was with Jacob. And Carolyn? Jacob said he was out to her. So she probably knew, too, because if the subject had come up at all, it wasn't as if he could hedge. I blushed harder and drank some soda, tilting the huge cup back to hide my face.

"Is he Caucasian?"

"He…." Lisa stared off as if she had to search for the *sí-no*.

"Is he Latino?"

Lisa thought hard.

Carolyn scribbled some notes and then looked up. "Is he of mixed heritage?"

"No." Lisa looked as if she'd surprised herself. "No, he's not."

Carolyn tried a barrage of ethnicities: Greek, Lebanese, Egyptian, every Asian type she could think of, and on and on. Jacob and I chimed in too, but all of our guesses were definite "no"s.

After fifteen minutes of hunting, Carolyn held up her hand. "Let's move on," she said. "We'll wear her out if we continue in a nonproductive vein. She's a resource, not a suspect."

"Unofficially," Jacob said.

"Unofficially." Carolyn turned to face Lisa, her hands on her knees. "Let's look at his history. Has he killed more than two victims?"

"Yes."

"More than two in this city?"

"No."

"Is he intending to kill again?"

"Yes, I think."

"Too vague," I said. "Maybe he's crazy and he doesn't even realize he's killing them."

"Right," said Jacob. "He's so sexy they just die from the touch of his dick."

I felt my face flush so red at that one I had to hide it in the napkin, but Lisa went pale.

"Yes," she said quietly.

"You're kidding," said Jacob. "Yes?"

"There's something paranormal at the heart of this," Carolyn said, mostly to herself, as she jotted some more notes.

"Yes," said Lisa, and I shivered.

11

We rested awhile, turning on the news, which nobody watched, and then they grilled Lisa again. I could tell she was getting fatigued, but she's a tough girl and she was willing to keep going with it late into the night.

If we couldn't get an I.D. on the killer from the witnesses, Jacob reasoned, we'd just have to get a look at him ourselves. We narrowed our questions down from, "Is he in the city?" to "Is he east of...?" "Is he north of...?" "Is he on this block?" "Is he in this building?" "This apartment?"

I think even Lisa was amazed at the power of the *sí-no* in the hands of a pair of relentless questioners.

"Does he live in this apartment?" Carolyn asked.

"No."

"Is he alone?"

"No."

Jacob stood up. "I think we'd better pay Casanova a visit. Right now. You go home," he told Lisa. "No gun, no badge—it's safer for you that way." He turned to me. "You riding with us?"

The image of me riding in the back seat like a little kid returned. "I'll...uh... take my car."

Carolyn verified the address with me and I nodded. "Let's go," he said, and we were off.

I turned off the GPS and drove there myself. We headed for the northern edge of Boystown again, not two blocks from the record store where the clerk I'd dated used to work. I wanted Maurice. Or Lisa. Or even to be sitting in that damn back seat. I turned the GPS back on just to have a little company, though since I hadn't entered a destination, its tasteful British voice was silent.

An SUV pulled away from the curb right next door to the apartment building and I pulled in, glanced around, and found Jacob parking across the street. We met up at the gate.

This gate actually locked, unlike mine, but Jacob ran a pocketknife down the edge and it popped right open. We trooped across the courtyard to the far right vestibule, and Jacob studied the apartment numbers by the beam of his penlight. "Here's the one," he said, tapping on the name "J. Barlow." "Get one of the neighbors to let us in."

Carolyn glanced up to see which windows were lit. "They're less likely to hide from her," Jacob explained. "Strangers don't realize that she's the one they need to be afraid of, not me."

"Ha ha," she said dryly, then pushed a button. A woman's voice said "hello." "Official police business, ma'am. Please buzz us in."

A crackle that sounded kind of like, "...*bzzt*...finally here...called..." came through the speakers and the inner door clicked open. Music with a heavy, thudding beat flooded out.

We jogged up to the second floor and stopped. Someone's stereo blared so loud that I could feel the vibration through the soles of my shoes. Carolyn gestured to me and I bent so she could talk in my ear, not that I thought the suspect would've heard her if she'd shouted aloud. "Loud music—like the first victim."

And maybe the second, for all we knew. The other half of Ryan Carson's duplex had been empty that weekend. That's why it'd taken so long to discover his body.

Jacob scowled at the unmarked doors. We were looking for apartment 2a. But there were three doors to choose from. Was 'a' on the far left or the far right? I touched one door, then another, but they were both rattling equally from the cranked up stereo. Jacob gestured for Carolyn to go with me, then pulled out his gun and approached the left-hand door—the most likely door, in my mind, if the lettering system went left to right like a western alphabet.

Of course, the right-hand door was closer to the stairs, and would be the first door you'd approach. I drew my gun and wished Maurice was there. He wasn't very quick, but he was accurate.

Jacob's hand was on his doorknob and he watched me to make sure I'd do the same. I put my hand on mine and felt the vibration carry right through it. Jacob nodded and we both tried our doors at once. Mine opened. I didn't have time to see if his did or not.

I held my gun at my side, camouflaged by my body. There was no need for the whole, "Police! Freeze!" business since we were acting out a routine noise call, but the thought of coming face to face with the mystery man gave me the creeps.

Carolyn had her gun out, pointed to the floor. She edged to the right, my usual position, so I went left. I passed by the stereo and saw it was on. Framed photos on top had fallen over. I swallowed. I'd picked the magic door—lucky me.

I wished I could turn the damn music down. The beat of generic technopop made my fillings rattle. But at least it hid the sound of our entry and would give us a chance to get a look at whatever we were up against.

Carolyn ducked into a doorway then came out signaling clear. We made our way through a sparsely furnished dining room. I glanced into the kitchen—empty. She checked a bathroom. There was one room at the end of the hall, the door open a few inches with yellow light shining through the gap.

Carolyn held my glance for a moment and then nodded. The bedroom. It was the only thing left. I nodded back and we burst in together, both our weapons drawn.

It was like a bad porno, only I was there, front and center. A dozen candles ringed the bed, lighting the room in a warm, inviting glow. The pair on the bed were kissing while they fucked, and the muscles of the top's buttocks flexed as he pushed in. The bottom was a tanned guy who clearly worked out. He lay back on the bed with his feet slung over his lover's shoulders. The guy on top was tattooed and sinewy, his amber hair cut in a shag like an early-70's glam rocker.

Carolyn stepped back, but I just stared. The tattoos were so strange, colors and whorls, and they seemed to undulate as the man moved, always moving, caressing, thrusting.

He couldn't have heard us over the music. Couldn't have seen us with his eyes closed. Yet somehow I could tell he knew we were there. He raised his head to look, breaking the kiss, and that's when I knew for sure that he was our killer.

Something stretched between his mouth and his lover's. It was thick, viscous, and thinner in the center than either end, like the tanned guy was full of syrup and the tattooed guy was sucking it out. It quivered there between them, glistening and slimy, and then it grew so thin in the middle that it snapped.

I know it was probably there just a nanosecond. But I saw what I saw. When this gelatinous funk snapped back toward the guy on the bed, there was a face in it, a stretched-out, human face. And it looked like it was screaming.

Then I staggered back, sickened by the sight of that ooze, but Carolyn was at my side with her gun leveled at the tattooed guy. "Freeze," she shouted, her voice hardly audible over the music. "Police!"

He cocked his head and looked at her as if she were the most peculiar specimen, and then he looked back at me, and somehow, into me. He opened his mouth.

I didn't want to know what was in there. I tried to look away, but the strength had leeched right out of me. I didn't have enough left to even avert my eyes. I'd rather see anything but that sickening maw. But there it was, filling my vision, opening wide.

He was displaying himself to me, I think. Showing me that inside him was nothing, an absolute void. Pitch black where teeth and tongue and throat should have been. Flat black and featureless, like a poorly doctored photo. Nothingness had never been so scary.

And then he screamed.

At least, that's the best way I can describe it. It was more like the shriek of a train trying to brake, hitting too many discordant, screeching pitches all at once. Horribly loud, even over the blare of the music, loud enough that it hurt, badly, and I shrank back and covered my ears.

I saw the dresser mirror beside me shatter, rather than hearing it. It was almost beautiful, like snow falling. A thousand shards glittering as they rained against my side.

Then the windowpane blew out, and gauzy curtains fluttered through with the force of the blast, like a gale had whipped up inside the room and sent them streaming toward the outdoors.

The guy with nothing inside him stretched, very quickly, until he was more of a rubbery line than a person. And he was out the window and gone before I could fully register how he'd even moved.

The beat of the music continued to pound through the soles of my feet, but I realized I couldn't hear it. My ears were still ringing from the sound of that metallic shriek the killer had made before he'd disappeared.

Carolyn was beside me, tugging at the sleeve of my sportcoat, but I was just too stunned to acknowledge her. Then she was gone and the music stopped reverberating, and the quality of the sonic aftershock changed somewhat in my own hearing. And then Jacob was there, shaking me by the shoulders, hard. "Vic," his mouth said, judging by the shape of it. "Vic."

I tried to focus on him. I think he was clutching me so tightly he might've actually been hurting me, but I didn't really care. Then Carolyn dragged him toward the bed and he left me there, leaning back against the closet door, standing amidst a spray of broken mirror.

12

The sun was up by the time I was coherent enough to talk to Jacob. The paramedics said I was in shock. Jacob had done CPR on the tanned guy, one James Barlow, until the paramedics arrived, but it had been no use. James was victim number three—in our city, at any rate.

We lingered in Barlow's courtyard, well away from the plainclothes officers and the techs who were starting to swarm the scene. "I couldn't hear anything over that music," Carolyn said. "But Vic held his head like he was getting split in two."

"All right," Jacob said. He pulled out his notepad. "So what did you see?"

"Well," Carolyn said, "the men were…together. Having intercourse. And the man, um…well, the killer, looked at us and opened his mouth, like he was yawning. And then the mirror and the window shattered and he was gone."

Jacob wrote very quickly. "Okay. But what did the killer look like?"

"Caucasian. About forty-five. Short hair, salt and pepper. Brown eyes."

Jacob frowned. "That's nothing like the other descriptions." He turned to me. "Is that how he looked to you?"

I shook my head. "Thirty, maybe less. Tattoos." I felt myself color. "Actually, I thought he looked like a young David Bowie."

Carolyn looked away. "George Clooney," she said.

Jacob's eyes narrowed as he considered Carolyn. "You got a thing for George Clooney?"

Carolyn scowled at Jacob as if he was a jerk for even asking. "Don't tease me."

"I'm not. I have a theory, and I know you can't lie to me if I ask you something directly. So. Do you?"

"I think he's attractive, yes."

Jacob looked at me. "David Bowie fan?" He wasn't making light of it, not in the least, but it still felt too personal to divulge that Bowie'd been my biggest masturbatory fantasy until I discovered flesh-and-blood boys who were willing to experiment with me.

I thought of making a snide remark anyway, but I figured if Carolyn could admit her crush, I could admit mine. "What she said," I echoed.

At least Jacob gave me the courtesy of not verifying my truthfulness by double-checking it with Carolyn.

"So our killer looks different to every person who sees him, tripping some part of the witness' neurological wiring and showing him or her the image of someone they consider to be extremely attractive," said Jacob.

Carolyn considered. "And so a majority of people are going to see the killer as someone of their own ethnicity. But different ages, different particulars. We haven't asked any of the witnesses whether or not they thought the suspect was attractive. But it might be a promising line of questioning to pursue."

Jacob stifled a yawn. "We've been at this more than twenty-four hours straight. I suggest we get some sleep and regroup at the Twelfth around two. That sound good to everybody?"

Carolyn was halfway to her car before I'd even had the chance to agree. Jacob blocked me with his body before I could follow. "Stay with me," he said, so quiet I almost couldn't hear him over the residual ringing in my ears. Or maybe it was my brain.

Relief washed over me, but it drained away as I realized that I really didn't want Jacob to see me that way—spooked by some killer psychically disguised as David Bowie who sucked souls out of men while he fucked them. Because that was the only thing that syrupy stuff could've been. A soul.

And the killer'd gotten too much of it before we'd arrived, and now James Barlow was on his way to the Coroner's.

"I really need to change my clothes," I said, squeezing past Jacob as I tried to recall where I'd parked.

Jacob fell into step beside me with a couple of long strides. "Then stop at your place first and then come over. You don't look so good."

I neglected to say that I had to buy a jacket, actually, since both of mine had doubled as splatter guards in the past two days. Damn the police department's dress code.

I found where I'd parked and we approached the spot. "Two o'clock," I told him, got into my car, and shut the door. I wouldn't say he looked hurt standing there beside the car while the morning commuter traffic flowed behind him. But his self-assured grin was nowhere in sight, either.

I pulled into the stream of traffic and gave the finger to some jagoff who honked at me. I'd wanted to stay with Jacob. In fact, I was kind of blown away that he'd even asked. But I felt like what I'd seen earlier had soiled me somehow, and taken a lot of the parlor-game fun out of my talent. And if Jacob figured that out, I'd go from being creepy and fun to just plain old creepy in his eyes.

I wasted a good twenty minutes getting to SaverPlus, only to find it didn't open until ten, and it was barely nine. Not having another hour to waste, I headed home and took a shower. I wish I could say it was a long one, but there just wasn't time.

And then I got into bed and closed my eyes. I'd been kinda scared that I might keep seeing that black, empty mouth again, the hole that led to nothing. But I could summon up images of lake skylines and whatnot to keep it at bay.

The ringing in my ears was another thing entirely. I got back up and swabbed them out with Q-Tips, which changed nothing. I found a pair of earplugs in the back of a drawer and put them in. The ringing changed in pitch, but also seemed to intensify. Finally, I turned on the radio, desperately seeking something other than asinine morning DJ banter. I found a Spanish language station, which seemed okay at first, if a little chipper and bouncy. But then a commercial came on and it was so jarring it nearly blew me out of my bed.

Finally, I flipped the dial until nothing but garbled noise came through, popped a Seconal, and passed out.

Two o'clock was ancient history by the time I woke up—two o'clock in the afternoon, at least. It'd be two a.m. in about fifteen minutes. Shit.

I checked my cell phone for messages. There were only a couple, both from Jacob. From two-thirty: "Vic. Your input would be helpful on this report—but if you can't make it until tomorrow morning, that'd be fine, considering the shock. I let both of our Sergeants know what the paramedics said. We've got Archives researching to try to figure out what this thing is, based on Carolyn's statement. Give me a call." He left his home number.

And then, from nine: "It's me. Look, I hope I wasn't out of line this morning. I just need to know that you're okay. Call me."

I decided it wouldn't be worth waking Jacob up just to tell him I'd overslept, so I texted him a note that said "SRY I MISSED U, WERE OKAY" It occurred to me that "we're" looked more like "were," but I was too lazy to find the apostrophe. I wondered briefly if SaverPlus was open at two a.m., and then considered that perhaps the shock hadn't worn off yet. My ears still rang, but just a little, and I turned on the white plastic 9-inch TV in the living room to drown it out. Infomercials.

Aside from the obvious concern in Jacob's voice, the thing that stuck with me most was the idea that he and Carolyn thought they could put a name to this thing, this seductive souleater with a big, empty void inside him. And what if they could? What if it was actually some sort of known entity—and what if there was some sort of method or charm we could use to stop it?

Each apartment unit in my building had a storage locker in the basement, behind the coin-operated washing machines. I kept my textbooks from Camp Hell down there. I figured I might need them someday, though I didn't want the evil I associated with them in my living space 24/7.

As I dug the basement key out of my kitchen junk drawer, it occurred to me that maybe I could wash the marinara off my new jacket. It was from SaverPlus, after all. Maybe it was made out of indestructible, machine-washable polyester. I checked the label. Wool blend. Dry clean only. I wondered how bad it'd be if I machine-washed it anyway. And then I realized that since I didn't own an iron, it probably wouldn't do me any good to even try.

I felt naked venturing down into the basement without a load of laundry to protect me. The narrow, dark stairs were a lot creepier at 3 a.m. than I'd imagined.

I stepped carefully to avoid pissing off whoever else lived in the building and made my way down into the cellar. The part that housed the furnace and hot water heaters was closed off with some newish looking drywall, but the exterior walls were nasty, old limestone slabs with crumbling mortar and greenish mildew between. A bare 75-watt bulb shone scant inches from the top of my head, but the unfinished wooden floor joists above it were so dark that they seemed to eat the light. Kind of like the mouth of a certain creature whom I was absolutely not going to think about until I was safe and sound in my white apartment with every single light turned on.

A gurgle sounded to the right of me and my glance snapped downward. I flinched back, thinking, "Rat!" But the thing that had caught my attention was barely visible, faint bluish lines that I had to squint to make out against a dark concrete floor.

And then it came together all at once. A spectral baby, fists flailing, with an umbilical cord still attached.

Jesus. Someone'd left a newborn to die down here. It could've been a month ago, it could've been half a century ago. I didn't care. Humankind just sucked. If I had a bottle of Auracel in my hand I would've downed the whole thing in hopes of never seeing another fucking revenant.

I stepped over the baby's ghost and unlocked my storage unit, too disgusted to try to keep quiet any longer. I let the metal door bang open and yanked out an old nylon gym bag. How many times had I stepped over that damn baby and never seen it? It'd probably died somewhere around 3 a.m. and that's when its presence was the strongest. Damn it all to hell. I was gonna have to start using a laundry service.

I stomped back up toward the first floor. A door swung open on the landing and a guy in a robe came out to see what all the noise was about. He stepped into my path, but then recoiled and shut his door. I guess I must've looked pretty pissed off.

Once I was back in my apartment, I turned on every damn light and left the TV going, tuned to a station I don't receive so that it played nothing but a staticky white glow.

I've never been booksmart, and I didn't pay much attention to what they tried to teach me at Camp Hell unless it brought about immediate relief. And nothing had really done that except pharmaceuticals. But I remembered enough, if I pressed myself, to recall that there was a section on paranormal creatures in one of my texts.

Vampires were the first thing that came to mind, but the two main categories I found were blood fetishists and psychic vampires. Since there'd been no blood at any of the scenes, maybe our killer was a psychic vampire, and that stuff I'd seen stretching between him and the victim was some kind of ectoplasm. I followed that line of thinking, about how the vampire was charismatic and seductive, and if he or she sapped a victim long enough, the drained person would eventually weaken and die.

Except that didn't make sense. The book said they'd die, not be utterly destroyed. It was a gradual thing, not the result of a one-night stand. And the thing we were hunting didn't just drain people of energy. It ate their very essence.

My eyes felt sandy. I closed the book and rubbed them, which made them feel worse, and went into the bathroom to see if I had any eye drops. I stopped in front of the mirror and stared hard, making sure the guy looking back was actually me.

Sure, my hair was a mess, as usual, and I was working on three days' worth of stubble. But my face itself was a wreck. Tiny red lines crosshatched my cheek, some crusted with dried blood, others just there, bled out. And my eyes were something from a bad horror flick, the whites all red with burst blood vessels. I'd always gotten some attention for my frost blue eyes, especially since they were set off by my black hair. But the red…it was a whole new look for me. Jacob had invited me over looking like this? Boy. He really did like his men creepy.

That'd teach me to let mirrors explode on me. But my eyes—crap, that thing must've burst the blood vessels in my eyes with his scream. I shuddered and twisted open the eye drops, only to discover they had evaporated, leaving nothing but a tiny, plastic bottle crusted around the tip with salt.

I watched the sun come up, then went to the drug store and grabbed some eye drops and sunglasses. After that I stopped off at the cleaner's, only to determine that they kept items no longer than 90 days. I left them to deal with the marinara sauce, and then sat in the parking lot of SaverPlus until they opened.

I bought two sportcoats. Both black. Tore the tags off and threw one in my trunk, put the other one on.

Everything I needed to do had taken a lot longer than I'd thought it would, so I figured I'd better let Jacob know I was on my way. I peered over my sunglasses into my rearview mirror while I waited for him to pick up the phone. The part of my eyes that was supposed to be white was blood-crimson, even more hideous in natural light than it'd looked in my bathroom. No wonder Jacob had sounded worried.

I got Jacob's voicemail. "Hi," I said. "I'm running a little late this morning, but I'll meet you over at the Twelfth. Unless that's not where you're gonna be. In that case, call me." Boy, was I slick or what?

As I pulled up alongside the Twelfth, I realized that I could've called Jacob earlier instead of sitting outside SaverPlus twiddling my thumbs. I could've called Lisa, too, and filled her in. Sonofabitch, why was my brain such a sieve?

I walked out and shifted my jacket, thinking that either I'd grabbed a different style or accidentally taken a 42. At least the sleeves were long enough. As I blew by the front desk, one of the plainclothes officers peeled out of his regular spot to intercept me. "Detective Bayne?"

I stopped and turned, and wished I didn't feel the need to wear my cheap new sunglasses inside. Between them and the overlarge jacket, the cop probably thought he was having an 80's flashback. "Yeah?"

"Sergeant Warwick called. He wants to see you at the Fifth Precinct."

I felt myself sag inside. I used to coexist peacefully with Warwick, but lately everything he said to me made me cringe. Or maybe it'd been Maurice who'd actually gotten along with him all these years.

"Okay. I'll just touch base with Detective Marks...."

"He's not here. I think you really need to see Sergeant Warwick."

My blood curdled in my veins as I wondered if something had happened to Jacob. I hopped in my car and slapped the police light on the roof, doing ninety all the way to the Fifth Precinct. I barreled through the front doors, up the stairs, past Betty's desk and into Warwick's office.

He stood up and glared at me. "What's with the sunglasses?" he demanded. "Are you on drugs?"

I stopped and stared, flabbergasted by his question, but too scared to challenge it. "Where are my partners?" I asked him. "Have you heard from them?"

"Marks and Brinkman are at the Commissioner's office, giving their reports about the murder scene you discovered last night."

"Oh," I said, and my heartbeat slowed. "Okay. Good."

"But they're not your partners anymore."

"What?"

"You're off the case. In fact, you're suspended." He tapped on the desk with one thick, callused finger. "Your badge and your gun."

"Suspended? What for?"

"I warned you not to leak information to Gutierrez—and who did you run to the second you left my office?"

I gaped at Warwick, wondering who could've possibly told him we'd gone to Gutierrez for help. Could he have a wire tap? Someone tailing her? Wouldn't he need a court order for any of that?

Whatever he had on me, I had no idea how to talk around it. I put my badge and my gun on his desk, thinking that I'd always imagined it would feel worse to give them up. It felt like nothing, like paying for the sunglasses or asking the pharmacist about eyedrops.

It felt mundane.

"And just so you don't get any bright ideas, Gutierrez is in police custody."

"You arrested her?" My voice cracked.

"She hasn't been charged with anything...yet. But the two of you are through playing psychic telephone."

"What the...? You can't just hold her. She can sue you. I hope she does."

"And then she and I can discuss the consequences of all those tests she cheated on."

Shit. I wished I was up on my legal rights, but I'd never even considered that I might be suspended. Never even known anyone who was.

Warwick sat down and took my badge in his palm. I thought maybe he looked regretful as he stared down at it, but what did I know? My eyes hurt. "Go home and get some rest, Bayne. You look like shit. Let Marks handle it."

"I need to give my statement," I said, grasping for some way to keep hold of the investigation. "I haven't given my statement."

"I'll tell Marks. But for now, Vic, just go."

13

I was glad that voicemail doesn't register hang-ups, because then Jacob would know that I called him approximately every ten minutes, although I only left him one message where I stammered something about being really sorry that I wasn't at the Twelfth like I'd said I would be, and that my text message was supposed to say "we're" and not "were," but that I was feeling much better and I really wanted to see him. I somehow managed to keep from apologizing for even being born. Barely.

As I thumbed through my Camp Hell textbooks yet again, I wished that I'd made a friend or two there, someone I could call and ask, just theoretically, what kind of supernatural beastie sucks out people's souls while they screw.

And then it hit me. A succubus.

I flipped my book open to the index and found a half dozen references to it.

Succubus: Lascivious female demon who takes the form of a comely young lady;

said to possess mortal men as they sleep and to sup on their essences. According to one

legend the succubus and her male counterpart, the incubus, were fallen angels.

Sup on their essences? I glanced at the date of the text and found it was written in 1964. Queer. And not in the way I like. None of the other passages were particularly enlightening, either.

So it was possible we were dealing with...what? A gay incubus, or a male succubus? Maybe. If I could just get in touch with the archivists at the Twelfth, I could give them my impressions. They had access to stuff that was written sometime after the dark ages, unlike me. Even databases. They'd know the latest research on entities that used to be called demons.

Because there had to be some sort of modern take on the demon. Red men with pointy ears and pitchforks: unlikely. Powerful psychic beasties that could pop all the blood vessels in your eyes by hitting the right note? Well, we had to call it by some name, and incubus was as good as any.

But I was off the case. The archivists at the Twelfth probably couldn't even talk to me. I glanced up at the clock. It was nearing seven p.m. They would've gone home by now anyway, I told myself. And I called Jacob's cell phone again.

"Marks."

"Oh! It's uh…you picked up."

"Hold on." I heard him cover the phone with his palm and excuse himself. A moment later, he was back. "Thank God, Vic. Are you okay?"

"I'm fine. But Warwick took me off the case."

Jacob's voice was an urgent whisper. "It came down from the Police Commissioner. They've been going over my statement with a fine-toothed comb all day. It's out of the bag that we used a psychic without a federal license to locate the crime scene, but I think that since we caught the guy in the act, they're gonna find a way to let it slide."

"But what about Gutierrez? Warwick said she was in custody."

Jacob sighed. "I can't talk now—this place is crawling with the Commissioner's elite officers. Meet me where we had dinner on Tuesday and I'll fill you in. Same time."

"Okay. But, Jacob…?"

"Gotta go. See you then."

In an attempt to clean up, I went into the bathroom and started shaving. The shaving cream stung as I smoothed it on, and even though I opened a new razor, it seemed to keep catching on scabs and hunks of dried blood as I dragged it over my cheeks. By the time I was through, I came to the realization that the stubble would've looked much better. And then I stuck a dozen little bits of toilet paper to my face. I wondered if SaverPlus sold welding masks.

I had half an hour to kill, so I got on the phone with the Fifth and tried to call around and find someone who could tell me where they were holding Gutierrez. An older cop who worked the night desk, one of Maurice's friends, told me she wasn't there—but that was as much as he knew.

Too bad I didn't have a touch of the *sí-no* or I would've tracked her down myself. But what did I have? I was a fifth-level medium. That was almost as high as you could go. There were a few level-6s scattered around and a single level-7, an old lady in France who could actually command spirits. But she'd died in her sleep a couple of years back and become one of those spirits herself.

So I could hear, and sometimes see, the dead. And they seemed to sense it and be sure they talked my ear off. Thing was, they never knew shit.

I needed to get going to make it to the restaurant by eight, so I slipped into the goofy new blazer and set out. The GPS managed to lead me, yet again, into the worst snarl of traffic I'd seen since the time I was late for a root canal. Eventually, I crept by an accident. A couple of glowing blue spirits gawked from the side of the road, but since they were dressed like they'd come right out of an off-Broadway production of Grease, I figured they weren't a result of the accident that they were rubbernecking.

I turned down an alley, out onto a main thoroughfare and picked up some real speed. Maybe Jacob would know where Gutierrez was. He'd help me get her out, or at least get me in there to talk to her, tell her it was gonna be okay.

I got to the restaurant ten minutes late, a miracle considering traffic, and didn't spot him anywhere. For once I wasn't the latest one. The maitre d', a thin Midwestern guy with steely gray hair, seated me. I wolfed down a bread stick, and then another, and then I realized that I hadn't eaten anything yet that day.

Eight twenty and still no Jacob. I ordered an iced tea. I flipped open my phone and tried his number, just to gauge when he'd get there. Maybe I could start with an appetizer. Maybe I could even finish it before he got there and order another one like I hadn't just inhaled one by myself. I'd have to pick up the check then, but fair is fair.

His cell went directly to voicemail. "Hey, Jacob. It's Vic. Let me know how long you're gonna be. I might need to start without you. Bye."

I ordered some soup—nothing that would stain my blazer too obviously—and scarfed down half the bowl. Jacob was probably talking to his sergeant, or maybe to Carolyn. Had her statement been taken separately from his? Likely, since the three of us had come up looking fishy. In retrospect, I was glad I'd overslept.

The iced tea caught up with me, and I flagged the maitre d' over so that he could tell Jacob I was there, in case he showed up while I was in the bathroom, which Murphy's Law said he would. "White male, olive complexion, six two or three, well built, black hair, brown eyes, short goatee."

The maitre d' frowned in thought. "One moment," he said, and flipped open his reservation log. "Jacob Marks. He was here earlier, sir. He left."

"Shit! Uh, sorry. How long ago?"

"Shortly before you arrived."

"Did he leave a message for me?"

The maitre d' shook his head. "I'm very sorry." He turned to greet some new customers that had walked through the door, but I caught him by the sleeve.

"Did it seem urgent?" I asked him. "Was he on his phone, in a hurry?"

"I'm sorry," he repeated, and turned toward the customers.

I grabbed him more forcefully and wished to God I had my badge. "Look. I'm a cop, and this is police business. What else can you tell me?"

The maitre d's eyes showed white all around. "He left with someone. A young man."

"What did he look like? Describe him."

"I...I don't know."

"Height, weight, race, hair color."

"Thin. Athletic. Blonde. He looked a little bit like Brad Pitt, actually."

Or maybe he looked an awful lot like Brad Pitt. And George Clooney and David Bowie. I hardly remembered letting go of the maitre d'. I was back in my car with the flashing light on the roof and absolutely no idea where I was headed.

I fishtailed into traffic and tried to think. Every crime had happened at the victim's house. And there'd been one every night, or every other. The incubus got around.

I swerved down a side street and headed toward Jacob's. I shut the GPS off and then flipped open my phone. "Information? Connect me to Carolyn Brinkman." Electronic noises came through as I begged that her home number was listed. "Douglas and Carolyn Brinkman," the computer voice said after an excruciating pause. "To connect, press or say one, now."

"One," I barked, and after some more weird, muted digital sounds, Carolyn's phone started to ring. "Thank God," I said. "Pick up, pick up, pick up."

Instead, a man answered. "Hello?"

I swerved around an overturned shopping cart that was laying in the road for no apparent reason. "Carolyn—I need to speak to Carolyn."

"Who is this?"

"Detective Victor Bayne. It's an emergency."

"Look, Mister Bayne, I know things look bleak, but you've got to see it from Carolyn's point of view. She's sorry about what happened, but it wasn't her fault. The poor woman can't lie."

"What? Yeah, I know about her talent. But I've gotta talk to her. It's about Jacob."

"She's finally calmed down enough to get some sleep, and she's on enough Neurozamine to obliterate The Amazing Kreskin, so she's not going anywhere tonight."

Jesus H. Christ on a bike. Coolhand Carolyn had doped out on us. Shit. That was usually my department. Jacob had told me on our first day together that Carolyn never took meds. I assume she hadn't been lying to him, considering Carolyn's double-edged talent.

"Look...ah, I get it. I'm a Psych, too."

Her husband sighed. "Then you know how hard it is. I'm sorry, Detective. But this business with Jacob will have to wait until tomorrow."

"Can I at least come and get her gun?" I asked. But the line was already dead.

You'd think I would've had some reason to buy a gun other than my service weapon during the last twelve, fifteen years. Then again, you'd think I owned more than one or two sportcoats, too. Shit.

But I knew someone who did have a gun, someone I'd been dying to see. I hit memory dial one, Maurice's cell phone.

"Hallo." A crowd noise swelled around Maurice, and I tried to imagine him among a sea of humanity, but couldn't place where he might be.

"Where are you?"

"Fort Lauderdale. Don't you remember? I told you on Sunday. I'm at the casino."

Shit. Oh shit. No. He couldn't be in Florida. I needed him here.

"Good thing you ain't a precog or I wouldn't even be able to talk to you in here. Nichelle just won five thousand nickels on a slot machine. You believe that? That's only two hundred fifty bucks, though. You say five thousand nickels, it sound like some huge jackpot."

The first vacation Maurice has been on since his fucking honeymoon and I call him, hardly able to restrain myself from begging him to hop the next flight home. What good would it do, other than spoiling his good time? It wasn't as if he could get back here any sooner than tomorrow morning. And by then it'd be too late.

I tapped my brake as I flew through a stop sign. "Look for a slot machine with a…a star," I said, pulling a psychic prediction out of my ass even though Maurice and I both knew I was about as precognitive as he was. "And don't let anyone know I told you."

"A star, huh?" Tinny ringing, jingling noises filtered through the murmur of the crowd. "You're all right, Bayne."

"Gotta go," I said, and hung up before Maurice could figure out how stressed out I was. The fact that he could barely hear me had worked to my advantage, but I wasn't gonna push it.

How much of a lead did Jacob and the incubus have on me? Maybe half an hour, but maybe less. They were probably driving like normal humans, not like me. I turned onto Jacob's street and swung into a spot by a hydrant, bumped the car in front of me and left the rear end of my car sticking out at an angle as I ran toward Jacob's condo building for all I was worth.

As I wrenched the vestibule's outer door open, a low, thudding vibration tickled the base of my skull.

Technopop.

14

I nearly rang Jacob's doorbell and then realized he might not be able to answer. I rang every neighbor's bell instead. "Police," I shouted to the first one who answered. "I'm here about the noise complaint."

They buzzed me right in.

Some little part of me must've been holding on to the hope that Jacob wasn't really with the incubus. That all the clues I was seeing—that he'd left the restaurant with Brad Pitt, that the same inane electronic beat buzzed through the floorboards of his condo and out into the hall—actually added up to something else. But when I put my hand on his doorknob and the door swung open, unlocked, my stomach clenched up and I felt numb all over. Because the unlocked door was just like every other scene.

I took in the entryway, the broad living room and the archway leading to the kitchen in one glance. Jacob's jacket was in a pile on the sofa, and his holster lay on top of it.

I grabbed his gun.

The stereo was right there. I could've turned it off and bought myself some space to think. The incubus probably already knew I was there, or would know before I had a chance to blow it away. But something about the music seemed inevitable, like I needed that throb to shift myself into the incubus' plane well enough to kill it.

They'd be in the bedroom. Because that's where all the other victims had been. I ran full-tilt toward the bedroom door, because if there even was a remote chance that I hadn't yet been detected, that damn music covered the sound of my approach. I held the gun at face level—none of that vertical-beside-the-head stuff you see on TV. That fucker took Jacob, and I was gonna nail him right between the eyes.

I hoped they weren't too intertwined. I'm not all that good of a shot.

I rounded the corner and—thank whatever powers there are to thank—the incubus was in the midst of peeling off Jacob's shirt. He himself was still fully clothed. Jacob wasn't moving on his own, but if the incubus hadn't gotten to third base with him yet, I still had hope.

If it was possible, the creature looked even more like David Bowie tonight, as if my brain had had a chance to peg him into some sort of category and was going all the way in reassuring itself that he fit. He was Ziggy Stardust, down to the glittery spandex outfit and the lightning bolt on the cheek.

"Freeze," I said, in a voice that would've sounded firm and clear in a normal situation. The music totally covered it, but I had a feeling the incubus could filter things like that out. "Police."

He looked up at me and started a little. Maybe he hadn't known I was there. Maybe I could've gotten right on top of him and squeezed off a few rounds before he'd been able to turn into spaghetti and fly out the window. Shit.

With just his head turned toward me, he started to open that black, empty mouth of his. I pulled the trigger. The shot sounded like a pathetic snap that hardly carried over the blaring music. I hit him...I think. I didn't see any blood, any bullet holes in either him or the wall, but he thought better of pulling that sonic scream crap on me again and turned to face me fully.

Jacob remained limp on the bed. I didn't have time to watch him and see if his chest would rise and fall, but I told myself he was just asleep—some kind of psychic trick the incubus had managed. Because the texts said that incubi struck while their victims were asleep, and damn it, something in that worthless book had to be true.

The incubus saw me glance at Jacob and smiled. His lips were closed, stretched over the blackness even more thinly. He reached toward Jacob. I squeezed off another round, aimed at his arm. A black bullet hole appeared in the wall behind him.

Ziggy Stardust thought that was funny. He stretched his arm closer to Jacob, going in slow motion to savor my reaction to it all the longer.

I was getting nowhere fast with the gun. I didn't fling it aside or anything melodramatic like that. Heck, I might still need it. But I used another weapon that I supposedly had in my arsenal, at least according to Camp Hell.

I shot a blue bubble of protection from a space between my eyes and above, a little outside my physical body. Third eye, pineal gland, seventh chakra, it's all the same. When you're psychic, it's where all your weird shit lives.

The bubble was so strong I actually saw it. Maybe nobody else would've, but I saw it in the same way I'd seen the dead baby in my basement or the spirits hovering around the accident. It sealed Jacob up tight. I let go of it, and it stayed there.

Take that.

The incubus saw it, too. He poked at the bubble and it stretched a little, but held. He looked back at me, his eyebrowless forehead hitched in the middle to show me his displeasure. He grabbed at Jacob more forcefully, but his hand glanced off the bubble.

I knew what I needed to do. Send him toward the light. I took a deep breath and then shot a sphere of light out toward him. It encircled him like a psychic spotlight, glowing beautiful and pure.

He touched it, and it shattered.

He smiled, showing Bowie-esque teeth a little square and crooked, but I could still feel the blackness lurking there behind them. "Aren't you just a breath of fresh air?" he said in a melodious English accent, his voice carrying effortlessly over the grinding cacophony of the electropop. "And what's that little trick you just tried to pull?"

I leveled the gun at his face.

"Now, now. Why so jumpy? I just want to talk. There's no harm in talking, is there?"

Probably. I didn't give him the satisfaction of a reply.

Instead, I made another white bubble, and I imagined it was a hundred times stronger, swirling with layer upon layer of psychic energy, impenetrable. And I flung it.

It engulfed him, pearlescent white whirling around him like a cloud cover. It held for a moment. And then it shattered.

"How did you do that?" it asked. "You're mortal. I can smell your soul. Come on," he coaxed, easing forward, "Let me get a better look at you."

I backed up a step. That was a good white bubble, a damn good one, and yet the incubus was just too strong for it. It was a stupid idea anyway, trying to scare off a demon by putting him in a bubble like Glenda the Good Witch. What I needed was a house to drop on him.

He took a dainty step forward, then another. "You don't need to be afraid," he said. "We'll just get to know each other a little better. I can make you feel very, very good. You're such a fascinating chap—I promise I won't kiss you until you grow tiresome."

He was on me now, his pale, slender hand reaching toward me. I didn't know how I'd respond to physical contact with him, since it was possible he'd trip some psychic synapse in me, maybe short me out. "Your pickup lines need a lot of work," I said, and then I pulled an image from the cop portion of my brain. I imagined something black, thick and suffocating, a shape that was man-sized, yet vague and featureless. I wrapped him up in a psychic body bag and zipped it up tight. And then I imagined it was totally lined with mirrors and sent that idea blasting toward him.

He just stood there for a second while I waited for him to shatter my shield. He flexed and wriggled, but my body bag stayed solid. I poured more energy into it, imagining the mirrors inside showing him a hundred thousand reflections of himself, except maybe there really wasn't anything to see, only blackness. He let his sonic scream rip, and the bag muffled it and made it even more shrill and ugly, psychic feedback. And I poured strength into the body bag until I started getting lightheaded.

And then I emptied the whole clip into it.

15

There was no body to recover, just a bunch of stringy slime—which analysis found to be inconsistent with human remains. And though I'd left twenty bullet casings scattered in an arc around my feet, only a single bullet was recovered, the one I'd aimed at the incubus' arm. That one had lodged in Jacob's bedroom wall.

Jacob's condo was now a crime scene. I'd invited him to stay with me and he'd accepted, though he was still too groggy from the incubus' sleep-whammy to shuttle me to and from the eye doctor's. I'd been about to call another cab for my trip home when Lisa called my cell phone and offered to pick me up.

Lisa waited right outside the clinic, idling in a little red hatchback. She'd walked right out of lockup and bought herself a used car. Not quite the reaction I would've had to incarceration, though she'd had the *sí-no* to keep her company, while I would've gotten a dead serial killer hanging by his shoelaces for a cellmate.

The clinic's automatic doors whooshed open and I stepped through, blinking against the glare of the sun. The ophthalmologist had dilated my pupils to look around inside my eyes, and he'd told me the residual blood in the whites looked much worse than it actually was and it wouldn't affect my vision in any way. I made him look inside again just to be sure. They say if you lose your sight, your other senses increase. And if my sixth sense got any sharper, I'd probably kill myself by tripping and falling on it.

Lisa gave me a big grin and reached to turn down the Mexican radio station as I climbed in. "It's okay," I said. "Leave it."

She ignored me and left the volume low anyway. "What do you think of my car? Is it haunted?"

I grimaced and took a quick look in the back seat before I buckled myself in. "Nope. Sorry."

"I didn't think so." She pulled away from the curb and swung around the U-shaped arc of the driveway, slipping into traffic with an ease that made me think she was learning her way around just fine. No GPS unit strapped to the dash. Maybe the *sí-no* was a more accurate way to travel anyway.

"I had a hard time deciding," she said as we idled at a red light. "I think I started out asking the *sí-no* the wrong questions. 'Is this car gonna last me five years?' I got a 'no' on everything, and was starting to think the lot was full of lemons." She put her left turn signal on and crept into an intersection. The oncoming traffic showed no gaps, but she waited for the end of the yellow light without any trace of anxiety and took a smooth turn just before the cross traffic gunned into the intersection. "Then I started worrying that maybe I was gonna be crippled in five years, not able to drive a car. Or maybe even dead."

I looked out my window at the line of orderly brownstones we passed. I didn't trust myself to attempt a reassurance that'd probably come out awkward and make things worse.

Lisa waited for a moment, maybe giving me some time to respond, and kept going when I didn't. "I talked to Carolyn. She told me I was reaching out too far. That I should ask questions like, 'Does this car have any mechanical problems?' Or, 'Will I enjoy driving it?'"

"Makes sense," I said. I noticed the leaves on a maple coming up were starting to turn gold. One more year just passing by.

"She's real sorry about leaking our plans to Warwick, you know."

I sighed. "Yeah. I know. I told her it wasn't her fault."

"When Warwick asked her what we were up to, she didn't even answer him, did you know that? He suspected, though, and when she wouldn't say whether you were talking to me or not, he just took it as a yes."

"I get it. I just said it was okay."

Lisa pulled into a space a couple blocks south of my apartment building. I assumed the *si-no* had told her there wasn't anything closer. "She thinks you hate her now."

"Jesus. I don't hate her. It just scares the shit out of me, how it happened. The thought that Warwick could use her own powers to manipulate her. The idea that maybe someone could do that to me."

Lisa cut the engine and slumped back into her seat. "Yeah. Me too. That's why I think I'm gonna get some training."

I swung around to grab her and shake some sense into her, but the seat belt caught me by the neck. I swore at it and clicked it open, but by then I'd calmed down enough to stop myself from acting like a lunatic. "Did Warwick talk you into it? He probably believes that fucking brochure that Heliotrope Station sends out, but lemme tell you...."

"Vic," she said quietly, putting her hand on my knee. "Calm down. Not Camp Hell. There's a new place in Santa Barbara. It's called PsyTrain."

I hated PsyTrain instinctively, but since I'm not precognizant, my instincts weren't worth much. "Sounds like a fucking disco locomotive."

"The department will pay for it. And when I'm done, I'll have a job waiting for me."

So that's how Warwick had talked her into it. He'd let her keep on being a cop. Shrewd fucking bastard. "Visit this PsyTrain first before you go," I said. "More than once. And make sure you talk to some people that've trained there, lots of them. And not just the ones they recommend, either. Find some on your own and...."

"Don't worry. Carolyn's going with me to make sure they're honest."

I didn't suppose Lisa could do any better than having the human lie detector in tow, but the mere thought of Camp Hell had sent adrenaline pumping through my veins and I think I wanted to keep on arguing just for the sake of it.

"If something doesn't feel right, I'll back out of it," Lisa said. She gave my knee a squeeze. "I promise. But Jacob's waiting for you. He's worried about your eyes. You should go tell him they're okay."

I swallowed back the urge to bicker and opened the car door. I hadn't told Lisa my eyes were okay—but she knew. I wondered how long it would be before HMOs started scooping up psychics to cut down on the cost of medical testing, and then slapping them with lawsuits whenever their diagnoses failed.

One last look at Lisa's back seat reassured me that the hatchback's former owners weren't along for the ride, and I gave her a brief, sullen wave as she cranked the Mariachi back up and pulled away from the curb.

I could've said something like, "Hi honey, I'm home," when I came in, but that would've implied that I was in a good mood. Which I wasn't.

My futon looked strange, small and a little bit cheap, with Jacob on it. He sat there in plaid pajama pants, hunched over the glass-top coffee table, shirtless and insanely buff, poring over one of my old textbooks. I suspected he'd already read the one about Psy-ethics. He looked up as I came in, his finger marking the spot on the page where he'd stopped reading.

"My eyes are fine," I said. "They just look bad. But they'll clear up in a week or two."

Jacob smiled his broad, infectious grin.

"I'm, um...gonna go lay down," I said, and ducked into the bedroom. Part of me wanted him to follow and help me blow off a little steam. And part of me was drained and exhausted and just wanted him to stay put. I guess I'd get my wish either way.

I kicked off my jeans, pulled on an old pair of sweatpants, drew the curtains and slipped into bed. A few minutes later I felt Jacob's weight settle behind me.

"So tell me about this third eye," he said.

I managed to not turn it into a dirty joke, since he was so earnest and all, and I didn't feel much like joking anyway. "What about it?"

"Does it feel like an actual eye to you? Does it blink? Did the incubus' scream affect it, too?"

"It's all a metaphor," I said. "It's not a real eye."

"But the text...."

"Is incredibly hokey and inaccurate. I used to think it was translated from Russian. They had a handle on Psych stuff a long time before we figured it out here. Them and the Chinese."

Jacob eased his arm around me and spooned my back into his chest. We fit our bent legs together, and his knees nestled behind mine. "I know you think I'm pushy for asking...."

"What? No, no I don't."

"I can tell. You sound disgusted when you answer me. But you're a difficult man to get to know. And I'm only trying to understand."

I felt bad. Just a little. "Look at the part on chakras in one of the newer books, the one with the guy on the cover who looks constipated. That's a little better explanation."

I think the cover model was supposed to be expressing some sort of psychic talent in action, but I'd always wanted to slip him an Ex-Lax. I half expected Jacob to leap out of bed to go find it since he was so into the whole Psych thing. But instead he just snuggled tighter into my back, his breath warm against my shoulder blade.

And his stiff cock hard against the back of my thigh.

All I had to do was reach back and take it in my hand, let him know that I was ready if he was. And yet I still felt peevish and out of sorts. He sighed and pressed a little harder, his fingertips fanning over my ribs as he held me. I felt a flutter of arousal at his touch, and his warmth, and the sheer solidity of him.

And yet.

Jacob pressed his mouth to my ear. He had a sexy voice and he was shameless about using it. "Make love to me," he said.

I turned my head toward him and his mouth covered mine, the light bristle of his short beard scraping at the criss crossed network of fine scabs on my cheek. His tongue traced my lower lip, drew my tongue out to meet it, but only reluctantly. I knew the incubus had used heavy psychic stuff to seduce him. Call it a glamour, or some kind of mesmerism. But I couldn't help it. I was jealous.

I turned my mouth from his. "I don't have any condoms or lube," I said, and did my best not to count the number of years it'd been since I'd dated someone steadily enough to need such things. The record store guy. Too many years.

Jacob's mouth went to my throat, and he traced a long lick down the sinew of my neck. "Who says I need them?" he asked, and I could hear the smile in his voice. "I just want to touch you. Taste you. Hold you."

His hand skimmed up my body and his fingertips found my nipple, took it firmly this time, and squeezed. Arousal surged toward my groin as if the two points were magically linked, and then he gave a little twist that made me whimper.

His lower hand slipped palm-down beneath the waistband of my sweatpants. My breath shuddered out, but I bit back the moan that threatened to escape me. It wasn't fair that he could make me so hard so fast. He cupped my balls with his palm and twisted my nipple again, and I writhed against him, feeling his hard cock settle in the cleft of my ass.

"Ready to lose the pants?" he asked me.

I wanted to give him a sulky answer, but he was stroking the skin behind my balls, just one fingertip, light and repetitive, and it was like all of my awareness surged into that one spot, leaving me helpless to reply.

He twisted my nipple again, and I arched and moaned.

"God, you're so hot," he said, and sank his teeth into the meat of my shoulder while he took his upper hand and jammed my sweats down around my thighs.

More shocks of arousal traveled down to my cock, which seemed very happy to be free and butting against the comforter.

I felt him against my lower body, thick black body hair, belly, groin and thighs, tickling against my ass and the backs of my legs. He pressed one of his knees between mine and spread my legs from behind. His thigh was so muscular and solid it felt like iron, and my back arched some more to allow him to spread me.

His lower hand slipped deeper between my legs, fingertips gliding feathery touches over my asshole that left me gasping.

"Touch my cock," I demanded, and my voice was a desperate rasp.

Jacob let go of my nipple and ran his upper hand down my ribs. He gave my cock a cursory stroke, then fondled my balls.

"Goddamn it," I said, but I wasn't mad, not really. Just so hard that it hurt— and he knew it.

His upper hand slipped around back to my ass, spread the cheeks while the fingers of his lower hand continued to swirl and tease. And then I felt his balls nestle against my ass, his thick, hard cock cradled again between my ass cheeks.

"Squeeze," he said, and I clenched up a little. He slid his cock within that cleft and shuddered against me. "Oh, God, yeah."

His voice was thick, not the usual controlled purr I'd come to associate with Jacob, the hottest cop in the city. And I dug that I could do that to him, make him all trembly and needy and hard.

He took my cock loosely in one hand while teasing my ass, my balls, the creases of my thighs with the fingertips of the one he'd wedged between my legs. It would've tickled, except he shifted his grip on my cock and gave it a long, hard stroke.

I arched and swallowed down a yell that would've carried to the next apartment if I'd let it out.

"Like that?" he said, gravelly in my ear.

"Fuck, yeah."

He pulled on my cock again, this time slipping a finger inside me.

I arched, hard, and stroked his cock with my ass.

He grunted and bit down on my shoulder, and pulled my lower body roughly against his on the downstroke. We caught a rhythm somehow, me grinding and clenching the length of his cock between my ass cheeks, him fingering me, stroking me, tearing at my shoulder with his teeth like some kind of beast.

I broke first, grabbing at the comforter, the windowsill, Jacob's wrist as he jerked off my cock, fingerfucked me, his leg between mine opening me even more, spreading me, taking my body and dragging an orgasm out of me.

I gasped his name as I came, my whole body twitching helplessly on his, splayed out wide like I'd been stretched on a giant rack.

He stopped pulling my cock and just held me for those final few twitches, so violent they rattled the bedframe against the floorboards.

"C'mere," he said, once I managed to draw a normal breath. He scooched back and helped me to roll over and face him. He took my trembling hand between his and wrapped it around his cock, and I felt my own come, sticky between his fingers. He moaned when I grasped him, and pressed his forehead into mine. He let go of my hand and brought his fingertips to my face, tracing the line of my cheekbone and jaw while I re-learned the shape of his thick, veined cock, learned how he shuddered when I thumbed the ridge under the head, learned how he groaned when I bore down hard on him and glided strong, even strokes down the length of him.

His top leg was thrown over mine and I felt his thighs begin to tremble as he got close. I slowed my strokes and he hissed, whether in approval or frustration, it was hard to say. And then his fingers wove into my hair and he pulled me forward into a slow, deep kiss as his breath hitched, and his hot, wet come painted my hand, belly and chest.

He kept on kissing me, long after he'd gotten off, until finally he drew his tongue into a gentle sweep across my lips, and he lay back just a few inches from my face and sighed.

I held him and felt his breath warm on my cheek, the weight of his leg solid and heavy just above my knee. It was so close to perfect. Except for that cold knot in my belly that told me my jealousy was still coloring everything.

"It's none of my business," I said, "but I can't help but wonder whose face that incubus was wearing for you. I mean, who's so great that you'd ditch me at the Cottonwood Lounge and run home with him?"

"You're kidding."

I closed my eyes so I didn't have to see him looking at me and decided it was best to keep my mouth shut, too.

"You are kidding, right?"

As if I would make a joke about something like that. I kept my eyes closed and refused to answer.

Jacob's sticky fingers traced the shape of my face yet again. "You really don't know, do you?" He pressed a gentle kiss onto one of my eyebrows, then the other. "It was you, Vic. He disguised himself as you."

CRISS CROSS

It was a pretty good day, for October in Chicago. The weather was warm enough that I could get away with wearing just jeans, a T-shirt, a flannel shirt, and my threadbare jean jacket. I could see my breath as we set the rowboat in the water, Maurice in his knee-high rubber boots, steadying the small aluminum boat so I could climb in. Water squished through my black Converse high-tops. Not the best shoes to wear fishing, I gathered.

But I'd never been fishing before, so how the hell would I know?

Maurice heaved himself over the side, thrust an oar into the slimy green water on the bank of the Calumet, and shoved off. And he did it with an ease that reminded me that even though he was graying, he was still in reasonably good shape.

Maurice Taylor had been my partner in the PsyCop Unit for a dozen years, and now he was retired. We'd been quintessential opposites when the force had matched us up: him, a mature black man without a lick of psychic ability, who'd inched his way up to detective with years of hard, honest police work. And me, an impulsive white kid with no friends, whose sixth sense was always tuned to eleven unless I was on an anti-psyactive drug cocktail.

Maurice was still old. And he still had his common sense, far as I could tell. Me? I wasn't a kid anymore, but at least I'd managed to make a few friends. Other than that, I couldn't really vouch for myself.

"Give that oar over here," Maurice said, stretching his hand out to me. "We be goin' in circles all day, if I let you just splash it all over the place like that."

I didn't argue. Maurice is more stubborn than I am. I know this.

Maurice took several deep breaths as he rowed us farther from shore. The Calumet's current wasn't particularly fast in the fall. It had pockets of reedy marsh along the banks that seemed like ideal places to just sit in your boat and while away the day. A train clanged by to the north of us and the scream of a siren drifted by from a stretch of elevated highway. Nature.

"Smell that fine air," Maurice said.

I grunted. It smelled like algae and exhaust fumes to me.

Maurice pulled a few more strokes with the oars and then eased our anchor—a hunk of metal that'd been part of a barbell in another existence—over the side.

"Shouldn't I have, uh…a lifejacket on?"

Maurice smiled and started fiddling with his rod. Or reel. Or whatever the fishing pole thing is called. "S'okay, Victor. Water ain't but waist high."

I glanced over the side of the boat. The water was opaque green. Hard to tell if Maurice was exaggerating.

He put the fishing pole in my hand and pulled out another. "Just set there and wait until I show you how to cast. Else you'll tear your eye out with the hook."

I looked down at the hook. Maurice had squished a worm onto it. A worm spirit didn't appear and immediately start telling me about the moment of its death, so I presumed I was safe from the spirits of bugs. But then it moved and I realized it was still alive. Gross.

Maurice cast his own line with a fairly straightforward explanation of what he was doing, then exchanged it with me for the first fishing pole, which he also cast.

I stared out at the little red floaty things that marked where our hooks had sunk and waited for more instructions.

Maurice wedged his fishing pole into a groove on the floor of the boat and unzipped his duffel bag. He pulled out a thermos and a battered plastic travel mug.

"What next?" I asked him.

Maurice poured some coffee into the mug and handed it to me. The early morning sunlight filtered through the steam that curled up from the surface of the coffee, and I felt like the two of us were in a Folgers commercial. Maurice poured another cup for himself, screwed the stopper back onto the thermos, and sighed. "We wait," he said.

I noticed he was smiling, a soft, kind of distant smile as he gazed out over the water, conveniently ignoring the beer cans and plastic shopping bags that floated around us. Retirement suited him.

We drank our coffees together in silence, and we stared at the water while I tried to control the shivering, me sitting there in wet canvas sneakers in October. It was warm for October, but not that warm. I wedged my fishing pole into the groove in the floor as I'd seen Maurice do and poured myself another coffee. I contemplated pouring out the rest of the contents of the thermos onto my freezing cold feet, but I figured it would only feel good for about a minute, and then the coffee would cool and pretty soon my feet would just be wet again. I saved the coffee for drinking, instead.

"So," Maurice said, after he finished his coffee. "Warwick find you a new partner yet?

"Yeah, a couple days ago. Some guy. His name's Roger Burke."

I really couldn't think of much to say about Detective "please, call me Roger," Burke. He was kinda like white bread. When I was a teenager, I would have been pretty eager to get him down my throat. But now that I was looking at forty, I found him a little bland.

Don't get me wrong, Roger was cute. He had a ready smile that he lavished on me at the drop of a hat. His thick hair was naturally blond, cut short and smart. His eyebrows and eyelashes were a darker blond, framing greenish hazel eyes.

I'd never seen him in anything less than a sport coat, but judging by the way it sat on his shoulders and buttoned smoothly over his nipped waist, I was guessing he probably exercised regularly, and was hiding a set of washboard abs under his perfectly pressed dress shirt.

It was difficult to say if he'd pitch for my team or not. Once upon a time I assumed that all the other cops except for me were straight. That was before Detective Jacob Marks cornered me in the bathroom at Maurice's retirement party.

I was still too fixated on Jacob to really give a damn if Roger Burke slept with men, women, or inflatable farm animals, for that matter.

"What's this Burke guy like?" Maurice asked.

I decided it would be far too gay to tell Maurice what color Roger Burke's eyes were. And besides, Maurice wouldn't give a shit. "He always buys the coffee. Seems decent enough. He was a detective for five years in Buffalo."

"New York?"

"Yeah."

"Huh." The plastic floaty on Maurice's line dipped beneath the water. He reeled the line in carefully but all that was on the hook was a drowned worm. He cast it back out. "What about that Mexican girl?"

"That Mexican girl" was Lisa Gutierrez. She'd been selected to be my non-psychic partner, or Stiff, after Maurice retired. Things had worked well between us, until our sergeant figured out that she was a psychic herself. She'd rigged her test scores to get the job.

"She's in California at some place called PsyTrain. Even if she decides to come back here once she's done, they'd never pair us up. They'd need to put her with a Stiff."

"Too bad. Heard the two of you hit it off."

I froze, and not just because ice crystals were forming on my sneakers. I'd been wondering if we'd have this conversation, just me, Maurice and a bunch of garbage floating around in the Calumet River. The little talk where I told him I liked men.

"We, uh…. She's nice."

Maurice reeled his line in a couple of turns and gazed out over the river. He didn't say anything more. I let my breath out slowly, relieved that I'd dodged the bullet, but maybe a little disappointed, too. A few moments of really, really awkward conversation, and then he'd probably never mention it again.

Heck, according to Jacob, Maurice probably already knew. Or at least suspected. Twelve years and no girlfriend? That might be significant if we were talking about an average guy—but it was *me* under the microscope. For all Maurice knew, I was just too messed up to have a woman in my life. I was probably too messed up to have a man in my life too, come to think of it. But since Jacob was a big, strong man with a gun, a cop who knew how to kick ass and take names, I figured he could hold his own.

The two cups of coffee I'd just sucked down roiled around in my stomach, and I hung my head over the side of the boat and tried to talk myself out of being sick. I'd swallowed a donut in three bites on my way out the door, but it wasn't doing a very good job of soaking anything up. Acid licked at the back of my throat and I swallowed hard.

"Don't tell me you're seasick," Maurice said, his eyes still focused on the floaties a few dozen yards away as if I wasn't turning green and gulping air.

I seized on the chance to blame my nausea on anything other than my own internal freak-out. "Maybe," I said. "Haven't been on a boat since I went on that horrible cruise when I turned thirty."

I stared down at the soupy green water sloshing against the side of the rowboat, and picked out tiny round shapes that were plants, or snails, or some other mysterious bits of life in the murk.

"Just set there," Maurice said. "It'll pass."

A larger pale, round shape floated beneath the murky water, probably a shopping bag, or maybe a milk jug. I tried to distract myself by imagining a homie out drinking milk with his posse and chucking the plastic bottle into the river, but I didn't find my own humor particularly entertaining.

It bothered me, not being able to tell what the thing was, and I leaned my face closer to the water and squinted at it. I noticed there was another one, about the same size and shape but maybe a little farther down, to my right. And another to my left. My vision seemed to open up and I realized these pale shapes were all around us, like cloud formations beneath the river's surface.

Some kind of algae, then. Or maybe even pale, sandy mounds, with the Calumet's bottom as close as Maurice had said it was, even closer, us bobbing in a couple of feet of water where we just could have waded instead, if I were dressed appropriately.

I pushed myself up on the side of the boat as my nausea receded. I was just about to ask Maurice about his trip to Fort Lauderdale when the underwater shape surged up toward me and coalesced into a pale, dead face.

I snapped up tall and the fishing pole leapt out of my grip. I managed to grab it before it fell into the water, but maybe I should've just let it drop. Maybe I wouldn't have looked like I was shaking so hard if I didn't have a big, telltale fishing line visibly quivering between me and the water.

The water that was full of dead people.

Maurice stared at me for a beat, glanced over the side, then took the fishing pole from my hands and wedged it into the bottom of the boat. "What you see?" he said calmly.

I knew what I must look like, whites of my eyes showing all around, face paler than usual. The Look. The one that said I'd just seen something. Maurice knew The Look.

I closed my eyes and images of pallid, distended faces bobbing to the surface filled my memory. Hundreds of them, eyes open and unseeing, a landscape of them stretching to the horizon—or at least the highway.

There wouldn't be that many there. Not in real life. It was just my own mind fucking with me.

"It bad?" Maurice said gently.

I opened my eyes and stared hard at his brown, gray-whiskered face. I took another breath. It wasn't that bad, I told myself. I'd just seen a handful of revenants and let my imagination run wild. It wasn't as if I'd never seen dead people before, I told myself. It wasn't like I'd never seen a ghost.

I peeked over the side.

A face peered back at me, rubbery mouth opening and closing like it was trying to talk—but the water didn't move and no bubbles came out. The face next to it blinked. A hand moved toward the surface of the water like a pale, bloated spider, reaching for me. And beyond it, another hand. And another beyond that.

"Jesus," I said. I jerked myself upright and started chafing my arms. "The water's full of them."

Maurice reeled in his drowned worm, and my empty hook, and then the anchor. I felt him shove the oar into the riverbed and give us a push toward shore.

"Should I make some phone calls, have 'em drag it?" Maurice asked.

"I don't know." Was anybody missing? Yeah, probably. But dozens of somebodies? Maybe hundreds? "I just…." I sighed and made a "whatever" gesture. "I don't know."

2

I helped Maurice load the boat into the back of his Ford Explorer and told him I was gonna go home, take an Auracel and have a nice, long nap. Actually, I was planning on taking at least three pills. So sue me, I lied.

My phone sat folded in the driver's seat and I flipped it open, hoping for a message from Jacob to calm me down. He's got this voice, low and sexy, more of a purr. And it'd be hard to keep dredging up the image of the river full of dead people if he was whispering sweet nothings into my phone.

There were two messages. Message number one: Roger. "Hi, Vic. Sorry to bother you on your day off. I'm settled in to my new place. It's not too far from your apartment, just a few blocks down, across the street from the supermarket. If you want to share a ride or anything, just let me know."

And message number two: Jacob. "Hey. Remember how I said the Governor was probably going to grant a stay of execution on Hugo Cooper? Looks like I was wrong. I've got to go and witness it. So...I'll be home late. Bye."

His voice dropped about an octave when he said "bye," sultry and inviting. It seemed weird to me that he could be so blasé about witnessing an execution, but that was part and parcel of the job. I'd put away plenty of guys who'd ended up on death row, but it was in my contract that I didn't have to watch 'em fry. Normally both the leads have to go. I only got out of it because I was a certified medium, and who knows what I'd see if I had to be present for the moment of death?

I slipped the phone into my pocket and headed back toward my apartment. Jacob and I didn't live together, not exactly. It was just that he was staying with me until he found a house or a condo. I'd killed this soul-eating incubus in his bedroom, and even though every psychic Jacob knew told him there was no trace of the thing left, he still refused to sleep there.

It'd been a few weeks, but since we both knew Jacob was actually looking at places—and because he thought my apartment looked like a hospital room in a charity ward—we'd never begun feeling too domestic together.

I parked my car, took three flights of stairs two at a time, threw open my front door and flipped on the kitchen light. I went through the living room, bedroom and bathroom and did the same, until the whole place incandesced. Everything in the apartment was white, from the cheap landlord-painted walls to the furniture to the bent plastic miniblinds. When my eyes settled on things that were not white, they invariably turned out to be shadows, nothing more. And that was the way I liked it.

I swallowed all three Auracel tablets at once, and sank down on the futon in the living room. And then I remembered: I'd meant to pick up rubbers on the way home, but in a few minutes I'd be flying too high to drive. It wasn't like Jacob had left a big note on the fridge that said "buy condoms" or anything. In fact, he hadn't said a word about taking anything further than blowjobs after the first time we'd spent the whole night together. It seemed like every day I set off with the intention of bringing home the goods, and then totally forgot about it. I thought it was fairly conspicuous that Jacob never picked any up, either. Since he's the poster child for organizational skills, I can only assume he was leaving the timing up to me. I'm not exactly sure how buying condoms—or not—turned into my issue. Maybe because all the issues in our relationship seemed to be my issues.

A woven blanket of Jacob's was draped haphazardly on the plain canvas futon cover, a splash of taupe, burgundy and black that looked far too dark amid all the white. I pulled it up to my face and inhaled. It smelled like Jacob and his condo, old wood and leather, clean man-smells. I liked Jacob. A lot. A whole lot. So what was this mental block I had about the condoms?

As the Auracel started throwing the room into soft focus, I decided that I was making a bigger deal out of the whole condom thing than I needed to. They still sold them at convenience stores, didn't they? I'd just have a little nap in my Jacob-smelling blanket, and when I woke up, I'd walk to the corner store and buy some. Problem solved.

—◆◆◆—

The drugs kicked in and I dozed. My miniblinds developed strips of black between the slats where sunlight had streamed in earlier. Jacob's blanket was twisted around my ribs.

I sat up and looked hard from shadow to shadow. Nothing moved. Satisfied that I was alone, I yawned and rolled a kink out of my neck. Nice way to spend my day off, doped up and asleep. I considered taking up drinking. But not very seriously, since the dead get really bossy when I drink.

And speaking of the dead...I thought of the floating faces in the river and shuddered. My triple dose of Auracel was still holding up, though, and hypothetically my sixth sense had a lid on it for the time being. But I hadn't been on Auracel when I'd seen them, and the images from before kept replaying themselves in my mind. Those faces. Hairless. Lips wormy and too mobile, forming soundless sounds, words. Hands reaching, trying to break the surface....

I grabbed the first thing I could lay my hands on and threw it across the room. You wouldn't think a plastic coaster would put such a big ding in the wall. Damn.

I looked at the clock. A little after nine. The state still does executions at midnight, as if deliberately and methodically killing someone isn't spooky enough as it is. Jacob would be gone until one, one-thirty. I wanted Jacob. I didn't want to be alone with the memory of those bloated bodies.

I called Lisa and got a message on her cell that said she wouldn't be available for the next couple of weeks due to her coursework, but to leave her a message and she'd be back in touch soon. She sounded perky, like just she couldn't wait to go meditate, or whatever they were teaching her. Couldn't she have phone hours, I wondered. Did she need to devote so much time to chanting "om" that she couldn't just talk to me for five fucking minutes to reassure me that the river wasn't really full of dead people?

I closed my eyes and breathed carefully, and told myself that I did not want to strangle Lisa. I debated taking another Auracel, but since I had to work the next day, opted for a Seconal to just knock me out instead. I tuned the living room TV to a station I didn't receive, slumped on the futon, and watched some static.

I think it's a white-noise kind of thing I'm looking for when I go between TV or radio stations. Something generic to shut out the dead. It's not anything they taught me at Heliotrope Station, better known as Camp Hell, the sicko place where I was supposedly being taught to harness my psychic ability. I'd just picked up static-surfing on my own.

Channel 8 was usually pretty good for a gray, textured nothingness. I hit zero-eight on the remote and settled in.

Except Channel 8 seemed to be tuning something in tonight. I wondered why that would be. Maybe another station had boosted its signal, or the hole in the ozone happened to be lining up with some broadcast satellite, or maybe Mercury was retrograde. Damn. I'd liked Channel 8 just the way it was.

I made out a face in the static and tried to match it with a familiar celebrity, without luck. I picked out the contour of a cheek, and an open mouth. A hand fluttered up, five fingers blurring. Sign language? I had no idea. But the Seconal was kicking in, combining with the grogginess brought on by all the Auracel I'd taken earlier, and my eyelids drooped despite the nagging compulsion to make sense of what I was seeing.

I wouldn't say I actually slept, at least not the whole time. Camp Hell called it a hypnogogic state, that window between sleeping and waking. Sometimes when I catch myself in that window I feel extraordinarily clear, like I've been going through the day wearing a pair of dirty, smudged sunglasses and it's just occurred to me to take them off. Other times I just feel like I'm falling.

It was in the middle of one of those sickening falling lurches that I snapped awake, as if I'd been caught. Jacob's face was right in mine, and he held me firmly by the upper arms. "Hey," he said when I woke up.

I cleared my throat. "Hey."

He stared hard into my eyes. "Were you…sleeping?"

I raised an eyebrow. Evidently he didn't think so, since he'd felt the need to grab me like that. "I dunno. Not exactly." I shrugged. He let go of me and settled down in a crouch between my legs, with his elbows resting on my knees. "Sort of dreaming."

"Your eyes were half-open, but they were fixed, not moving."

Oh. That must've been really attractive. Good thing anything paranormal, ugly or not, makes Jacob horny. But still, there had to be a limit somewhere, and I wasn't eager to find it. I wondered if he'd had any luck with househunting. And then I remembered he'd been at an execution all night, and it was probably somewhere in the wee hours of the morning. "I took a sleeping pill," I said as I pushed off the back of the futon. He eased back and stood, and gave me a hand up.

I glimpsed Channel 8 but didn't see any more staticky people. Jacob turned off the television, poking the manual on/off button as we went by. The lights in the bedroom were already on; in fact, all the lights in the apartment were still on. I waited for him in the bedroom doorway while he swung around to flick off the kitchen and bathroom lights. I usually left the kitchen light on all night, since it was far enough away from the bedroom to leave my sleep undisturbed, yet it ensured that I wouldn't awake in total darkness and see…well, I dunno what I might see, but I didn't want to find out. But for the past two weeks with Jacob there, I'd been sleeping with the lights out. All of them.

I didn't move as Jacob approached the bedroom. For someone who made me feel so safe, he sure looked like hell. A deep, vertical scowl line I'd never noticed before was wedged between his dark eyebrows, the laugh lines at the corners of his eyes just looked weary, and his mouth was pressed into a grim set. "Are you okay?" I asked. And I felt a little stupid for taking so long to ask it, but at least I'd figured it out eventually. I'm really not accustomed to having to worry about anyone but myself.

Jacob fit himself into the bedroom doorway with me, one of us backed against each jamb, and propped his wrists on my shoulders. We were both a handful of inches over six feet tall, but his solid mass dwarfed me as he pressed his forehead into mine. "That guy they put down today, Hugo Cooper. He was a monster."

"Yeah," I said, as if I knew it all. Cooper had kidnapped three women. Kept them alive in a hundred-degree attic. He probably wouldn't have murdered them if one hadn't escaped and run for help, which caused him to panic and try to erase the whole thing in a brutal, frenzied massacre.

Those were the basics, but I'm sure Jacob would be able give me every last detail, the location of every scattered body part. I hoped he wouldn't.

"No matter how evil they are," I said, "it fucks with your mind to watch 'em fry."

I felt Jacob's breath, warm, on my cheek. He kissed me, a chaste brush of his lips, and my heartbeat sped. "It was lethal injection." He turned toward the bed, and sighed. "But, yeah. It was no picnic."

The little flutter I'd taken for pleasure felt more like panic as Jacob pulled away from me. Faces in the river, dark house, and Lisa unreachable in Santa Barbara. I slipped around him and got into bed, pulling him down beside me. He didn't respond as quickly and eagerly as usual, but he seemed willing enough.

I pulled Jacob close to me, arms around his neck, and pressed my mouth against his. He's got full lips, normally set in a slightly knowing grin; nothing arrogant, just an I-got-the-joke-five-minutes-ago type of look. He worked his way out of his suitcoat as I clung to him and ran my tongue back and forth over his lower lip. His jacket slid from the bed to the floor and he settled himself against me. I ran my hands down his back, which was hot through the fabric of his shirt everywhere it'd been covered by the coat. I could feel the cut of his muscles, even on his back, and even through that shirt. Jacob works out—religiously, I'd learned since he'd been staying with me. And aside from pumping iron, the man takes a run after work if police business doesn't keep him late. *A run.*

Jacob broke our kiss and narrowed his eyes. "Why are you smiling?"

I realized he'd probably still been thinking about the execution and promptly attempted to look serious, even though I was totally busted. "You make me happy. That's all."

Jacob scowled harder. "I don't trust you when you smile."

I pressed myself more firmly into his chest, and wished my psychic powers could also make our clothes disappear. "Really." I loosened his tie. "I had a lousy day too, and I'm glad to see you."

"You had a lousy day…fishing?"

Boy, nothing got past him. "Let's not talk about it." I stripped his shirt off, then pulled my ratty sweatshirt over my head. I knew the perfect thing to take Jacob's mind off the crap day we'd each had. But of course I'd forgotten the condoms—again—so I'd just have to make do. Not that I've ever known anyone to complain about getting a blowjob.

I pushed Jacob onto his back and got to work on his belt. His expression grew less pensive as he watched me unzip his fly and start tracing the muscles on his abs with my tongue. Maybe he even grinned a little, too. Or at least he'd stopped scowling. I ditched the rest of my clothes fast, then finished stripping Jacob a little more respectfully. He wears expensive tailored suits that don't appreciate being torn off and wadded up on the floor. The Seconal—not exactly a modern sleeping pill, actually a barbiturate that used to be a party drug in the seventies—had made me mellow, more apt to finesse his clothes off than tear at them.

Once I'd undressed Jacob I ran my palms down his thighs, feeling the swell of hard muscle beneath the skin. He lay back and watched me taking him in, and he definitely looked less stressed than he had when he'd gotten home. I always thought of him as fearless, but maybe I made him feel safe somehow, too.

I settled myself between his legs with my feet sticking off the bottom of the bed and I kissed him on the stomach again, but now Jacob's cock was brushing against my chest and I let that contact happen, almost as if it was accidental, and felt him swell against me.

I slid my hands over Jacob's hips and held onto them as I worked my mouth lower. His skin was pleasantly salty; the hair on his thighs was soft against my cheek. My mouth found its way to the base of Jacob's cock, and he let out a low groan. His hands covered mine, and our fingers meshed together. He squeezed my fingers encouragingly.

I ran my tongue higher, licking along the underside of his cock while it rose up to meet my mouth. It's a big, wide cock, but it looks right on him. And there's something dirty about trying to cram it into my mouth and going to work the next day with an aching jaw that really gets me off.

"Mmm, yeah."

Speaking of dirty: Jacob's a talker. And keeping my mouth full of cock has the added bonus of me not having to answer him. Not that the words aren't sexy as hell—I just worry that I'll sound like an idiot if I'm the one saying them.

"Uhn, that's right, Vic. Yeah…sweet mouth."

My cock gave a throb into the bedspread, but I couldn't grab it since Jacob was holding my hands tight. The thought of that made me even harder. I got his cockhead into my mouth, and the slick salt of precome touched the back of my tongue.

Jacob gave a sharp gasp and squeezed my fingers.

I felt the girth of him with my lips and slid back, wetting Jacob's cock so it'd slide a little easier.

"God, Vic. Yeah."

I bore down on it on that first good stroke so I took him all the way into my throat. I could appreciate why Seconal was so popular if it made me that relaxed and still let me get hard.

Jacob moaned louder.

I was digging the thought of a big slab of cockmeat invading my throat—probably that was the residual high of the Auracel talking—so I did Jacob hard and fast. Lots of suction, lots of speed. His hands clenched hard at my fingers and his body arched up off the bed.

"Oh God! Oh my God!"

He was loud enough for the downstairs neighbors to hear and I loved it. I humped myself into the bunched-up covers while Jacob's cries grew wordless and louder still. He yanked my arms, dragging me onto his cock, battering the back of my throat against its stiffness. I sucked hard and let him guide me, no, slam himself into me.

And suddenly he was still, a yell escaping him that was more like a long, hard breath, too intense even for sound. Hot bitterness surged over the back of my tongue and my gag reflex was gone in a haze of prescription meds, and I welcomed Jacob's shot, let the come warm me and fill me up. His fingers had gone slack, and I jerked my hands away and grabbed my own cock, fisting it with quick, efficient strokes.

I wanted to just let it rip, but there was the ghost of a dead newborn in the laundry room, and I only had one change of sheets left. At the last moment I clapped my other hand over the tip, and caught my own load as it shot.

I looked up and Jacob was watching with heavy-lidded eyes, and definitely grinning now. I leaned over him to get a tissue from the bedside table and wiped my wet hand with it.

"You should've come on me," he said. I don't know how he can look me in the eye and just say that. Even with the drugs, it wasn't anything I could speak out loud. "You'd look hot, really hot."

I didn't feel like talking about the real reason why I hadn't, so I threw the tissue into the wastebasket and snuggled up beside him instead.

Even though it was three in the morning and Jacob had to be exhausted, he didn't let it go. "Do it next time, okay? I want to see it, shooting all over my chest."

I sighed.

"Okay?"

I rolled over, pulled a pillow against my face and spoke into it. "I have this hangup about the laundry room," I said. Good thing the pillow was there. It sounded even dumber aloud than it had in my head. No wonder I worried about talking dirty; talking in general seemed to escape me.

Jacob pressed himself into my back. His body was much warmer than mine, tacky with sweat, and his chest hair tickled against my shoulder blades. "Okay," he said, and kissed the nape of my neck.

———⚮———

I woke to a slender ray of sunshine streaming through the miniblinds and nailing me directly in the eye. A sharp twinge of pain flared behind my eyeball, somewhere in my brain. "Fuck."

I sat up and looked at the clock. Eight thirty-eight, and my shift started at nine. Not good. I vaulted over Jacob while the pain, apparently fueled by my movement, flared again. I staggered a little as I went into the kitchen and retrieved my cell phone from my jacket pocket. I'd be late, and I was in no shape to drive. I hit memory dial seven, the last programmed number on my phone. Roger Burke.

"Burke here."

I squeezed my eyelids together. Couldn't he just answer with his last name like every other cop? I chalked up my annoyance about the word "here" to my Auracel hangover. "Hi, Roger. It's Vic."

"Oh, hi, Vic!" He was way too happy for a Wednesday. "What's up?"

"Listen, I uh...." I realized I probably should have rehearsed the way I was going to say it. Damn. And then I remembered his phone message from the day before. "I wanted to take you up on your offer and get a ride from you today."

He didn't miss a beat. "Sure, no problem."

As I searched for a way to end the conversation without explaining any further why I couldn't just drive myself like a regular person, I realized I heard the ambient noise of the Fifth Precinct behind him—the peculiar phone ring and the sound of male laughter as the uniformed cops joked around the water cooler. Christ. Roger was at *work* already and he'd leave to come back and get me? I shook my head. "Gimme, like half an hour," I said, and hung up.

I figured I should at least take a shower so I didn't smell like sex. I washed a couple of aspirin down with a slug of orange juice from the carton and turned the shower on. The room filled with steam. I got under the scalding spray and the pain in my head seemed to lessen a little as my capillaries all opened up.

The shower curtain rustled as Jacob slid in behind me. His chest pressed into my back and he wrapped his arms around my middle. "Morning," he purred.

My cock stirred a little at the feel of a big, hot body behind me, but the pain in my head was more insistent than my groin was. "Hey," I said, and clapped my soapy hands over his to keep them north of the border.

He seemed to pick up on my body language, the way he picks up on everything; he massaged my shoulders, not my cock, as the hot water tumbled over me. "I'm looking at a condo on the lake today," he said. "Why don't you come with me?"

"To make sure it's clean?"

"Clean is good," he said, and his soapy hands slid down my back, grazed my ass, then slipped back up to work the knots out of my shoulders again. His voice was light and teasing, and I wondered if he was angling to move in together—for real, and not just a temporary, stopgap arrangement.

Jacob nuzzled my wet hair aside and dragged his lips along the back of my neck. My cock started swelling. "Roger's picking me up," I said, and the regret was plain in my voice.

Jacob's lips lingered for a moment, then his hands gave my shoulders a squeeze and he pulled away and reached for the shampoo. "I could've given you a ride," he said.

I felt guilty for not having asked him, but it was just far too gay to have my boyfriend dropping me off at the precinct. "It's your day off." I turned to face him, since it felt too weaselly to lie with my back to him. He seemed fine, concentrating on soaping up his hair.

I rinsed off and slipped out of the shower, and found a week-old towel in the hamper. I left the clean one for Jacob. He climbed out a minute later, water beaded on his olive skin, muscles rippling...with red scratches criss-crossing his thighs.

"What's that?"

He glanced down. "Don't you remember your own handiwork?"

I squinted at the marks. They looked almost as if they'd been made deliberately, like Xs. "Um. No."

He grinned and dried himself off lazily, flexing for me all the while. "Right before you jerked off last night, you got a little rough."

I did? I stared at his thighs. They were just scratches. But still. It really didn't seem like something I'd do, even buzzed. I considered kissing them as some sort of penance, but if I knelt down in front of him on the bathroom floor I'd be asking for a big naked porno scene for Roger to stumble into. I shuddered at the thought.

Which was weird. Roger wasn't bad looking, and a threesome should have been interesting fantasy fodder. I watched Jacob watching me as he dried off. Maybe I was falling in love. I shrugged and finger-combed my hair, dropped my towel on the floor and went to find a clean shirt.

3

Roger had stopped at Starbucks on the way to pick me up. He'd even put cream in my coffee. I wanted to be leery of him for being so nice to me, but I chalked it up to his enthusiasm at landing such a prestigious job. Being a PsyCop didn't pay as well as private psychic work, but then there wasn't any call for Stiffs in private work, either. Maybe he was making better money than he had in Buffalo. Or maybe he was a Psych groupie like Jacob. Hard to say until I got to know him a little better.

I looked at him out of the corner of my eye while he drove and tried to get a bead on him, but he was difficult to peg. A regular guy. Probably straight. "So," I said. "Are you, uh, married or anything?" Smooth. Really smooth.

He probably could've put me in my place by responding, "Why, are you? I guess not. The whole station knows you've been shacked up with Detective Marks from the Twelfth since Detective Taylor retired." But, of course, he didn't.

Nope. Roger was the picture of mildly interested surprise. "No, not married. Not seeing anyone." He smiled. "I mean, I just moved here from Buffalo last week."

"Right," I said, wondering how far a straight guy would pursue it.

"You?" he asked.

"Me? Uh, no. Mediums aren't exactly marriage material." Class-five mediums like me, anyway.

"That's a common misperception," Roger said. "In fact, Psychs are just as likely to be married as Non-Psychs, and they have a significantly lower divorce rate."

I considered telling him that the divorce rate was so low because the psychics' spouses probably killed themselves to get away, but I didn't know if he'd appreciate my sense of humor. Not that I even knew if I'd be kidding or not.

Thankfully, I don't live far from the precinct, and we were there before Roger could tell me any more fascinating facts about being psychic.

We reported to Sergeant Warwick's office for the day's assignment. I let Roger lead the way since I was the cause of our lateness. I figured he'd be more difficult to ream out than me, given his cheerful demeanor. Warwick looked up from the files on his desk and motioned for us to sit. No threats, no accusations, no nothing. I made a mental note to use the Roger-goes-first tactic the next time I screwed up.

"Since this is Detective Burke's first day with you in the field," Warwick said,

"I'm starting you off with a cold case."

I felt something unclench inside me. Cold cases were a walk on the beach. Maurice and I would grab a box of donuts and take a leisurely drive from scene to scene, me staring out into space and him working on his grocery list. I'd never gotten a hit from a cold case. I'm not really sure why, given the persistence of murder victims. Most likely I was looking in the wrong spots.

Of course, if Lisa had still been my partner, we could've used her precognizant ability to figure out where to focus our energies. Ever since Lisa was a little girl she's played this *sí-no* game, where she could answer any yes or no question correctly. To say the *sí-no* would save us a little legwork would be the understatement of the year. We could figure out which scenes still contained any clues before we'd even left the precinct. Hell, we could figure out if the spirit was even lingering around at all, or if going out to look for it would be an exercise in futility.

But, departmental policies being what they were, Lisa and I would never be partners again. I gathered the files from Warwick and stomped out of his office more sulkily than I'd meant to, but damn it, I thought the policy of pairing a Psych and a Stiff, no matter what the circumstances, was shortsighted and just plain stubborn. The theory is that psychics' energies are complemented by the total sixth-sensory void of a certified Non-Psych, or NP. And while Maurice had been my partner, that had seemed to make a lot of sense.

In retrospect, I think I just got along with Maurice.

I threw myself into the seat at my desk and flipped open the first file. The case involved a child-killer, Terry Lawrence, who'd confessed to a slew of murders and then recanted his confession, saying the police promised him they'd push for an insanity plea if he'd just help them clean house a little by fessing up to a few more missing children. The body of one eight-year-old girl had been found, but five others had never resurfaced. Lawrence's thirty-year sentence was coming up for parole, and the state was hoping that PsyCops could shed some light on the validity of Lawrence's earlier confessions.

"Where would the spirits be most likely to be found?" Roger asked.

"Where they died, or where they were buried, especially if it was a hide-the-body situation. They get testy when they're not planted right."

Roger took a file from the desk and scanned it. "Since we don't know where they're buried, I'm guessing we need to look at Lawrence's residence."

I shrugged and tried not to let my shitty mood leak out all over Roger. He was a nice enough guy, but he was no Maurice. And he was certainly no Lisa.

Roger seemed unfazed as he did a little typing on his computer. I stared down at another missing child's file and pretended to read. I took a long pull of my coffee. At least the coffee was good.

"Lawrence had a bungalow on Argyle near California."

I pinpointed the area in my mind. "Two blocks from the East River Park."

"That's the place."

If I were Lawrence, I would've dropped the bodies in the river. No doubt the officers working the case had thought of that, even in the seventies. I flipped open the file, and yes, they'd dragged the river as soon as they'd fingered Lawrence as their man. But it'd probably been too late.

I remembered the gape-mouthed face rising up out of the Calumet and shuddered.

Roger's keys were clicking away. He hadn't noticed. "There's a strip mall where the bungalow used to be," he said. "Looks like it's either a gyros place or a cell phone dealer now."

I gulped the rest of my coffee, which had been getting cold anyway, and felt it churn around with my stomach acids. I dropped the cup into the wastebasket. "Let's go and have a look," I sighed.

We pulled up to the cell phone store and found it didn't even open until three. Athens Gyros next door was an uninspired strip mall greasy spoon with a stained acoustic drop ceiling and paneling that dated back to whenever Lawrence's house had been razed. There was a klatch of old ladies nursing diner coffee toward the front of the restaurant, a dark-skinned guy of indeterminate ethnicity reading a paper against one wall, and toward the counter, a mother who looked to be about twelve years old trying to make her squalling kid drink some soda.

"Let's not flash our badges," I told Roger. "Not yet, since we're not investigating anyone here, or even this building. We'll just get…lunch."

It was early enough in the day that the oil in the deep fryer was probably still fresh, so I ordered an extra large curly fry and a couple of Polish sausages. I tacked on a coffee, since I'm a sucker for diner coffee. Roger went with a Greekburger, a side salad and a lemonade. The salad was a little suspicious, but at least he was eating red meat; he probably wasn't some kind of health nut. Did straight guys eat salads? Maurice never had one unless his wife made it. That was about the extent of my knowledge of the eating habits of the heterosexual world.

We slid into an orange plastic booth, me with my coffee and him with his lemonade, and tried to look like something other than cops. I'm usually pretty good at that, since I'm such a slob. And I suppose Roger could've passed for a businessman in his perfectly fitted suit.

Roger stared at me hard as I sipped my coffee, and not a come-on type of stare, either. God. He expected me to be tuning in my pineal gland even as I waited for my lunch. I wondered how explicitly I'd need to tell him to relax.

I excused myself and went to the bathroom to gather my thoughts and take a piss. The tile was brown, the countertops were orange, and the old light fixtures cast a weird, yellowish illumination on everything. I aimed at the pink urinal cake and peed, focusing on the wall when my piss looked orange in the sickly light. I stared up at some cobwebs in the ceiling corner and thought it would be in my best interest to just lie to Roger and say that it took me a while to attune myself to new situations. PsyCops are like marathon runners. They've got to pace themselves. The rookies have to learn how to take it easy or else they burn out.

Not that he was all that young. I was guessing early thirties. But I was also guessing that he was out to prove something on his first run as a PsyCop. Yeah, lying was the ticket.

Two big Polishes and a steaming platter of fries were waiting for me at the table. Roger hadn't started eating yet, out of some sense of etiquette, I guess. I quelled the urge to roll my eyes. Maurice would've had a hunk of curly fry on his lapel by now.

I sat down and gulped half my coffee, hoping the sixty-something Greek guy who'd taken our order would come around with refills soon. In fact, I was betting on it, since the old ladies looked like they'd been settled into their booth for quite some time and they still had something to sip.

I stuck a fry in my mouth, burnt my tongue, and switched to a Polish instead. It was almost as hot, but there was at least a bun to buffer my tongue. I ate about half of that, leaning over the table so that the mustard and diced onion landed on the tray rather than my sportcoat, and then finished off the rest of my coffee.

I was full already.

Huh.

I hadn't had any breakfast and had hardly touched the fries. Two Polishes with fries should have been about right.

Roger worked on his salad in a quiet, methodical way. I finished my first Polish, then went up to the counter for a glass of water to help me keep the thing down. I almost asked the guy to come around for a refill on my coffee while I was at it, but a rumble in my gut told me to give the coffee a rest.

I walked back to the booth with my red tumbler of water and slid in, my gaze focused inward. "What is it?" Roger asked in a hushed voice. "Do you see anything?"

Oh, that again. I shushed him. "It takes time," I lied.

Roger dutifully clammed up while I figured how many coffees I'd had so far. Two. Okay, the Starbucks was a grande, so maybe it'd counted a double, or even triple. So the cup at the diner would make four.

Shouldn't have been a problem. I'm a cop. Coffee runs through my veins. I wondered if I could convince Roger to let me run into a grocery store to get some antacids without him tagging along to see what I was buying. I didn't know him well enough to let him see me laid low by a few cups of coffee.

It probably wasn't even the coffee. Maybe it was food poisoning. I tried to remember what I'd had for dinner the night before and came up blank. Lunch, then. I thought back.

Crap, I'd slept through lunch and dinner on an Auracel/Seconal cocktail. And I'd had a donut for breakfast. Could I get food poisoning from a donut? It seemed unlikely, and yet I had felt queasy in the boat.

I glanced up at Roger and he was staring at me like I had the moon landing playing in my eyes. "Anything?" he whispered.

I finally did roll my eyes at his ridiculous persistence—I just couldn't quell it—when I saw a little girl with a pageboy haircut, wearing an atrocious plaid dress. She stood beside Roger, facing me from across the table. The back of the booth practically bisected her from left to right, and her head and shoulders poked out over the top.

I tried to recall if she'd been one of the files I'd scanned earlier, but it was too hard to tell. The photos I'd had were school pictures, kids against garish seventies backgrounds with freakishly fake smiles plastered on and their hair slicked into strange shapes that probably didn't resemble its normal state.

I looked harder at the little girl ghost and there was something off about her. Most ghosts are off in some way, which is why people are scared of them. I looked harder at the girl. Her eyes were too intense, piercing, almost. And her neck looked mottled. When I realized what I was looking at were finger marks, she reached out toward me as if she wanted to hold my hand.

That was different. Usually they talk. I wondered if maybe she'd been a deaf-mute in life.

I hadn't actually expected to feel her touching me, since all the ghosts I'd ever seen were totally noncorporeal. But her fingers were clammy and dead against the back of my hand. A wave of revulsion swept over me and I fought to keep my lunch from coming up. I jerked my arm away, then ran my fingers through my hair in an attempt to cover up the gesture. I had no desire to try talking to her, and even less desire to explain my reasoning to eager Roger. "Let's get out of here," I told Roger calmly. "There's nothing to see."

The kid's ghost followed us but I walked fast, slamming the car door and hoping Roger would get a move on it, too. I pressed my thumb into my forehead but then thought better of it. Some Psychs do that to stimulate their crown chakra; mine was plenty hyper on its own.

Roger fastened his seat belt and started the engine. The little girl ghost stood in the parking spot we'd just backed out of with her thin arms reaching toward the car. "Where to next?" asked Roger. "The park?"

I nodded, while I wondered how I could get him to stop off so that I could get something for my stomach. I racked my brain in an attempt to find something innocuous to purchase, but couldn't think of a single thing I needed. Maybe water. The human body's made up of something like ninety-nine percent water. Water was a perfectly normal thing to need, right?

"Hey," I said as we neared a teeming supermarket. "I need to stop here a second."

I must've sounded casual, since Roger turned on his blinker and pulled into the lot without any questions. "I'll just be in and out," I said, opening my door as he passed by the entrance while his car was still moving, so he'd need to wait for me rather than park and follow. "Need anything?"

He looked a little perplexed at my sudden burst of motion, but he didn't challenge me. "Nope," he said. "I'm good."

Thank God. I jogged through the automatic doors and swerved around a woman who seemed to have twenty or thirty kids in tow. At least six, anyway, and most of them howling. But none of them were trying to put their hands on me, and that was good enough for me.

I trailed along behind them until I felt grounded enough to move on to the drug aisle. I picked up a few rolls of antacids, the small ones that you can hide in your pockets. I remembered a time when I hid more interesting things than antacids in my pockets and I felt sorry for myself. Then I grabbed a water from a refrigerated unit at the end of a checkout line, and rejoined Roger in the car.

"Thirsty," I said, and I toasted him with the water. And then I drank it so I wouldn't have to talk to him while he drove the rest of the way to the park.

I was thankful that the East River looked nothing like the Calumet. It was deep and rushing, and its surface started about twenty feet below street level. Not the type of slow, shallow river in which a guy would bob around in a rowboat.

It occurred to me that if I just hurried up and talked to a dead kid and found out where it was buried, we could go back to the Fifth. Heck, maybe I could even go back home. I turned off my phone so it wouldn't disturb me and started looking in earnest.

We hiked up to the guardrail at the edge of the river and looked down. Someone had drunk a twelve pack of Busch Light and dumped all the cans and even the cardboard box onto the riverbank below. If the river had been higher the litter probably would've floated away by now, but instead it just sat there in the dirt, an unsightly reminder that most people suck.

I bent at the waist and hung over the rail, looking hard for ghosts in the water. But the surface was just grayish, greenish rushing water. Nothing more.

Since a ghost could theoretically hang out on the banks, just like those empty beer cans—great analogy—I hiked up the river, pausing periodically at the guard rail and squinting down into the river. After walking what probably amounted to several city blocks, we came across a black metal footbridge.

I trooped to the center of the bridge with Roger tailing me and stared down, fully expecting to see faces flowing past twenty feet below. Nothing.

We crossed to the other side and combed through that for at least an hour. My stomach continued to churn, and I surreptitiously opened the antacid wrapper inside my pocket with my thumbnail. I crunched on the tablets whenever I could sneak one into my mouth without Roger noticing. I wished I'd eaten something a little blander for lunch, like maybe gruel. It's hard to try to pick out ghosts with your stomach screaming for your attention.

Eventually I spotted a park bench half-hidden among a cluster of scraggly shrubs and made my way over. I sat, and Roger sat beside me. He pulled out a notepad and started writing, presumably detailing all the areas we'd scanned and come up empty.

I cast my mind back to the files from the morning. I'd memorized the kids' first names: Michael, Lucy, Dawn, Hubert… who the hell names their kid Hubert, even in the seventies? Must've been a family name. I pressed my thumb into my forehead. I stared in the direction of the river and actually *tried* to see the kids. Nothing.

I let my breath out and sagged against the park bench, draping my elbows over the back. The cell phone store would be open. I figured we could go back there, scan the place, and call it a day.

I looked at Roger and was about to say as much when I saw it. There was a face in the bush behind Roger's head.

I focused on the face and it grew clear. A man, late thirties-early forties, with the top of his head sliced off.

I wanted to jump back and yell out the first swear word that popped into my head, but there was Roger. I have no idea why, but I just couldn't let Roger know I'd been spooked, just like I wouldn't tell him about my stomachache. Probably it's a guy thing. I just blinked.

The shallowly-decapitated guy's eyes widened, as if he'd just realized that I could see him, or maybe as if he'd just seen me. He'd probably want to tell me what'd happened. Industrial accident. Gruesome mob hit. Whatever.

A hand appeared in the bush beside the face and reached toward me.

"Don't you fucking dare," I snarled, and it was Roger who jumped.

I ignored Roger, went around him, and grabbed at the bush, tearing off a branch. The ghost with the shave-topped head groped at me again.

"What the fuck do you want?" I said, swinging the branch like a baseball bat. It passed right through his hand. "Talk to me, you stupid fuck."

A second head coalesced. It was mutilated like the first, but its scalp flapped from the side of its skull like a bad toupee. Another hand reached out of the bush toward me, and another.

"Stop it," I yelled, swatting the bush with the branch I'd torn off. Another mutilated head appeared, and another. They weren't exact copies of each other, either. Like a bunch of different, unrelated guys got clipped by a ceiling fan on a rampage.

Another pair of hands sprouted out, and another, and something cold and psychically slimy trailed over my wrist where a spectral hand touched me.

I whirled away and ran toward the river, the branch still in my hand. I was screaming, but I didn't give a fuck. I barreled into the guardrail, which clipped me right at hip level, and flung the branch into the rushing water.

"Aaaaaaghhh!"

And then I threw up.

4

I think if I were anyone else, they would've taken me to the hospital. But… think about it. A guy who sees dead people, and a hospital where people are dropping like flies. Bad combination.

There's a special clinic in the near north suburbs where I fill out inane psychological tests every four months to see if I'm crazy yet and get my prescriptions. It's a low, blond-brick building, constructed ten years ago at the end of a residential street. There's no signage on the building, so I've always just referred to it as "The Clinic." And no one had ever died there. Not yet, anyway.

After my freak-out and apparent collapse, Roger called Warwick, who rushed over in person to take me to The Clinic.

There was a Paranormal Psychiatrist on staff who I'd been seeing so long that he called me "Mister Bayne" instead of "Detective." Dr. Morganstern, man of a thousand sweater vests. He was the one who'd gotten me into the Auracel trials a year before the FDA gave the drug a stamp of approval. I wondered if he had any fun new drugs that would help me hold it together.

A nurse drew a couple vials of blood, took my vitals and ran through my physical symptoms without going into my psychic experience. I've always gotten the impression I was only to discuss those things with Morganstern.

I lay back in a comfy bed, in a room that looked more like a very small hotel suite than a hospital room. The bedspread and curtains were done in a muted floral pattern, and there were a couple of live plants on the dark wood nightstand. I peeked into a cabinet expecting to find a television, but the cabinet was empty. No big deal. If there had actually been a set in there, it probably would've had cable, and so my static station would've been playing all-day soap operas.

There was a brief knock on the door, and a woman in her early thirties who I'd never seen before let herself in. She was slim and pretty, with ash blonde hair cut short and just a little spiky, with glasses so delicate I could've crushed them in the palm of my hand. She wore a boxy sweater over brown corduroys. "Hello," she said, glancing down at a clipboard she carried and then back at me. "I'm Doctor Jennifer Chance."

Oh God. I had a big breakdown in a public park and I had to deal with some doctor I'd never even met? Great, just great. "Is Dr. Morganstern around? Did you page him? Not that there's anything wrong with you—I just want to talk to Dr. Morganstern."

"I'm sorry," Dr. Chance said. I thought I could detect some genuine sympathy there. "Dr. Morganstern is in Japan."

"Oh," I said. And that seemed to be all there was to say about it. I wanted to argue with her, to try to put off doing anything until Morganstern was back, but I wasn't sure my problem, whatever it was, could wait. I didn't realize how attached I was to him until he wasn't there.

Dr. Chance took my account of what had happened to me, what I'd seen, what I'd done. It seemed odd to me that she wasn't wearing...oh, I dunno. Scrubs. A lab coat. But then again, neither had Dr. Morganstern.

Chance questioned me for nearly an hour, writing notes even as she spoke. I wondered if that was something like being ambidextrous, the ability to speak and write at the same time. I'm lucky I can walk and breathe simultaneously without choking.

Chance shuffled some papers. "Your intake sheet says you vomited and then partially lost consciousness. What have you eaten today?"

"A Polish sausage, a curly fry, some coffee."

"And earlier?"

I felt like a lecture would be coming but there was nothing I could do to avoid it. Then again, I had no reason to think Dr. Chance was the lecturing type. I sighed. "Coffee. And coffee the day before. A donut yesterday morning. That's all."

"Is it common for you to skip meals?"

"No. I don't know. Yeah, I guess." She wrote some notes. "It's a cop thing," I added lamely.

"I'm scheduling an upper G.I. for you first thing in the morning. Eat bland foods as your appetite allows, then no food after midnight, no water after two a.m., and no more coffee today. Got it?"

"You think I have an ulcer, don't you?"

"It's too early to say. But given your medical background, we have to take more precautions than we do with the general public."

Right. It was more likely that the force wanted to keep me alive so they didn't have to go through the trouble of finding and training another Psych.

"Drugs?" she asked.

Shit. I wanted to lie about how much Auracel I'd taken the day before. I always lied. But they were testing my blood as we spoke, and lying wouldn't get me anywhere.

"Auracel, ninety milligrams about twenty-four hours ago." Chance recorded the number without making me repeat myself, or mentioning that it was triple the highest recommended dosage, or doing a spit-take. I probably should've told her about the Seconal, but Seconal's been discontinued for some time and I didn't exactly get it through a reputable connection. If it showed up in the tests and they called me on it, I could just say I'd forgotten.

"Would you be able to sleep if you stopped your medications until tomorrow morning?"

"Yeah. Of course. I mean, I'm not dependent or anything. I don't take them every day." Just on a bad day. Like a day in which I've seen a bush full of scalped heads.

Just thinking about it made me crave an Auracel with a Seconal chaser.

I made an appointment to return at seven a.m., an ungodly hour, but since I wasn't likely to sleep and couldn't eat, it was probably for the best.

"About the sleeping," I said, wondering if I could get my hands on some barbiturates legally. "If you knew of something that could take the edge off—maybe you could write…."

"We'll see after your blood work comes back. Good night, Detective."

Was it night? I checked the clock on my cell phone. Quarter past seven. I wanted to be home. I wished I'd been born with the ability to teleport instead of hearing the dead. And I wondered if Roger'd bought another cup of coffee for me while he was waiting.

I opened the door to the lobby and nearly bought the idea that my desire to teleport had made it happen; Jacob stared at me from a seat directly across from the door. He had on a pair of jeans, one of his incredibly form-fitting black T-shirts, and a plain leather jacket. He was on his feet and halfway across the room before I even cleared the doorway. "What happened?" he asked me.

I blinked and looked around. A yellow streetlight shone through the thick safety glass on the doorway. The receptionist's window was dark and he was gone for the night. We were alone—except for the surveillance camera that was trained on us. They don't take any chances at modern Psych facilities.

I shook my head. "I dunno. They're doing some tests." I took Jacob by the elbow and steered him toward the door. Despite the fact that there were no faces swarming in the popcorn texture of the walls, no spirits popping out of the philodendrons, I really, really wanted to be home.

Jacob's car was parked in a handicapped spot next to the front door. He opened the passenger door for me and it felt like we were going to the prom. I wondered if anyone was watching. "How'd you end up here?" I asked him. "Did Roger call you?"

Jacob closed my door and got in the driver's side. "Maurice did."

My struggle to figure out how Maurice figured into everything must have shown on my face. "Maurice is your emergency contact," Jacob told me.

"Oh," I said, because that was true. I wondered how Maurice knew to tell Jacob—and then I realized the whole "I'm gay" conversation wasn't going to be necessary at all. "Oh."

5

"Are you sure you don't want to go to the emergency room?" Jacob asked me for the third time. He was driving with both hands on the wheel and he looked like he'd be happy to run down anyone unlucky enough to get in his way.

"I don't go to hospitals," I said. "I can't. Not without something to block out the ghosts."

Jacob pressed his lips together in a grim line and glared through the windshield.

"This is the same clinic I go to for everything except dental and vision, Jacob. It's fine. It's…it's more than fine. It's the only place qualified to deal with Psychs, and besides that, it's state of the art."

He didn't say anything else for the rest of the ride home, and I was worried he was pissed off at me. I almost apologized to him, except that he was the type of guy who'd probably ask me what I was sorry about, and I wouldn't be able to answer him.

I left Jacob in the kitchen while I flipped on all the lights in the apartment and checked the closet for spectral heads. All clear.

I turned around and found Jacob blocking my way out of the closet. I wondered if he'd appreciate the irony. He stood with his arms crossed, biceps bulging. It was a pose he'd struck when I'd first met him, in which he'd looked all buff and sexy. Now he looked mostly mad.

"Any idea why Lisa called me from Santa Barbara and told me to leave?"

I eased forward, and Jacob reluctantly allowed me into the bedroom. I sat on the edge of the bed and tried to remember if the message I'd left for Lisa was anything that should've sent her into a tailspin, but I didn't think it had been, even if I had just seen a bunch of submerged heads right before I'd called her.

"No."

Jacob sat down beside me and the bed creaked. He let his breath out slowly. And when he spoke his voice was soft, as if he'd just let all the anger out of himself, too. "I couldn't figure out what she was trying to tell me, and on top of that she was whispering so that I could barely hear. She said you were in danger. From the living and the dead."

Lisa. Did she know how to leave a melodramatic message, or what? Not that

I didn't believe her—which is saying a lot, since she was off consorting with the Moonies of her own free will. But until she could give me some specifics, there really wasn't much I could do.

I could feel Jacob staring at me from the side. "That's why I'm worried about that clinic," he said. "What if they don't have your best interests at heart?"

I laughed before I could even control it, an ugly little bark that was too loud and sudden in my stark bedroom. "Christ, Jacob. I'd lay money on it that they don't. The force, the government, whoever…they want a medium. A level five. Can I expect them to keep me comfy and cozy and safe? No. But I can count on them to do what it takes to keep me upright and babbling."

"…and that partner of yours?"

"Roger? You think I need to worry about a guy who buys me Starbucks?"

"Look," said Jacob. "Here's what you should do. Take your cash card, and mine, and withdraw the maximum amount from each account. Then go to the train station and buy a ticket with cash…."

"What? Why should I go anywhere? I don't know what this supposed danger even is. And where would you be in all of this?"

Jacob stared at the side of my cheap white laminated dresser. "Here. Figuring out what's going on."

"You expect me to go somewhere without you?"

Jacob's jaw worked for a moment, and then he put his elbows on his knees and his face in his hands. "You've got to get away from me. Lisa said…."

"Lisa said? You told me you couldn't even understand her!"

"She said I brought it."

I stared. I tried to piece something into that phrase that would make sense of it. What did he bring me? A stomach virus? What about something more insidious… like hope?

I really, really wanted a Seconal.

"Look," I said, doing my best to put on a voice that was incredibly reasonable sounding. I did a pretty good job. "She didn't give you a full message, so we can't act on it. I don't know what she meant. Do you?"

Jacob looked at me sideways.

"That's what's wrong with Psychs," I said. "The sixth sense doesn't match up with the other senses, so anything we describe comes out flawed. It's like trying to describe how purple smells, or what pain sounds like."

Jacob stared at my knee as if he couldn't quite bring himself to look me in the eye. "But we can't just sit back and do nothing," he said. He'd quieted down, but his voice still held a clipped urgency. "You didn't hear how panicked she sounded."

Good thing. I'd already thrown up and sort of fainted. I didn't need something else to worry about. "It's not going to help for me to go running off," I told Jacob. "If The Clinic, or whoever, is as dangerous as all that, they've probably got some kind of chip in me already."

Jacob finally did look me in the eye, and his face went ashen.

I shrugged. I'd been on a short leash ever since I can remember. That's how I've turned out to be such a liar. "Lisa did her job," I went on, trying to calm Jacob down. "She warned us. Now we know to look out."

"Look out for what?"

I sank back onto my bed and stared up at the ceiling. "Who knows? But if we just play dumb and keep our eyes open, we'll find out."

—◊◊◊—

Jacob made me some eggs and toast and I ate it, and washed it down with orange juice. Breakfast at eleven thirty p.m., since I wasn't supposed to eat after midnight. We curled up on the couch together and watched an old rerun of Ghostbusters. It probably shouldn't have struck me funny, the idea of green, gooey ectoplasm and a bad guy made of marshmallow, but it did.

And the next thing I knew, Jacob was shaking me. And not very gently, either. "Say something," he said.

"What?" I mumbled, struggling to orient myself. "What?"

"Can you hear me? What day is it? Who's the president?"

"Yes, I don't know, and a horse's ass."

Jacob let go of me. We were on the living room futon with all the lights on and a re-run of Three's Company on TV. Dark showed through a gap in the miniblinds. The VCR blinked 12:00—no help there—but I couldn't have been asleep for long. My heart fluttered in that nervous rhythm it gets when I'm ripped out of the early stages of sleep.

"Were you having a nightmare?" Jacob asked.

If I was, it hadn't been very impressive. I actually didn't have many nightmares. My waking life probably gave my subconscious an inferiority complex. "Uh-uh. Why? Was I talking in my sleep?"

"No. You scratched me."

I gave Jacob a look like I couldn't believe he'd be such a sissy over a scratch, when he turned toward me and I saw the arm of his T-shirt hanging off, a line of bright blood slipping down his arm. "Holy shit! I did that?"

Jacob wadded the remains of his sleeve against his upper biceps. "You're awake now?" He stood cautiously. "I don't want to get blood on your white couch."

"Fuck the couch." I jumped up. "Let me see."

He shook me off and went into the bathroom, where I crowded in behind him. "How bad is it?"

"You're blocking the light," he said. He sounded too calm for someone who was bleeding.

I reached up and flicked on the fluorescent bar over the mirror. It hummed a little, but it was good enough to shave by. "C'mon," I said. "Show me."

Talking to Jacob was like talking to a brick wall. He turned on the cold water tap and then tore his bloody sleeve the rest of the way off. Although he didn't turn so I could see the cut, I got a good look at it in the mirror despite him. It wasn't just one scratch, it was two. They almost looked like a sloppy, upside down "T."

"Shit."

Jacob splashed some water on it and took a look at it in the mirror. It showed up plain for a moment, and then more blood oozed out of it, mixing with the water and running in a rivulet down his arm.

"What did I do that with?" I demanded. I wondered how I could've possibly been asleep while something like that was happening. "Was I sleepwalking?"

Jacob sighed, splashed the cut again, then pulled a big handful of toilet paper off the roll to blot it with. "You weren't sleepwalking. I thought you were...you know...just putting your arms around me in your sleep. And then you scratched me."

"What—with my nails?"

Jacob didn't answer.

He had to be wrong. Not that he'd lie about something like that, but I was sure he'd been mistaken. I must've had something sharp in my hand that I'd dropped while he was shaking me. My fingernails weren't capable of inflicting that kind of damage. I looked down at them with the intention of saying so, and saw they were caked with blood.

I spun out of the bathroom and into the kitchen. I wrenched the kitchen faucet on and thrust my hands beneath it. My vision started tunneling like I was going to have another fucking fainting spell, and I gulped air to keep myself standing. I told myself it was just some congealed blood and not a shred of skin I was pushing out from under my fingernail as I tried to scrub away what I'd done.

I was still washing my hands when Jacob came out of the bathroom. He'd tied a handtowel around the "T" I'd gouged into him.

"Maybe I should go to a motel," he said.

I glanced at the clock. Almost five. "No, don't," I said. "I have to go to the clinic in an hour and a half anyway. I'll stay awake. I'll have some coffee."

Jacob reached over my shoulder and turned off the faucet. He sighed and leaned back against the sink, crossing his arms loosely over his stomach. "It's not me that I'm worried about. It's you."

"Which is why you should stay. We'll watch the early news."

Jacob pinched the bridge of his nose, a weary gesture. He'd been up all night. "Lisa made it sound like I was the problem here, not you. That I needed to get away from you."

"She said that? Specifically?"

Jacob knuckled his eyes, sighed again, and sat down on a kitchen stool. "I don't know what she said specifically, Vic. She took me off guard."

"And then what did you do?"

"I tried to call you," he said, in a "duh" sort of way. "But it went to voicemail."

I looked over at the jacket hanging from my back door. The phone was in the inner pocket and it hadn't made a sound in ages. Cripes. I'd turned it off at the park.

I pulled the phone out of my jacket, flipped it open, and winced. Fifteen phone messages. Lisa, eight times. My own land line: Jacob, I guessed. Maurice, twice. Jacob's cell. Warwick. Maurice again. And Roger.

"Aren't I Mister Popularity?" I said. I hoped I sounded as disgusted as I felt—with myself for leaving my phone off, or with everyone I know waiting until I was at The Clinic to call me, I don't know.

"Did Lisa call?" Jacob asked.

"Yeah."

"Then see if you can make heads or tails of it," he said, and went into the living room.

I wanted to tell Jacob to come back, but there was something so determined about the way he'd walked off that I didn't bother. I looked at my phone in my hand and wondered if it would make a bigger ding in the wall than the coaster had.

But I was the one who'd called Lisa first, back at the river when I'd first seen a cluster of ghostly underwater heads. So I should probably listen to what Lisa had to say.

I accessed my voicemail. "Vic," she whispered. "Shit, I gotta talk to you."

The next message was a hangup. Actually, it was more like a half second of panicked breathing, but I was trying not to think about it. The next four, more of the same. On the seventh message, she finally said something.

"I shouldn't be calling you. I'm not supposed to be talking to anyone. And they told me not to use the *sí-no* on anyone by myself until I take these ethics seminars, but you sounded so bad in your message. Vic, something's really, really wrong. And I can't figure out what it is without knowing what's going on with you. I don't know what to ask…shit."

It cut off abruptly, then picked up again with her next call. "The only person you can trust is Carolyn." There was a second of shaky breathing, some tinny, intercom-sounding announcement whose words I couldn't make out, and a little chime. "I gotta go to the cafeteria or they'll find out I called you. Look, not even Jacob, okay?" She sighed. "Especially Jacob."

I looked at the doorway to the living room. How could she tell me not to trust Jacob? And how was I supposed to explain that to him? I heard cloth rustling and followed the sound into the bedroom. He was doing exactly what I was afraid he'd be doing: packing a duffel bag. Less than twenty-four hours ago he'd been hinting at getting a place together, and now this.

"She didn't say anything specific," I told him, hoping that I could distract him by talking. "I'm not supposed to trust anybody. That was the gist of it."

He glanced at me and then focused again on tucking a T-shirt into his bag. "She called me up and told me something was wrong and it was because of me. She was pretty pissed off. I tried to get her to go into the *sí-no* with me to prove I wasn't doing anything—at least, nothing that I knew of—and she wouldn't even go there. Then she said she was going to get kicked out of the program if they caught her and hung up."

Jacob wasn't going anywhere. That's all there was to it. I stuck my hand into his bag and pulled out the shirt he'd just packed. He stared at it but didn't move to stop me. "Look," I said. "You're here and Lisa isn't, and this *sí-no* shit is just too fucking vague. Don't leave."

Jacob fiddled with the duffel bag's strap.

"Please." I took him gently by the chin and turned his face toward mine. When I stared into his eyes, I felt the L-word threatening to come out, but it was too soon, way too soon. I pressed my mouth against his to stop myself from saying anything stupid and he kissed me back, slow but sure. There was a slight hesitation, then Jacob deepened the kiss, his tongue sliding over my lower lip as his fingers abandoned the duffel bag to tangle in my hair.

He got his arm around me and pulled me against him hard, and I had his lower lip between mine, sucking on it, raking it with my teeth, and despite all the horror show it seemed like my life had become, I was hard for him, rocking myself into his hip while his breathing grew rough.

Jacob pulled back from the kiss and looked at me, and his hand tightened in my hair. His eyes looked black, his face flushed and intense. Then he glanced at the clock radio, and I did too. Five thirty. There was enough time before my appointment.

He dragged me down onto the hardwood floor, yanking off my undershirt while I unbuttoned my pants, the same ones I'd worn to work yesterday. Sometime while I'd slept, Jacob had changed into sweatpants and a T-shirt (now missing a sleeve and splattered with a couple drops of blood), and he stripped out of those in no time flat.

We knelt together naked on the floor. My hands moved over the muscles of his chest and belly, brushed against the hardness of his hipbones and clutched him there. I told myself not to scratch him and wondered when exactly I'd turned into Freddy Krueger while I did my best to ignore the towel wrapped around his arm.

Jacob's hands dropped to my ass. He took a cheek in each hand and squeezed, and his fingers pressed into the crack like he could open me right up. My cock must've liked the idea. It stood up straight and poked him in the hip.

Jacob groaned and let go of my ass, swaying back enough to get his hand between us and wrap it around my cock. I gasped, and his mouth covered mine, tongue hot and wet, pressing in.

His hand moved on me, that demanding stroke of his, and my hips flexed in time with his pumping. And then he let go, took me by the hips just like I had him, and eased us apart. "Suck me" he said, his voice low and oh-so-edible, "while I suck you."

I dropped down onto my side and Jacob lowered himself the other way, one hand stroking my thigh while he tucked his other arm under his head. It was a stupid time to have sex, I told myself, what with the disembodied heads and freaky phone calls…and then Jacob's lips slid onto me, just covering my cockhead, and his tongue did a slow tease at my slit.

I pressed my face into his thigh and let out a trembling breath. He sure knew how to make me forget my problems. I dragged my lips downward until my chin settled into the crease of his thigh, then slid my mouth over the musky skin of Jacob's balls. He made a low noise in his throat and took my whole cock into his mouth.

I found the base of Jacob's cock and pressed my lips into it, and felt it swell and harden. I let my breath play over it as I eased my mouth slowly up its length, and ran my tongue carefully over the broad head, and then my own lips, getting everything nice and wet.

Jacob's hand slid around me and grabbed me by the ass again, squeezing me like he really meant business. I wondered if I'd end up in a backless hospital gown at the clinic where the whole staff would get a good look at my white ass with red fingerprints all over it, or maybe even bruises. Jacob nudged my mouth with his cock, and I hoped he did mark me up, fingers, teeth, hickeys, the works. The idea made all my blood surge down to my groin.

I took him by the ass too, squeezed it hard and used it to pull myself against him, stuff his cock as far into my mouth as it would go. Jacob made another inarticulate noise and pulled at my ass again, and then one of his fingers was there, stroking my totally exposed hole.

I pulled my face back a little and then ground it into him hard, clutching at him just as brutally as he grasped me, and the two of us fell into some sort of rhythm, grabbing and squeezing and rocking into each others' faces. I broke first, crying out around his fat cock as he managed to hit all the right nerve endings just at the same time, tongue and lips and fingers all making me crazy. He swallowed like he always did, and his sucking turned from insistent to gentle as he drew my orgasm out, relishing every last twitch he could pull from me.

I got my hand around the base of his cock and started pumping it into my mouth. I felt the cold inrush of air as Jacob gasped around my wet cock, felt his thigh start trembling against my shoulder. It occurred to me that I was going to have stomach tests an hour later, so I pulled off at the first hint of bittersweet, jacked off Jacob's spit-wet cock and felt his hot come splash over my neck.

I settled my head on Jacob's lower thigh and simply lay there with my arm draped over his hips while his breathing evened out. No scratches. No grabby ghost hands. No phone calls. Jacob and I were fine.

6

I called the Fifth Precinct on my way to The Clinic and had them list Jacob as my emergency contact along with Maurice. Jacob wanted to come into The Clinic with me, but I made him promise to go to work. He'd only do that after I swore I'd call him to pick me up after the GI series. He gave me a good long look before I got out of the car, and a squeeze on the knee. I forced a smile.

The receptionist's desk was occupied this time, same guy as usual whose name I can never seem to remember. I think of him as, "Nerdy, Horn-Rimmed Glasses," but I doubt he'd appreciate knowing that. I asked him about altering my emergency contact at The Clinic, and he said he'd get the paperwork ready for me while I was having the procedure.

I didn't much care for the word "procedure." I swallowed hard and quelled a Camp Hell flashback. The same nurse from the night before took my pulse and temperature, and instructed me to strip down to my socks, don the pale blue hospital gown and have a seat on the paper-covered exam table. I tried to see if I actually did have Jacob's finger marks on my ass but my neck didn't turn far enough, and there wasn't a mirror in my room.

Moments later, Dr. Chance knocked once and strolled in wearing a very undoctor like peasant blouse, denim skirt and cork-soled burgundy clogs that I couldn't keep from staring at. She was so focused on her clipboard that the urge welled up in me to flash her my ass and ask if she saw any bruises. And then I assumed that I must be getting panicky if I was fantasizing about doing something that'd probably get me committed. Again.

"How are you feeling this morning, Detective?"

I thought about it, kind of. Actually, it was more like I thought about what to say that would sound normal. "Tired." I said, finally. I figured that'd be reasonable.

Chance kept scanning notes. "Any more alarming sixth-sensory experiences?"

I thought some more. "Uh. Nope."

"Good. And did you have any coffee this morning?"

Oops. I almost had. But then I had this fight with Jacob and we made up in the best possible way. What were we freaked out about again? Lisa? No, something else.

Oh. The scratches.

My stomach churned its own acid. I wondered if I should tell Chance about the scratches. I decided to hold off, since once I said something I wouldn't be able to take it back. Besides, I reasoned. The scratches weren't sixth sensory. They were just fucking weird.

"Detective?"

"No. Nothing since midnight."

Dr. Chance gave me my choice of strawberry or chocolate barium milkshake, with the warning that they tasted like neither. I chose the strawberry. I was then given a club soda-like drink and told to swallow it but not to burp. And then they took a bunch of X-rays.

After I dressed, a nurse offered me a bottle of orange juice and a plastic-wrapped bagel from a vending machine, which I accepted in hopes of flushing the barium out of my system.

By ten o'clock I sat waiting in an exam room for Dr. Chance and her cork-soled clogs. There was a small desk with a chair for the patient beside it. I preferred that chair to the paper-covered table. Chance came in with her clipboard. "We've called the radiologist in and so far your stomach looks normal."

At least some part of me is.

"Your blood work is another story."

I sat very still to keep myself from bashing my head into her desk.

"We're going to have to reconfigure your meds," she said. "Your liver enzymes are high and your liver itself is slightly inflamed."

"Okay." I had no idea what that meant, but I seriously doubted it was anything to mess around with.

"No acetaminophen. If you need a pain reliever, take plain aspirin, and no more than the recommended dose. I see here that you don't drink alcohol. Is that correct?"

"Yes."

"Good. Don't start."

I nodded.

"And no Auracel."

I blinked. "Were you listening when I told you I was seeing heads in the bushes yesterday?" I asked her. I'd also gotten to my feet, somewhere in my panic of having my precious pills taken away. I towered over Chance, who simply looked up at me from the rolling stool at the small Formica desk.

"Regardless of that, Auracel is not an option for you until your liver enzymes come down."

"And how am I supposed to get my liver enzymes down?" I asked her. Actually, I yelled it.

"We'll take some more blood today and try to determine if you've been exposed to hepatitis, or if this is your liver's reaction to Auracel at such high doses."

"This is bullshit," I said. I'd begun pacing in the narrow aisle between the exam table and a small metal sink on one side, Dr. Chance and my empty chair on the other. "I am a level five medium. You can't just tell me to go cold turkey on the Auracel."

"Detective? Sit down."

I couldn't. I was too pissed off. But I did stop pacing and instead planted my hands on my hips and glared at her.

"I can prescribe a mild sedative in the short term, and remove you from active duty until we determine a course of treatment."

I glared at her some more.

"But right now, all of the FDA-approved anti-psyactives are metabolized by the liver, and we can't risk you taking them until we find out what's going on."

"Even at lower doses?" I asked. And what I meant by that was, the actual dose I was supposed to have been taking all along—one pill twice daily, not three and four at a time.

"Detective," she said, gesturing again toward the chair beside the small desk. I was exhausted, so I gave in and sat.

"You need to be careful specifically because you *are* a level five medium. As such, you are not a candidate for an organ transplant."

I tried to imagine marching around with a dead guy's liver inside of me and my brain nearly leaked out my ears. Dollars to donuts the sonofabitch who'd lost it would be dogging my steps trying to get it back until I was pushing up daisies.

"I want to see Dr. Morganstern," I said.

"He's arranging his return flight, but in the meantime, we're both agreed on this course of action."

I glared at the paper-covered table. Chance kept talking. "And another thing." She slipped a pamphlet into my hands. On the cover was a triangle with a rainbow inside and I nearly spewed the bagel the nurse had given me. Jesus Christ, how'd she know I was gay? It was the blowjob. They'd found traces of semen in my mouth. Oh God, I was so fired. And then I'd lose my health coverage, and then my liver would explode.

"In addition to changing the meds, you'll have to start watching your diet," she said.

I stared at her.

"The USDA modified the food pyramid to reflect their most recent guidelines," she said, as I scrambled to figure out what my diet had to do with being queer. Chance pointed at the pamphlet. "You'll note there's no donut group. And no coffee group either. Limit coffee to one cup a day. Two, at the most."

I looked back down at the pamphlet and read the title. *My Pyramid Plan: a Guide to Healthy Eating.*

———✺———

Once Dr. Chance and her clogs left, I sat in my backless gown for several minutes staring at the summer-green wall. No anti-psyactives. I could do it. I could. In fact, I was straight most of the week (in the drug sense, anyhow) because it made working easier. And my apartment was clear, as long as I didn't go in the laundry room. And then my liver would stabilize, and everything would be just great.

I ignored the way my hand was shaking when I called Jacob for a ride home.

"Good timing," he said. "We're eating lunch about a mile away at Palatzo. Want me to pick anything up for you?"

I thought of the not-gay brochure I'd stuffed into my back jeans pocket. "Chicken calzone. And a…salad."

"Sure. We're on our way."

Apparently Jacob didn't know me well enough to know I hadn't had a salad in over a year.

But I knew him well enough to figure out that he'd lunched well outside his precinct so he'd be nearby when I called for my ride. Palatzo was okay, but it wasn't worth making a special trip for.

The whole "we" business was a little unsettling, since it meant his partner, Carolyn Brinkman, was with him. Carolyn's only a level two Psych, but she can smell a lie a mile away. At least she paid for her talent by having to be truthful herself, but that price wasn't much consolation for me when I was freaking out about the prospect of life without Auracel. I wished I'd called a cab instead, but it was too late. Jacob had probably already paid for my salad.

I dressed slowly and tried to compose myself. I'd just have to scour my old Camp Hell textbooks and figure out how to deal with unwanted spirit sightings on my own. The books were written before anti-psyactives even existed, so they had to have something I could use. And people ditched ghosts all the time, right? That's what exorcisms were all about.

Okay, maybe not all the time. But it was possible.

I stopped by the receptionist's desk on my way out. Most of it faces the hallway that leads to the exam rooms, but a little window gives access to the waiting room. I noticed the reinforced glass in the little window, like I always did. I wasn't sure if it was to protect the Psychs from the public or the public from the Psychs.

Nerdy Horn-Rimmed Glasses was typing as I tried to slip by, but he snapped-to when my hand touched the doorknob. I don't know why I thought I could get past him anyway; he had to buzz me out.

"Detective Bayne," he said, and I made myself turn toward him. It wasn't his fault I had to reschedule, but who else could I blame? "I have a prescription for you," he said, and suddenly I liked him a whole lot better.

I took the little white bag from him. It felt light. Damn it.

"You're scheduled for fasting blood work for the next five days. Would you like to keep your appointment at seven?"

I ran my hand over my face. Being psychic was such a pain in the ass. "Make it eight," I said. No reason for me to be up with the pigeons if I wasn't on active duty.

The guy clicked around on his computer. "Eight a.m. tomorrow," he said, somehow managing to make it sound incredibly nerdy, and buzzed me out.

I nearly tripped over Roger Burke as I flew out the door. "Oh," I said, since I'd expected Jacob.

"Victor!" He grabbed my hand and shook it vigorously in both of his. He was so happy to see me I almost regretted being off active duty. "How do you feel? Are you okay?"

"Just, um...y'know. Hangin' in there. They took me off active duty for now... tests."

"C'mon." He clapped me on the shoulder in a straight-guy kind of way. At least, I think that was what it was. I wondered if the Auracel had killed my gaydar along with my liver. "I'll drive you home."

"Um," I said, feeling weird about refusing a ride from someone so eager to please. "That's okay...."

"I picked up some Starbucks on the way here."

Every cell in my body said, "woo-hah." Chance had said I could have one a day, right? And if I had to limit myself to one, it might as well be Starbucks. I wondered how rude it'd be to just take the coffee and decline the ride.

"Well, I've got a friend coming to pick me up," I said. "He's on his way."

"Oh," said Roger, still cheerful, far as I could tell. "Okay." He walked side by side with me to the front door. "But you might as well take the coffee. If you want it, I mean. They'll get cold if I try to drink 'em both myself."

Yay. He offered. "Well, uh, sure. Since you went through the trouble and all. Can I give you anything for it?"

"Nah, it's my 'get well' present." I pulled the door open for Roger as he said this, and he nearly walked smack into Jacob.

7

Roger did a little double-take when Jacob didn't step back and apologize like a regular guy might. Jacob stood his ground instead and looked from Roger to me, and raised an eyebrow.

"Oh, hey," I said. "This is Roger, my new partner. Roger, this is Jacob, my, uh…." God, could there be a worse word than "boyfriend?" It made us sound like Barbie and Ken. Or Ken and Ken. Or Ken and G.I. Joe. I told my mind to stop stalling and think of a way to say it. "My partner…at home."

There. I'd said it within the first week of knowing Roger. Now we wouldn't have any awkward conversations looming over us. Or not as awkward as this one, anyway.

Jacob's lips curved into a smile and he held out his hand. "Good to meet you," he said, a teasing lilt to his voice. I had no idea he'd be so tickled about being introduced as my boyfriend. Or whatever.

"Right," Roger said brightly—my guess was that his brightness was covering some discomfort, but that was fine, as long as he wasn't gonna be a dick about it. "Jacob Marks from the Twelfth Precinct. You and your *work* partner are a very well-known PsyCop unit."

Jacob inclined his head graciously. He could take a compliment like royalty. Then he turned to me. "Ready to go? I think Carolyn's been eyeing your salad."

I didn't particularly care about ditching Roger. I just wanted to get home. "Yeah, okay. Thanks for stopping by to check on me."

"Wait!" Roger dashed to his Crown Vic, a carbon copy of Jacob's, except that it was midnight blue instead of black, and pulled out the Starbucks. "Don't forget your coffee."

"Thanks," I repeated, giving him a salute as I took it. Jacob smirked at me a little as he held the passenger door open for me yet again, but I ignored it.

Carolyn was in the back seat when I climbed into the car. Her tweed suit fit her perfectly, and her blonde hair was swept back into a neat French twist. I couldn't say if she was eyeing my salad, or not.

"I'm not mad," I told her, protecting my coffee as Jacob closed my door for me. We hadn't really talked since a conversation she'd had with Sergeant Warwick resulted in Lisa not only being suspended from duty, but locked up somewhere—"unofficially," of course. Not that Carolyn could've done anything different. She hadn't been able to lie, and Warwick had figured out exactly how to read her silences. She'd been pretty quiet after that.

I peeked over the headrest and she met my eyes. "I know," she said. Good thing I'd actually meant it instead of just saying it to make her feel better. "I just didn't like being the weak link."

Jacob climbed into the driver's seat, shut his door and pulled away from the curb. Roger was still parked, drinking his coffee, and he waved at us as we passed him.

"So that's the guy who's wooing you with coffee," Jacob remarked.

I was about to snap back that I certainly wasn't being wooed when I noticed he was grinning. I calmed down. "Yeah, that's Roger."

Jacob glanced at Carolyn in the rearview. "You'll have to talk to him and ask if he's maneuvering to steal Vic away from me."

"That's really ethical," she said.

I rolled my eyes and concentrated on my coffee. It was good, really good, a bitter, earthy taste that spread through my mouth despite the liberal helping of half & half Roger had added. If I could be bought with coffee, that'd be the right kind.

"I think we should stop by Crash's," Carolyn said, and the smile on Jacob's face died.

"We need to talk about it first," he said.

"We are talking about it—right now. Vic, I have a friend who's an empathic healer. Maybe you'll get better results from him than from Western, pharmaceutical-based medicine. I think you're trying to treat the metaphysical with the physical."

And the physical wasn't even available to me anymore. Not the physical Auracel, at least. I only had a few pills left and my prescription was history, so I'd have to give it up whether I agreed with Dr. Chance or not.

"I dunno," I said. Jacob didn't seem too keen on the faith healer, and I trusted his judgment. "It's kinda physical, too." Jacob looked at me sharply, and I wondered how to avoid talking about what the Auracel was doing to my liver without actually lying, since Carolyn would know. "My meds aren't working out."

"His techniques work on the physical, too," Carolyn said. "It's just a different approach."

Typically I'd scoff at anyone calling themselves a healer. If they had real talent, they would have been scooped up by the pharmaceutical companies, or the government, or some big TV star like Oprah. And if they didn't have real talent, why would I get my hopes up?

But Carolyn was real, and this guy was a friend of hers. And maybe if he could get my liver set right, Chance would let me have my Auracel again. "I guess I'll check it out," I said.

Jacob pulled onto the highway and said nothing, but the way he glared at the car in front of us, I thought laser beams were gonna shoot out of his eyes.

I didn't feel like getting into an argument in front of the Human Polygraph so I concentrated on my coffee. Still good. I sipped and sipped until it was gone, and then I mourned the fact that I had to wait until tomorrow to have any more.

Jacob exited the highway in a neighborhood that had once been Mexican, had then been infiltrated by art school students, and now held an uneasy mixture of poor people and yuppies. We passed a crowded grocery store, a packed arcade, and a tire shop whose entire front was covered in shiny hubcaps.

"There's nowhere to park," Jacob said, and I jumped at the sound of his voice.

We were in front of a Laundromat marked *Lavanderia* when the traffic started to creep. The figure of a Hispanic man coalesced in front of the business, arms crossed over his chest in a defiant stance. He unfurled his arms and reached toward the car, and I could see the outline of the bricks behind him through his arm. Another Hispanic guy with a scraggly mustache appeared beside him, same posture. And another beside him, barely a teenager. And then a big, round Mexican woman with gigantic permed hair. All of their hands grasped at me like they were doing the wave.

"Never anywhere to park," Jacob muttered.

Another group of reaching ghosts waited for us at the intersection. The only time I'd ever seen a group so large was at a blind turn where a whole vanload of tourists had bought it. Jacob's head snapped around as he looked at me, still glaring. "What?"

"Nothing," I said, and then wondered if Carolyn would be morally obliged to pipe in and say that I was lying. Although maybe I was so transparent she didn't need to. "There's a lot of activity around here," I admitted.

"You keep flinching," Jacob said, turning a corner to begin the old no-parking-spot shuffle.

I held myself very still as a guy with half a face ran toward the car, the wreck of his mouth open and his twisted hands extended. Not only had my reality become more *Dawn of the Dead* than I was accustomed to, but suddenly all the hungry cadavers were acting like I was in possession of the world's last brain.

What was with the grabbiness? I was accustomed to ghosts complaining a lot and being insufferably redundant. But the whole touchy-feely thing was fucking creepy.

I knuckled my eyes. "It's kinda bad," I said. I wondered how Carolyn's talents responded to my excessive minimizing.

Jacob rounded another corner with a big mob of ghosts clustered on it and pretty soon we neared the *Lavanderia* again. "I'll drop you off." He pulled over a block down from the *Lavanderia* crowd of specters. "Maybe Crash *can* help you." The laugh lines at the corners of his eyes looked deep, as if the sleepless night he'd had with me was really catching up with him. "Just be careful."

Carolyn and I hopped out during a break in traffic and she steered me onto the sidewalk. Jacob drove away in search of a spot before I could ask him exactly why I needed to be careful. First Lisa, now him. Nonspecific warnings that told me absolutely nothing.

The block we were on had a couple of decrepit storefronts interspersed between a row of sagging three-flats. Latin music floated out of one window and mingled with rap from another. And the storefront we stood before had a cracked plate glass widow dominated by "Tarot - Palm Reader" in flashing blue and pink neon with a big blinking neon hand beneath it.

"You're kidding me," I said.

Carolyn pulled the door open and motioned to a tiny vestibule inside. Its ancient paneling had been painted glossy red and dotted with lavender thumbprints all around. Since there was nobody there, corporeal or otherwise, I went in and headed for the palmist's, telling myself to keep an open mind.

"Not there." Carolyn closed the outer door behind her. "The shop's upstairs."

I looked up the narrow staircase and saw the thumbprints wended their way up. I climbed the creaky stairs with Carolyn right behind me. As we neared the top, I saw a haze of smoke around the single bare bulb. It smelled of burnt sage, incense and cigarettes.

On the second floor landing, the stairs turned and went on to a third floor, but the thumbprints stopped at a frame-and-panel door. The wood was painted yellow with blue stripes, and a sign hung in the center that read "Sticks and Stones" with the words formed out of twigs and semi-precious tumbled gems.

"Here," Carolyn said, but I'd figured that from the stink of burnt herbs that lingered there. Did the sage keep the ghosts at bay? If so, I wondered if I could manage to use it without burning my apartment building down.

I opened the door into a small shop packed with exotic stuff. A threadbare

Oriental carpet covered a hardwood floor that was scratched and dull with age. Racks of scarves and other gypsy-like clothing ran along one wall. Shelves covered with devotional candles—from Saint Agnes to XX Double Cross—covered another. Plexiglas cases full of herbs, trinkets and stones blocked a bead-hung doorway from the rest of the one-room store.

Despite the onslaught of colors, textures, and smells coming from the shop, I turned my focus inward. The little hairs on my arms had stopped standing on end, and my heart was pounding hard more from climbing a flight of stairs than from panicking at the sight of the grasping dead. My panic started to ebb, a little.

Carolyn came in behind me and closed the door. "Crash?" she called.

Latin brass band music drifted up from the street, but a more pleasant *a cappella* number played from somewhere behind that doorway; bluesy and soulful, like a woman with a knockout voice humming to herself while she worked in her kitchen.

The soul music quieted as a hand parted the beaded curtain. A man's hand, wrist covered in black O-ring bracelets and silver on every finger.

"Carolyn!" he cried, and the rest of him (which was equally as decked out as the hand he'd led with) burst through the curtain. Crash was maybe thirty, with spiked-up bleached white hair and a ring through his nose. He wasn't what I'd imagined one of Carolyn's friends would look like. He was hot. Not that I thought anything would happen between the two of us—cheating is the top entry on my "no" list, and I was in a relationship. "I had a premonition that I'd see you today," he said.

"No you didn't," Carolyn said dryly.

Crash clucked his tongue, then looked at me, crossed his tribal-tattooed arms over his chest and raised an eyebrow. "Hey," I said, doing my best to seem like I wasn't in a ghost-panic.

"Hey, yourself."

"This is my friend, Victor," said Carolyn. "We came to see you about healing."

Crash pulled a rough, handmade-looking bowl out from under the counter and placed it on top. It was full of sand. I tried to imagine what he'd use it for: some kind of ritualistic cleansing? And then he lit up a cigarette and flicked the spent match into the sand. "No 'Hi, how are you, I haven't seen you in, what, a month? What've you been up to?' That's so cold."

"I'm sure you're devastated," Carolyn said.

I wondered if all of their friendly banter was this chipper. If so, I hoped I'd never get either of them mad at me.

Crash crooked his finger at me. "I take it you're the volunteer from the audience?"

The humming resumed from beyond the curtain, loud and clear, and although I've never been much for R&B gospel-type music, I really liked it. I stepped forward, just as much to catch more of that music as to let Crash have a look at me.

Crash held up a hand. "That's close enough," he said quietly.

I stopped and wondered if I was so contaminated that even a guy named "Crash" couldn't deal with my proximity.

"What is it?" Carolyn demanded. "Do you see something?"

"Don't get your panties in a twist, Little Miss PsyCop. I'm not in high gear all the time like you are."

I tried to settle myself. If he thought Carolyn was in high gear, then I was practically in orbit.

"Vic is psychic," Carolyn said.

"Do you mind?" asked Crash. He held his hand palm-out toward her, instead. "I can do it myself."

"I'm just trying to help," Carolyn said, a trace of poutiness in her voice. Crash stared at me, alternating between gnawing at his thumbnail and taking drags off his Camel Light. I stood there like a lump. Carolyn watched Crash watching me.

"He's a medium," she muttered, like she just couldn't keep it in.

"A big overblown TV antenna. Yeah. I get it."

Well. It was the first time anyone'd ever called me *that*.

"Something's unusual about his reception," Carolyn told him. "That's why we came to see you."

"Maybe you should've taken him to Radio Shack." He squinted at me, considering.

"If you're not up to it, just say so," Carolyn said. "It's not like you've got the only metaphysical store in Chicago."

Crash huffed a little and then looked at me. "Only the best one," he said, his eyes boring into mine. "Okay, c'mere."

I shuffled forward another step and he grabbed me by the sleeve of my jean jacket, and dragged me halfway across the Plexiglas countertop. "Hold still," he said. "It's not like I can see the problem written on your forehead."

I was close enough to see his eyes, pale green, like jade. The bluesy humming seemed to intensify as I stared into them. He flashed a tongue stud at me, grazing it across the ridge of his lower teeth. I couldn't tell whether he'd done it on purpose or if it was just a habit.

"You're not right," he said. I thought he'd let go of me with that, tell me to get the hell out of his shop and stop dirtying his vibe.

And then he grinned.

I swallowed. He probably liked it dirty.

He leaned the cigarette into the bowl of sand and slid his fingers down to my bare wrist beneath the sleeve of my jacket. I assumed he'd do something theatrical, but instead he closed his eyes and tilted his head like he was listening to a faint whisper.

Even Carolyn stayed quiet.

Crash let go. "I'd do a gemstone cleanse first," he said. "And once that's done, take a look at fine-tuning."

I snorted before I could even censor myself. Here I was, swarmed with dead and my liver about to explode, and he wanted me to play with crystals? "That's it?"

Crash found his cigarette, took a drag and exhaled slowly so that the smoke drifted around his face. "What did you expect—the numbers for tonight's lottery? You'll have to go downstairs for that. Actually, that's not a bad idea—pretty soon they're gonna replace mediums with radios and video cameras that'll let everyone see spirit energy. The government's got it in the works even as we speak. And then you'll be out of a job."

"Listen," I said. I caught him by the wrist this time, the non-cigarette wrist, and pulled him forward. Not only did he allow it, but he smirked about it like I'd invented some fun new game. "I have a health problem. Can't you tell me something I can use?"

Crash's smirk slipped a little. "I was serious about the gemstone cleanse. If you really are a medium and not just a bullshit artist, it might even help you shield. Unless you live beneath high tension wires, in which case there's nothing to do but move. It's all energy: particles and electrons."

The thought of shielding appealed to me. I'd done it once before—on Jacob, not myself—to keep an incubus from feeling him up. I imagined myself learning to shield so well that I'd be surrounded by an aura so strong and pure that the grasping dead just dissolved on impact.

And then I realized Crash had just called me a fraud. I think.

I suppose I could've flashed my federal license at him and told him I was a fifth level medium, and in fact that was my initial impulse, but I stopped myself before I did. It just felt lame. "How can crystals help me shield?"

I heard the shop's door open and Crash looked over my shoulder instead of answering me. "Well, well, well," he said, and his eyes narrowed.

How could I not turn and look, too? It was Jacob.

Jacob crossed his arms. He was in his suit so he looked reasonably imposing already, but his sleepless night had left him with a don't-fuck-with-me expression that I personally wouldn't have challenged.

"Are you here to tell me you're sorry," said Crash, "or are you just tagging along with Carolyn today?"

Jacob's eyes narrowed. "I'm only the chauffeur."

"How ridiculous, thinking an apology might come out of you, seeing as how you're always right."

I crossed my arms and wished someone had given me a heads-up on the bad blood. I felt vaguely guilty for noticing Crash's looks, but that was stupid. Jacob wouldn't read anything into the wrist-grab. Would he?

"So can you help Victor," asked Jacob, "or is this just another waste of time?"

"I can do plenty," Crash said. He huffed into the back room and left the beads clanking behind him.

I looked at Jacob and he glowered at me as if he dared me to say anything.

I wasn't going there.

Crash knocked the bead curtain aside with a heavy box woven from some kind of cane or bamboo. He slammed it onto the Plexiglas and Carolyn and I winced. Jacob was motionless.

A black woman with a flowered scarf covering her hair followed him out into the main room. She was big, well over two hundred pounds, and looked to be at least sixty. A blue caftan covered her body, hanging loosely over the mounds of her breasts and wide curve of her hips. Her skin was dark and shiny, and she fanned herself with a cheap paper fan printed with the likeness of Saint Anthony. I realized she was the one who'd been humming in the back room. Crash didn't introduce her, and I was too freaked out about the state of my liver and Jacob's big, bad attitude to ask.

Crash pulled a sheet of paper, copied on both sides, out of the basket, and a few baggies of polished stones. He unzipped the baggies and dumped the stones onto the counter, and then considered them. The black woman pointed to a particular stone, and he pulled it out. "I made up this chart that'll tell you how to place the gemstones," he said, working fast as if he just wanted to get our visit over with. "Turquoise, hematite, citrine, rose quartz, sodalite—pay special attention to this one since you're psychic. It'll keep your third eye clean."

He went too fast for me to follow. I hoped the chart was color-coded.

The black woman pointed at a pile that Crash ignored as he scooped every-thing into a small paper bag. The woman shook her head. "The corresponding colors are on there so it shouldn't be a problem." I tried not to wince outwardly at the thought that maybe he'd read my mind. He began to roll up the bag, and then stopped and looked to the pile the woman had indicated.

She pointed again. "And here," Crash said. "Take this double-terminated smoky quartz, too." He pulled the instructions out of the bag, scribbled something on them, and stuffed them back inside along with the final crystal. The black woman nodded and went back to fanning herself. "Use that one on the brow chakra along with the sodalite."

He thrust the bag into my hands. "That'll be twenty-six fifty."

8

The swarms of ghosts seemed thinner when we left Crash's shop, and though none of them came running at me, there were still a lot more of them roaming around than I was accustomed to. Jacob, Carolyn and I walked five blocks to the car in silence.

The ride home was pretty quiet too, until Carolyn spoke with a suddenness that made me jump. "Crash was Jacob's last boyfriend."

Well. The animosity between them made sense. I wasn't jealous, exactly, but the thought of Jacob in bed with someone younger, wilder, and much more self-assured than me didn't do much for my mood. I closed my eyes and sighed.

Jacob didn't say anything.

"They were together for quite a while, six months or so."

"Seven," Jacob muttered.

"That's a long time for Crash."

It's a long time for me, too. Once the truth had been stuffed into the car with us like a big, reeking sack of garbage, Carolyn stopped talking. I wondered how she could deal with so much truth without taking out her service weapon and swallowing a bullet.

We pulled up in front of the apartment and I made a break for the courtyard gate with my chicken calzone and my bag of rocks. Jacob's quicker than I am, and he was right on my heels. "Carolyn shouldn't have to be the one to tell you what's going on—it should be me. It just never seemed like the right time to go into all of that."

I clutched the bags to my middle and knocked my gate open. The hinges were rusty, and it never rewarded me with a satisfying bang no matter how hard I shoved it. A young black woman materialized to my right, with long blonde hair that was obviously a wig. She wore a pair of short shorts that let her ass cheeks hang out and a lavender tube top. A knife handle protruded from the center of the tube top, right between her breasts, with dark blood seeping out in a big, black circle around it.

"Hey, white boy. You want a date?"

"Jesus," I said, and walked faster. "Go away."

Jacob, who didn't see Jackie, the World's Most Irritating Dead Prostitute, thought I was annoyed with him. Come to think of it, I'd never seen her before, either. I usually just heard her. I tried to look on the bright side; at least now I knew where she was.

The three of us were almost at the vestibule door when I spun around to talk to Jacob. I held my bags out between me and Jackie, and she stared at them, puzzled.

"Jacob, whatever. We've obviously both seen other people. Fine."

He stopped close to me and stared into my eyes. "It doesn't feel fine right now. I'm sorry."

"Don't you be wavin' no bags at me. All I was ax-in' was did you want a little company, and here you go wavin' that shit in my face...."

I turned toward Jackie. I was fairly sure she couldn't care less about the calzone, but Crash's bag was another story. "That bother you? Huh?"

"Why you be so rude? What I want your skinny white ass for, anyway?" She backed up.

Jacob, meanwhile, had frozen. He was looking in Jackie's general direction, but I doubted he saw her.

I took a step toward Jackie. "What bothers you about it?" I said. "What's it feel like?"

Jackie flung a hand up, palm toward me, dragon-lady fingernails splayed. "You be trippin'," she said, and she backed up some more, the boxy evergreens that bordered the building passing through her thighs. "I ain't gotta take this shit."

And she disappeared.

I looked back at Jacob. "I think this stuff is for real."

He looked at the bag and the furrow between his eyebrows deepened. "I don't doubt it. Crash is for real. I just wish we could've turned to anyone but him."

"Why, what's the matter with him?"

"Nothing's the matter. Just..." he looked over his shoulder at Carolyn in the car. She waited patiently, flipping the radio stations. "Who likes to go crawling back to their ex for a favor after a breakup? It wasn't pretty."

I tried to imagine what anyone I'd dated in the past ten years could possibly do for me and came up empty-handed. "Look," I said. "You get back to work and I'll be here figuring out these stones." And thinking of ways to avoid mentioning my liver. "I'll be fine."

I turned toward my door but Jacob sidestepped and blocked me with his body. He cupped my jaw with one hand, ran his thumb down the side of my cheek, gave me an intense look that I had no idea how to interpret, and then left.

I went upstairs to try and find some way to survive the night without Auracel.

Crystals seemed like a pretty lame substitute, but they were all I had. My kitchen counter didn't seem like a sacred enough space to work with them, but I figured it was cleaner than the floor. I upended the bag and let them slide out, then fished around inside for the directions.

What I'd assumed was some kind of fancy computer font turned out to be extremely small, evenly-spaced, cramped handwriting. There was a diagram of a body with the chakras drawn in a row up the spine, starting with the tailbone and ending over the top of the head. That, I remembered from my Camp Hell textbooks. But they had different names than I remembered from my training, and each one had a bunch of other words written around it: wind, metal, water… stuff I'd never associated with chakras.

If that wasn't bad enough, the instructions were clear as mud. "Activate each crystal singly by placing in the receptive hand. Assume *padmasanda*. Avoid clavicular breathing."

Shit.

I left the instructions and rocks on my table and decided to work on my calzone instead. At least I could understand that, even though it was cold and I was too lazy to throw it in the microwave. I tore a chunk out of the middle and threw out the crusts. Then I forced down the salad. It tasted okay, but I wanted to figure out the stupid rocks instead of nibbling on bunny food.

One of my old textbooks was in the living room. Jacob had been reading it and we hadn't gotten around to putting it back in the basement. Or, more accurately, I hadn't been back to my storage closet in the basement since I'd seen the baby's ghost there and so the textbook was gathering dust on my fake mantle.

With the help of the old textbook I made some headway in figuring out how to "activate" the stones. It probably took me ten times longer than it would've if Crash's instructions had been written in plain English.

I muddled through to a point where I was supposed to place the hematite (a.k.a. the black stone) on my crotch and imagine a chakra spinning clockwise. I laid down on the floor, put the hematite in place, and then wondered how to determine clockwise. Was the clock facing me? Or was the clock laying on my crotch for the world to see?

I should probably call Crash. And say what? "Hi, I'm Jacob's new boyfriend, which nobody's told you yet, just to make things as awkward as humanly possible. I'm too retarded to figure out this whole crystal cleanse thing and I'm hoping you'll take pity on me."

Right.

My jean jacket hung over one of my kitchen stools. I glanced at it from my spot on the floor and saw the edge of the white paper pharmacy bag sticking out of its pocket. Still on my back with a rock on my crotch, I reached over and pulled it out. No printed warnings on the bottle like regular people get from real pharmacies. My name, the name of the pill, and the dose. One tablet three times daily with or without food.

I swallowed one of the new pills and thought about taking a nice, long nap, after which everything would all be better.

Sleeping didn't seem to do the trick. It was mid-afternoon when I woke up, and if Jacob was working a case, I probably wouldn't see him until early evening at best.

I sat down in front of the TV and tuned in to Channel 8, figuring that it might help me concentrate on the textbook/cryptic instructions combo. I stared at the static, and let my mind wander. I'd have to talk with Jacob about Crash. I let it go. I should probably tell him about my liver. I let that go, too. It was just me and a speckled blue stone, unactivated, that I thumbed absently while I watched the soothing gray snow swirl on the screen.

And then a face appeared.

I took it for some kind of ghosting from another frequency, like the jazz-hand guy I'd seen the night before. The face's mouth opened and the figure reached toward the camera, and I wondered if it even had been a TV transmission, or a bunch of these dead, grasping fucks in my own living room?

My living room.

My personal space is my sanctuary.

If I didn't have a ghost-free zone to come home to, I'd go nuts. As it was, I could barely stop myself from putting my foot through the little TV. I reminded myself that it might feel good to kick it now, but I'd only have to clean up the broken glass later.

I called Lisa and got her voicemail. Again. I snapped my phone shut and ground my molars together for a while, but that didn't provide any inspiration.

I wanted answers, and Crash was the only person I could think of who might have any. I could have just called him, I guess, but thanks to Lisa, I didn't have much faith in my phone anymore. My meds didn't have any warning about not driving—not that they had any warnings on them at all—so I set off for Crash's neighborhood in person to see which way my clock was supposed to face.

Jackie was sitting on the hood of my car when I went outside. She filed her nails, pointedly ignoring the bloody shank sticking out of the center of her tube top. She didn't say anything as I got in, but she gave me a nasty look and shook her head as if she'd never seen anything so pathetic. She disappeared when I started the engine.

I took the surface roads to Crash's, not trusting myself on the highway at speeds over thirty miles per hour. The ghosts at the intersections were thick, not just the normal car crashes I was accustomed to, but new ones as well. Little howling kids in hospital gowns with sticklike arms reaching toward me. A screaming couple decked out in full wedding regalia, reaching toward me like they expected me to toss the bouquet. A bunch of moaning guys in uniform with riding boots and bandoleers who grasped at me like a dead army.

They started wandering into the street as I passed. They weren't particularly fast, but they weren't slow like horror movie zombies, either. I swerved around a couple of them but decided it would only get me killed. I started just driving through them, doing my best to make sure that I wasn't plowing into any live pedestrians.

Parking still wasn't fantastic by Crash's store, but I figured it probably never was. It was a neighborhood that'd been built before cars, and had too many people crammed into it today. To claim my spot, I drove though a bag lady with a high-stacked shopping cart. I hesitated at first since she might just be panhandling, then pulled right through her when I saw her arm pass through a lamp post.

A couple of women arguing in Spanish blocked the door to the palmist's shop and I barely stopped myself from trying to walk through them. One of the women flinched as I veered away from her at the last moment, then snapped, "What is your problem?"

I could've pulled my badge on her and given her attitude, but my heart just wasn't in it. I mumbled, "Excuse me," and squeezed into the thumbprint-painted vestibule.

The door closed behind me and something inside me quieted. No more dead. Just me. Crash's building was a safe zone—safer than my own apartment, evidently. I stood there in the vestibule for a second and enjoyed the stillness until I felt more like myself again, and then I took the stairs two at a time and let myself in to Sticks and Stones.

The black woman looked up from the counter and gave me an easy smile.

"Hi," I said. "Is Crash around?"

"He in back," she said, her African American accent thick and kind of soothing, with a little bit of a Southern twang to it. "He playin' on that computer." She shook her head, a little like the way Jackie had shaken hers about me. "He do that all day long."

"Maybe you can help me," I said, thinking that I might not need to deal with Crash at all. I'd expected to be relieved about that, but it felt strangely like disappointment, instead. I swept that idea under the rug for the time being. "I tried to follow these instructions to the letter but I feel like I'm screwing it all up."

I had Crash's diagram in my hand, folded a bunch of times now and a little sweaty from the way I'd been clutching it.

The woman waved it away. "Don't you worry none 'bout that, chil'. It real simple." She pointed to a hematite that Crash had left spilled out on the counter with a bunch of other rocks. "Take that up in your left hand."

I picked it up.

"Now close your eyes, and be still. See the sky, right through the roof of this building. And see the light come down from heaven. That God's love, and it all around you, all the time."

I'm not exactly an atheist, but I can't say I have a clear idea of what "God's love" would look like, if I could actually see it. Still, I dug the idea of something positive and pure around me for a change. I imagined white light surrounding me and the stone.

"All right, now. Hold it. And breathe. And know that God loves you."

I kept my eyes shut for a moment and did my best not to overthink her statement. She probably lived in a world where God loved everyone. Must be nice.

She smiled when I opened my eyes. "It ready now. You put it on your base for protection. Your pants pocket'll do just fine."

I looked at the black stone in my palm. It looked the same, felt the same. But maybe belief was all I needed. "And I just do the same for the rest?" I asked, wondering why there was a need for such an elaborate set of instructions if that was all there was to it. Maybe the word "God" was just too loaded nowadays.

The beads clacked open and Crash flew out of the back room, startling me. "Back for more?" he said.

I looked to the black woman for moral support, but she wandered toward the far end of the counter, fanning herself.

"I, uh…." Something told me that he'd think I was the biggest idiot in the world if I admitted that I couldn't figure out his instructions. "This crystal thing is new to me."

"Carolyn said you were a Psych. I just assumed you'd gone through the whole certification deal so you could suck off the government's teat."

If that was what I had done, I'd gotten the raw end of the bargain, for sure.

"I'm certified, yeah."

"And you can't do a simple crystal cleanse?"

Could he make me feel like even more of an idiot? "They didn't teach that where I trained." Or maybe they did, and I'd been too doped up to notice from huffing spray paint to block out the visions.

He sighed and lit a cigarette. "Okay, fine. I'll go through it with you step by step."

"That's all right." I backed away from the counter and gestured toward the end where I'd last seen the black lady. "Your assistant helped me figure it out."

"Assistant?"

I heaved an inward sigh and wished it were politically correct to say "the great big black woman" without coming off as a jerk. "Your partner?" I tried.

"Partner," he repeated.

"The lady who works here," I said. "I didn't catch her name."

Crash took a long pull off his smoke and crossed his arms. "Don't fuck around."

My mouth worked stupidly in reply.

He glared at me and took another long drag from his cigarette. And then he said, "I'm the only one who works here."

9

"Whoever the woman in the flowered scarf is—her. She explained how to activate the stones without all the counterclockwise spinning chakra crap."

Crash blinked at me a few times. "What woman? Where?" he asked, as if he was talking to a small, very stupid child.

I pointed toward the end of the counter. "There. She was working over there." I gestured at a narrow doorway beyond. "She's probably in that room right now."

"That's a closet."

I was starting to get annoyed with him. "Fine, I don't know where she went. The woman who helped you pick out my crystals earlier today."

Crash jabbed his cigarette into the sand and leaned on the counter with both palms flat, eyes narrowed. "Look. I'm not some Stiff you have to wow with the whole psychic routine, got it? I'm a legitimate businessman selling legitimate products. You came to me for help. At least give me the courtesy of dropping this 'Ooh, I'm such a powerful medium' shit."

"What do you mean, shit?"

Crash rolled his eyes and whispered, "I see dead people." He threw his arms wide and his voice went loud. "Come on, man. You get impressions and you know how to read them. So do two to three people out of every hundred if you believe the pabulum that good old Uncle Sam's trying to stuff down your throat. My guess is it's more like seven to ten."

I tried to figure out a defense while Crash ranted at me, but I couldn't quite find one. He wasn't saying I was crazy, and he wasn't exactly saying I was fake, both of which I'd heard too many times to count.

"Look. I do see dead people."

"Okay, you have a perception, I get that. But you've got this terminology that's just designed to feed into the whole 'us and them' mentality that's gonna come back and bite you in the ass the second the right-wing fundamentalists get a chance to burn you at the stake. Instead of 'see' you could call it 'sense,' or 'perceive.'"

"No. I see them."

Crash smirked dismissively and tapped another smoke out of his pack. "Okay, pal. Whatever pays the bills. But don't keep up your act for my benefit. I know how these things work and I don't buy it."

"Christ Almighty," I said, banging my fist on the counter. "Dead people are fucking swarming me and you're trying to tell me I don't see them?"

The black woman appeared again at the end of the counter. I'd been so wrapped up in Crash that I hadn't seen her come in. "No need to be takin' the Lord's name in vain, chil'."

"I'm sorry," I told her. "But he won't listen."

Crash blew smoke in my face. "What—you want me to believe you're seeing ghosts right now?"

I looked at him, and then back at the black woman. She clucked her tongue at my swearing. I wondered why she was so solid and so real it hadn't even occurred to me that she might not be corporeal. And she wasn't grasping at me like the ghosts outside, or telling me over and over how she'd died. "What's your name?" I whispered.

"Miss Mattie," she said, fanning herself. "Short for Matilda."

"Hi. I'm Victor."

"I know," she said, smiling a little sadly. "Be nice to Curtis, all right? He a good boy at heart."

"What's next?" Crash asked me. "Are you gonna tell me I was Cleopatra in a previous life?"

"Who's Curtis?" I asked him.

His eyes narrowed. "So Carolyn told you what my driver's license says. Big fucking deal."

"Oh," I said. I'd stopped yelling back at Crash as soon as Miss Mattie spoke. I guessed she'd had a civilizing influence on me. "Um, who's Miss Mattie, then?"

Crash stared at me, his pale eyebrows knit together in the middle. "Who told you that name?"

"The...um...full-figured African American woman told me. The one in the flowered scarf."

"In my day it was all right to say 'Negro,'" Miss Mattie said. She turned and walked slowly toward the narrow closet door, wide hips swaying beneath her big blue caftan. She disappeared through the door.

My phone vibrated in my pocket.

"What color is her scarf?" Crash asked me.

"I don't know," I said, debating whether or not to take the call. "Lots of colors. She went into your closet and I can't see it anymore."

"So you don't actually *see* her," he said.

I decided I'd better check just in case Dr. Morganstern was back in town. I flipped open the phone and found a text message from Lisa.

"Someone told you about her—who, Carolyn? Jacob? You're all in this PsyCop bullshit together, aren't you?"

"You could say that," I said absently, scrolling down Lisa's message.

DANGER – YOUNG BLOND MAN NOT WHAT HE SEEMS. SORRY CAN'T TALK.

Shit.

Heart thudding, I turned on my heel and headed toward the door, which was only a few steps away.

"Where are you going?" Crash demanded.

"Police business. Gotta go."

"Oh, shit, you're a cop, too? You don't act like a cop—I thought you were just a consultant or something. Get the hell out here and leave me alone; I've had enough bacon to last me a lifetime. And tell Carolyn I don't want to meet any more of her pig friends."

I briefly considered telling him I was also sleeping with his ex-boyfriend, but decided it might make him mad enough to come after me and deck me. I went back to my car, pretending that the people full of bullet holes and tire tracks weren't swarming all around me, and pulled out my phone. I dialed Lisa's cell.

"Lisa Gutierrez speaking. I won't be available for the next couple of weeks due to my coursework, but leave me a message and I'll get back in touch with you soon."

Damn.

10

As I unlocked my front door, I heard someone on TV murmuring in a low, reassuring voice punctuated by sporadic bouts of refined applause. Good thing I hadn't drop-kicked the set. I would've had to explain about it to Jacob.

Then again, if I'd done that, I could've avoided talking about my liver. Or Crash. Or Lisa's weird text message.

The light on my answering machine was solid. "Anyone leave a message while I was out?" I called in the direction of the living room doorway. I opened the fridge to see if food had appeared inside, and lo and behold, it had. The crisper was full of leafy green stuff and there was milk in the milk compartment of the refrigerator door. Also, beer. You know there's a man in my life when there's beer in my fridge, since I can't drink it myself.

Jacob walked to the threshold of the room and stood there framed in the doorway. His black hair was damp, and his olive skin glistened. The gray T-shirt he wore had a vee of sweat at the collar. His expression was neutral, a cop-stare that could mean anything.

"Exercising to PBS?" I asked him. "If someone's gotta do it, I'm glad it's not me."

He broke into a smile that lit up his face. "How are you?" he asked. His tone said, how are you, really?

I shrugged. "Something's up," I said. "I don't know what. But my talent's in overdrive." And I'm not supposed to take Auracel anymore. I didn't say that part out loud, because if Jacob knew why, I could see him enforcing it. I just wasn't in the mood for tough love.

"I saw the stones from Crash in the living room," he said. "Did they help?"

"I dunno. I don't think I did it right." I wondered if I was obligated to tell Jacob I'd just been at Sticks and Stones. If I asked about Miss Mattie, I'd obviously have to get into it.

Jacob had crossed the kitchen and backed me into the refrigerator door before I had a chance to decide whether to talk about my second visit with Crash or not. He seemed to loom over me, broad and hard and radiating heat. Maybe he'd make a move on me and I'd be excused from a conversation I didn't even want to have.

He stopped just in front of me, his body filling my whole field of vision, strangely comforting. I leaned into him for a kiss, but he turned his head just enough to nuzzle his cheek against mine instead. The salty new-sweat scent of him was dizzying up close and I felt my breathing pick up speed.

"I probably should have mentioned Crash before now," he said in my ear, and my rising anticipation flagged.

"Do we have to talk about it right this second?" I asked. I found a vein in his forearm and traced it as it wound around a thick, ropy muscle. I wondered if he'd been bench-pressing the futon.

"I don't want you to think I'm keeping secrets," he said.

"What secrets? I haven't given you a laundry list of the guys I've been with." And then I wondered if he was actually fishing for just that—my history.

"I can count the guys I've been serious about on one hand," I told him. "The last one was Ben and he worked in a record store. We were together four months. Before then…." I cast my mind back through a string of one-night stands and then settled on the boy with the blue hair who'd seemed like he'd be fun. "Mike. He was a hair stylist."

It seemed inadequate to compartmentalize Mike simply by mentioning his job. He'd also had a wicked sense of humor and made a mean omelet. But in the end, I felt like my ghosts brought him down.

"So was Crash," Jacob said. "Before his store. That's how he met Carolyn."

All roads seemed to lead to Crash that night. Did he try to get all of his customers to bleach their hair or was that look reserved especially for him? And did he spin out conspiracy theories while he waxed women's eyebrows? Plant seeds of anarchy while setting permanent waves?

I couldn't picture it.

"Unless you have kids or anything, I really don't need to know," I said.

"He's an empath," Jacob said, veering the conversation yet again towards Crash. "I'm guessing a strong level one. Didn't test high enough for government certification."

I tried to imagine Jacob being with a lover who always knew how he was feeling. Maybe most people possess mundane empathy of a sort, even if it's just an interpretation of their standard five senses. And then I tried to imagine Crash taking a test that could land him an actual job where he might have to take the ring out of his nose and cover up his tattoos with long sleeves, and I didn't doubt that he'd bombed the test. I had no idea what'd possessed him to take it to begin with, since he must've loathed the entire process and everything associated with it.

My own test had been a cinch, at least the medium section. I was high as a kite and the dead guy they brought me to wouldn't shut up. The other parts—clairvoyance, precognition, empathy, telekinesis? Zip. Zilch. Nada.

"I'm gonna work on this crystal cleanse thing." I slipped out from under Jacob's massive gravitational pull. My apartment felt too small, like there wasn't enough space in there for the two of us unless we were having sex.

As a Stiff, Jacob's about as empathic as I am. But he read me well enough anyway. He showered while I set myself up in the bedroom with the diagram and the gemstones, and stayed out of my way for a good couple of hours.

The smell of food brought me out of my cave. I'd cleansed each of the stones and done my best to envision God's love shining on down. It felt stupid, but I figured I didn't have anything to lose by trying.

Jacob had been busy putting my kitchen through paces it'd never seen before. There was a big salad, broiled chicken and even warm bread waiting for me on the countertop. "Wow."

He motioned to one of the tall stools. "I miss my dining room table just now," he said.

"I never had a reason to own one. But look at it this way. You get to sit next to me."

We pulled up to the kitchen counter and ate. I imagined the world's gayest food pyramid would've been proud of me for getting so many real food groups in.

When we were done, I took the plates and headed for the sink. "I hope you don't mind cleanup detail," Jacob said. His eyelids looked heavy.

"Fair's fair," I said. "You cooked, I'll do the dishes."

He gave me a small smile and headed for the bedroom. By the time I joined him, he was fast asleep, sprawled over most of the bed.

I stripped down to my boxers and reached for the light switch, taking one last look at the man in my bed. He wore only spotless white boxer briefs, and the stretchy material was molded to his impeccable body. The shallow scratches I'd made on his thighs the night before were still visible, though not serious. The T-shaped welt on his upper arm was red and scabbed. I wondered if I should sleep on the futon to make sure I didn't scratch my initials into his chest while we slept. I wondered if maybe he should lock the bedroom door.

That scratching thing had to be some sort of fluke. It probably had something to do with all those needy ghosts I'd been seeing. A stress reaction.

I went back into the kitchen and got another sedative out of my jacket pocket. I'd only taken two so far, and Dr. Chance had said I could take three a day. I wondered if maybe I should take two more; it was nighttime, after all. And maybe the second one would count toward my next day's allotment.

The liver business had me spooked, though, so I took just one, turned off the lights, and squeezed into bed beside Jacob.

As I stared up at the ceiling and waited for the drug to kick in, I considered taking one of my remaining Seconals along with it, worried some more about my liver, mentally smacked myself for not taking the damn Seconal instead, and then wondered if I could make myself throw the new pill up so I could take a Seconal.

Somewhere in there I guess I fell asleep.

I woke up alone in a darkened room, dead center of my bed with my arms and legs splayed wide. My head was fuzzy and my vision blurred. I forced myself upright while the room tilted around me.

I staggered to the door and threw it open, and was dazzled by the blinding whiteness of the room beyond. Roger's midnight blue Crown Vic was there, with him thrown over the hood. His dress shirt and suitcoat were scrunched up around his ribs and his bare ass showed off its pretty curve where it tilted up to meet Crash's hipbones.

Crash wore a stretched-out old wife-beater with a cracked band logo on the front, and the tribal tattoos covering both arms stood out in stark contrast to his skin. A battered pair of jeans pooled around his ankles.

Crash leered at me like my arrival was just what he'd been waiting for. He grabbed either side of Roger's ass and slammed in hard. "Hey, PsyCop," he said. "How's this for sticking it to the man?"

While I tried to look anywhere but at Roger, the vanishing point of the universe seemed to center on his hazel eyes. "Hi, Victor," he said, and he stretched his far arm out over the hood and held out a Starbucks cup toward me. "Would you like a cup of coffee?"

My knees buckled and there was a roar. My first thought was that I'd been shot. But then I realized I was in my bed, and the room was dark except for the illumination that leaked in from a streetlight outside. And Jacob was shaking me, hard.

"What?" I said, trying to piece together what was real and what wasn't.

Jacob stopped rattling me, but he held me at arm's length, his fingers digging into the meat of my shoulders.

"What?" I asked him again.

"Are you awake?" Jacob growled.

"I'm awake." I wished I didn't need to know the reason for him waking me, but I supposed there wouldn't be any way out of it.

Jacob let go of me and my shoulders throbbed where he'd grabbed them. We both knelt in the center of the bed, and as he sat back on his heels, I made out a big black "X" through the hair in the center of his chest. I squinted at it and saw a dark trickle ooze down from the corner of the X and spread along the waistband of his immaculate white boxer briefs.

"Holy shit, you're bleeding!" I lunged for the reading lamp on the bedside table and realized I was clutching a cheap plastic ballpoint pen so tightly that my nails had dug into my palm hard enough to break skin.

I stopped and stared at my hand in the dark, unable to grasp the significance of the pen.

Jacob reached past me and turned the light on. The pen tip shone dark red with his blood.

"What the fuck?" I threw the pen in disgust. It picked up no momentum at all and just clattered to the hardwood floor. I glanced wildly at the digital clock. Five after three in the morning. I looked at Jacob, who was poking through his chest hair at the red X I'd gouged into him.

"Were you having a nightmare?" he asked, inscrutably calm.

Images of Crash's tattoos and Roger's earnest face and firm, rounded ass spewed into the forefront of my memory. "Yeah. I mean, no. Just fucked-up dreams."

Jacob grabbed a tissue and blotted his stomach. The tissue turned red.

"I'm sorry," I said stupidly. "I'm so sorry."

He seemed exhausted when he finally stopped smearing the blood around and met my eyes. "How much do you know about the execution I witnessed the other night?"

"What?" I tried perform some sort of check to see if I really was awake this time without doing anything too obvious like pinching myself. "Um, I dunno. Lethal injection, you said."

Jacob held the wet, red glob of tissue to a spot on his ribs where the blood soaked it through. I grabbed another handful of tissues and handed them to him. "Hugo Cooper," he said. "What do you know about him?"

"The murderer?" Given our profession, I would've felt like an ass if I admitted that sometimes the cases start blending together. It wasn't a crime I'd personally worked, it wasn't in my precinct—and it had happened so long ago that I was still trying to figure out how to act like a cop when it was all going down. "He kidnapped three women and he killed them."

"Details," Jacob prompted.

"I dunno. One got away. I guess that means he killed two, right? Or were there four to start with?"

Jacob stared at me hard but I could only shake my head; I had no clue what he was getting at.

"We had a nickname for him down at the Twelfth. I was thinking maybe you'd heard it."

"It was a long time ago." I wished he'd get up and see to the seeping gashes in his middle. "I really don't remember."

Jacob sighed. "It never went to the press. We're careful things like that don't leak out, otherwise there'd be melodramatic headlines, copycats, the works. But just among ourselves, we called him the Criss Cross Killer."

I looked at the giant bleeding X on him and my stomach sank.

"Oh."

Jacob stood and made his way toward the bathroom. I sat on the edge of the bed and did my best not to puke.

11

Jacob and whatever few clothes he kept at my place were out of the apartment by five. He didn't seem mad, exactly, but he had his cop-face on and my nonexistent interpersonal skills were no help in figuring out if he was leaving for now, or leaving for good. He said he was just going to go figure some things out. But how many guys have gone out for a pack of smokes and just kept on going?

Telling Jacob I was sorry didn't do any good. And begging him to stay didn't help. Punching the wall didn't solve anything, either. So I took the handful of stones Crash had sold me and flung them out the living room window.

That felt good for about two seconds, but afterwards I was still me, and my life still sucked.

I wandered from the living room to the kitchen to the bedroom and back about a dozen times, and then it occurred to me that Lisa could help me figure out what was going on. In fact, when you think about it, Lisa owed it to me to help me sort this shit out. It was her half-assed warnings that made Jacob leave.

I called Lisa's cell phone and left her about twenty "call me" messages. Okay, maybe thirty. I texted her. "NEED HELP," and "CALL ME BACK," and then I couldn't think of anything else to say that I had any chance of typing successfully with my thumb.

I called the operator in Santa Barbara and found there was no listing for PsyTrain, the illustrious program that evidently didn't let its participants have a shred of contact with the outside world. Convinced that they were turning Lisa into the next Patty Hearst, I called the night detective at the Fifth, a tough nicotine-stained broad named Alice who you don't want to rub the wrong way. I talked her into tracking down PsyTrain's phone number with a promise of a case of Diet Coke and a raspberry twist coffee cake.

I called PsyTrain.

Apparently they weren't impressed enough with my credentials to put me through to Lisa. I realized that I probably should have lied and said I was Sergeant Warwick, or maybe even the Police Commissioner, but now it was too late.

I stared at my phone. I put on a pot of coffee and paced through my apartment. In the bedroom, my sheets were rumpled and splattered with Jacob's blood. I wadded them up and stuffed them under the bed. I swallowed a scalding cup of black coffee in one long gulp and then poured myself another cup. Compared the Starbucks I'd been drinking, it tasted thin and sour, even though I'd brewed it up strong.

I admitted to myself that I had no idea what to do next.

I had to know why I was cutting up Jacob. And I had to know why ghosts were on me like flies on shit. It seemed like Crash might be able to help me, but for every reason I could think of to call him, there was another why I shouldn't. He was legitimate—both Jacob and Carolyn vouched for that. But he never seemed to get a handle on the way my sixth sense actually worked, since it was obviously different from his. And did I really think I could get Jacob back by turning to his ex-lover for yet another favor? Oh, and to top it off, Crash hated me.

There was always Carolyn. She seemed…smart. And blunt. Mostly blunt. It might be good to have the Lie Detector in my corner, but then she'd pipe up whenever I let one loose. Which was probably more often than even I realized.

The only one who could tell me was Lisa. I had to see Lisa.

The idea of driving to Santa Barbara alone was ludicrous—I couldn't read a map to save my life and I'd probably end up in Canada. But finding someone who can drive is a lot easier than figuring out why psychics do the fucked-up things they do.

Maurice. I trusted him enough to help me out. Sure, he'd ask questions. You don't just drive someone across the country without asking questions. I paced back and forth in front of my bay window, and the glaring overhead light bounced my reflection back at me through the slats of my miniblinds as I tried to figure out how to approach him. I'd have to tell him that I was playing tic-tac-toe on Jacob in my sleep. He'd already figured out Jacob and I were together, but I'd have to come right out and say it. Awkward. But who else could I turn to?

My cell phone buzzed and I nearly tripped over a Camp Hell textbook trying to get to it. It was Lisa, it had to be. She knew how badly I needed to talk to her. She'd tell me what to do.

I flipped open the phone and my heart sank. It was Roger. "Hey," he said. "I hope I'm not bothering you. But I was out jogging and I saw your lights on. Are you up for Starbucks?"

I nudged the blinds aside and looked out past the courtyard. A reversed image of my living room overlaid the gray pre-dawn street below, but if I shifted my focus, I could pick out details. Traffic was sparse but regular, commuters who needed to be downtown by seven. Roger stood on the far sidewalk in sweats and a T-shirt, waving.

Roger—stupid Roger. I didn't want Roger, I wanted Lisa. And yet, there Roger was, always willing to lend a hand. Or give me a ride.

I wondered if Roger was so eager to please that he'd take his midnight blue Crown Vic on a little spin to California. Then I wouldn't have to burden Maurice with the gruesome details of my sex life.

"Coffee sounds great," I said. "I'll be down in five."

———∿∿∿———

Roger did his best not to look surprised when I asked him to drive me to California. He suggested flying, but commercial airlines were out of the question. All it would take was one airplane-bound ghost to turn me into an air-rage psycho.

"Driving it is." He toasted me with his espresso. "I'll need half an hour to get my things together. Bring a suit. We'll want to look official when we get to the PsyTrain facility."

I had a jacket that didn't look like it'd been slept in, I thought.

"And your prescriptions—have you got a couple of weeks' worth?"

"I dunno. I'll just have to make whatever I've got last. I'm not going back to The Clinic and announcing that I'm going out of town. I'll just have to call them and reschedule my fasting bloodwork. I don't want them involved. Warwick, either."

"Warwick's easy. You're on medical leave. Just check in with him on your cell phone and act like you're still in town."

Hooray for the cell phone. If Maurice was looking for me, he'd try that number, too. I could just tell him I was on a lot of meds and he wouldn't ask any questions. If Jacob was looking for me....

I didn't know if Jacob would be looking for me or running as fast as he could in the opposite direction. He'd told me he just needed to get some rest so he could think clearly. I had no idea what that was supposed to mean.

Roger and I were packed up and on the road by noon. He went over the route to Santa Barbara with me and I glazed over somewhere in Oklahoma. I hadn't taken one of my new pills since the night before. I figured I'd better save them in case things got ugly in the motel and I needed to knock myself out.

City traffic was spotty, as city traffic tends to be, but in another hour we'd hit the highway, passed through the suburbs and were driving through cornfields and skirting small, rural towns and the occasional strip mall. Rural Illinois: corn country.

"I don't want to pry," Roger said, reaching to turn down the top-forty station that played more ads than music, "but why didn't you ask Detective Marks to go to PsyTrain with you? He's a lot more intimidating than I am. And if they're being stubborn about letting you see Detective Gutierrez...."

Miss Mattie was more intimidating than Roger was. But I doubted he was fishing for a validation of his manliness. He wanted to know what was up with me and Jacob. "He'd probably want to go through the proper channels," I said. "And I don't have the time."

"Really?" We passed a field dotted with cows. "I heard he wasn't above bending the rules. Take that case with the shapeshifter where you used Detective Gutierrez' abilities even after you were specifically told not to."

Shit. He'd done his homework. No big surprise. "I dunno. I guess I just don't want to get him any more tangled up in this."

"In what, Vic? What are we doing?"

I sighed. We'd been on the road for a couple of hours. He could turn the Crown Vic back around and be rid of me easily enough. Heck, he could pull over and dump me by the side of the road, too. "Something's up," I said. "You know how my talent's been a little...overly sensitive lately?"

"Yeah?"

"There's something else, too. It's gonna sound a little crazy..." like anything having to do with PsyCops sounded rational. "But it's almost like I'm contaminated. There was this murderer who was executed a few nights ago, and it's like I'm acting out his M.O. in my sleep."

"You're channeling?"

My third cup of coffee lurched in my stomach at the thought of a spirit using my body like a wetsuit. "I dunno. I've never done any channeling. Not on purpose, anyway. I think you need really solid defenses to mess around with that shit."

"And you don't have them? Solid defenses, I mean?"

I pressed my tacky forehead against the passenger window. "I thought I did. I mean, the dead used to just stick to the places where they died—if not that, then their graves, or some other place that meant a lot to them. But now it's like they're coming out of the woodwork and following me."

Roger drove in silence for a while. I fished around in my pocket for a sedative. The thought of all those cold, pale, grasping hands was making me antsy.

"What do they do? When they follow you."

I had a pill on my tongue, so I swallowed before I answered him. "I...I dunno. They grab at me."

"Have you tried talking to them? Asking them what they want?"

"Look, Roger, the dead aren't rational people," I said. Maybe he was just playing

Devil's advocate, but I felt my adrenaline surging as if I needed to protect myself. "You can't just have a conversation with them. It's not like they're gonna give me a message and then be satisfied and go away—that's Hollywood bullshit. They don't have a message and they don't have a purpose and they don't go anywhere."

"So when there's an earthbound spirit, it's around forever?"

"Jesus, I don't know. There aren't enough mediums around to help the researchers come up with a solid theory. And it's too fucking subjective."

Roger glanced at me. He looked concerned, in a mild and boyish way. "But what do you think, Vic? You've had this ability your whole life. You must've put some kind of logic to it."

Actually, I'd had it since I was twelve. Close enough. "I guess they disappear over time," I said. "Otherwise I'd be fighting my way through mobs of Neanderthal spirits."

"Makes sense."

"Sometimes I think that ghosts are people who were unhappy in life," I said. It wasn't very scientific or very accurate, but it was an idea I've always had in the back of my head. I'd never really voiced it, since I couldn't help but think of what it would mean for me once my time was up.

12

We hit a big snarl of traffic in Saint Louis around six in the evening. We stopped to pick up some burgers, but I ended up getting swarmed by dead in the drive-through line and making Roger hit the road again before he had a chance to order.

The spirits thinned out once we were on the highway again. I offered to take the wheel for a while, if Roger could keep me on our route, but he told me there really wasn't anywhere to pull over.

I took another pill since Roger didn't need me to drive, and soon we'd gone past all the suburbs and made our way through more farmland again. I stared out at the stubbly, shorn fields dotted with gargantuan rolls of hay, glad that we were in an area that wasn't particularly populated since I'd had my share of ghosts for the day. A transparent hitchhiker with hollow eyes appeared just as I thought that. He reached out toward me as the Crown Vic sped past him.

It'd been dark a couple of hours by the time Roger pulled up to a B&B some-where in the middle of rural nowhere. I would've preferred a Super 8, a newer construction that had less potential for ghost activity, but every time we passed by a likely motel, Roger waved it away and said he was still good to drive.

"I dunno about this place," I told Roger. "An old farmhouse, probably full of dead...farmers."

"Just take a look," he said. "We'll ask to see the rooms before we commit to anything."

Nobody swarmed me as I got out of the car; a good sign. We knocked on the front door and stood shivering on the porch for a good ten minutes before a burly guy with a gray crew cut came to let us in. He said that a double-occupancy room was available, if we wanted it. It felt funny to think of sharing a room with Roger, but since we'd just spent the past ten hours together in a much smaller space, I told myself there was nothing weird about it.

The room was kind of goofy and overdone, with hunter green wainscoting and wallpaper with a fishing motif. At least it wasn't all hearts and flowers; it would've been way too weird to wake up next to Roger in a room that looked like a honey-moon suite, especially since I'd had that dream about him and Crash.

There weren't any spirits lingering around, and that's what mattered the most. Roger booked the room while I got our overnight bags out of the car.

There was a television tucked into a bureau at the foot of the two double beds, but I hadn't been interested in TV since I realized I was getting reception from the other side in my own living room. An ancient rotary phone sat on the table between the beds, black plastic with a fat, curly cord connecting the handset to the phone. I wondered if it even worked. Maybe, maybe not. But it gave me an idea. "Do you need anything?" Roger asked me, reaching for the remote.

I needed lots of things, but I figured Roger was already doing everything he possibly could for me.

"I'm fine." I wished the new pills were as strong as Seconal. Dr. Chance had said they were sedatives, but they didn't seem to be relaxing me at all. I pulled the plain bottle out of my pocket and looked at it, and wondered if it was just some kind of placebo. Lisa would be able to tell me if they were real or not without a shadow of a doubt.

I went into the bathroom, ran the water to cover the sound of my voice, and flipped open my phone. Years of acting secretive had stuck with me, and even though Roger and I were neck deep in the whole California plan, I still only wanted him to know only as much as I absolutely had to tell him. The reception bars on the phone's screen were tall, which was a relief since we were miles from civilization as I knew it. My thumb was poised to hit the memory dial to Lisa's cell when the phone vibrated in my hand, startling me. I dropped it and it made a huge sound against the hunter green tile floor.

"Everything okay?" Roger called.

I gnawed at the inside of my cheek and quelled the impulse to tell him I was still "fucking fine," since I could hardly get testy with him given everything he'd done for me. Still, the mother hen routine was starting to get old, and fast.

"Dropped my toothbrush," I said, wishing I could've thought of something heavier on the spur of the moment. "Unlisted" showed on the screen, and I debated letting it go to voicemail. It could be Warwick checking up on me. It could be Jacob, who I was dying to talk to—and yet if he knew what I was doing he'd probably try to talk me out of it. And it could be Lisa.

I picked up. "Bayne," I said, keeping my voice low.

"This is Victor, the medium, right?" A man's voice, definitely not Lisa.

"Yes."

"Okay, yeah. I was just wondering about Miss Mattie."

Recognition clicked in. It was Crash. He'd probably gotten my number from Miss Can't-Tell-a-Lie.

"Now is really not a good time."

"I acted like a dick before, you know? But it just blew my mind when you said you were talking to Miss Mattie."

The mirror started fogging up. I turned the cold tap higher. "I'm right in the middle of...."

"I've been thinking about her all day. She was our next-door neighbor—died when I was just a kid. But she always said I had the 'gift.' Like she did."

Shit. I wanted Crash to go away. I wanted to talk to Lisa. "Uh huh."

"So is she, like, watching me all the time?"

I sighed and drew a big happy face on the fogged up mirror with my fingertip, then smudged it out with my palm. "No. She comes and goes."

"That's a relief. 'Cos I know a few moves that'd probably kill her all over again if she saw 'em."

I did my best not to imagine him naked.

"I can show you some, if you wanna come over."

I closed my eyes and wished he hadn't just said that. "I don't think so."

"C'mon, man. I know you want to." He said "know" in such a way that I was sure he'd picked it up from me while we were grabbing wrists.

I sighed. "I'm in a relationship right now," I said. I wasn't sure whether or not that was actually true, since Jacob had left. A huge pang of loss swept over me, and I perched on the edge of the clawfoot tub so the emptiness didn't bowl me over.

"No one has to know," he said, a smile in his voice.

"With Jacob," I added, because maybe if I insisted that it was the case, he'd come back.

At least the statement was enough to take the wind out of Crash's sails. "Well, well, well. Didn't take Jacob very long to find himself a shiny new psychic to show him some parlor tricks, did it?"

I had no idea. I just wanted to talk to Lisa.

"I'd invite you both over, but he's kind of a prude about three-ways. And besides, he's pissed off at me."

"Looked like it went both ways," I said.

"I never told him I was a saint. He just expected me to act like one and got all high-and-mighty when I didn't."

Good to know about the cheating. It just confirmed what I already believed: that it's pretty low to polish your rod on the side, and Jacob wouldn't have any of it. Sure, I was busy racing across the country with another guy, in an attempt to get a straight answer out of Lisa as to why I was turning Jacob into mincemeat. But it was still good to know.

Maybe Crash had called for a reason—other than the fact that he wanted to get in my pants. Maybe Miss Mattie was guiding his hand. Or fate.

"Listen," I said, glad for a reason to change the subject. "Is there any way to shield if you haven't got any crystals or stuff like that?"

Crash snorted. "Like what, the 'white balloon' trick they teach in KinderPsych?"

I closed my eyes and wished I hadn't even asked. I might have been better off not knowing my training was about as advanced as a five-year-old's. I really, really wanted to talk to Lisa. "Okay, then. I gotta go."

"Whatever. The invitation still stands. With Jacob or without."

He hung up and left me staring dry-mouthed at the ugly tile floor.

Roger knocked softly. "You okay in there? Do you see something?"

I stood and looked at the mirror, half expecting to find a ghoulish apparition reaching for my reflection, but I was alone. Odd, considering the age of the building, but after all I'd been through, I wasn't going to complain. "Nope," I called. "All clear." I tried Lisa's cell phone again and got the same damn message I'd gotten since she'd settled in at PsyTrain. I texted "CALL ME" yet again. And then I splashed some water on my face so I looked like I'd been doing something other than hiding with my phone in the bathroom.

Roger lay back in one bed with ESPN playing on the TV when I emerged, a cloud of steam trailing behind me.

"You sure you're okay? You don't look so good."

I ran my fingers through my hair. "I think it's this new medication," I said. "It's supposed to calm me down, but I'm totally wired." I'd also had six more cups of coffee than I was supposed to that day. Not that I was counting.

"What is it?" he asked. "Is it an anti-psyactive?"

"Just a sedative."

"I've got some muscle relaxants for a shoulder spasm I had a couple of months ago. They're not very strong, but maybe they'd take the edge off?"

I was about to decline, but Roger was already up and rifling through his bag. It couldn't hurt to try, I figured. Muscle relaxants didn't seem to amp up the ghosts like alcohol did, and maybe a mild dose really would help me get some rest.

Roger set the bottle on the table between the two beds. I lay down on my bed, picked it up and read it. The pharmacy's address was in Buffalo. One-half to one tablet as needed, up to four per day. That seemed like a pretty broad range. How strong could they be?

I opened up the bottle and tapped a round orange pill onto my palm. There was a line down the middle where it could be broken in half. I considered taking half, briefly. Then I swallowed a whole pill. I've never been the kind of person to do things halfway.

Roger handed me a bottle of water from a tiny refrigerator beside his bed. I took a swallow and lay back on my pillow and stared at the ceiling. I didn't feel anything. But it'd be too soon. And it probably wouldn't be all that dramatic, anyhow. Just a little something to help me sleep.

The ESPN sportscasters droned on over the squeak of sneakers on a basketball court, and I wondered where they were broadcasting basketball from in October. Was it basketball season in China? Did they even play basketball in China? The sportscasters didn't sound Chinese. I considered opening my eyes to see who was playing but it felt like way too much effort. I drifted off to the sound of rubber soles on hardwood.

13

My dreams were vivid, floaty, and downright pleasant. I was drinking coffee in a coffee shop full of hot young men. Crash was behind the counter with his spiked blond hair, giving me a knowing come-hither look every time he caught my eye, and flashing the tongue stud to make sure I knew that if I consented to spend a little naked time with him, I wouldn't be sorry. Some of the murder victims from my last case were there, too: the guy with the Scotty dog collection was yukking it up with the buff architect. At a table in the far corner, the goth boy who'd broken my heart in the mid-eighties was licking the foam from a latte off his black-painted lips in a way that sent a major rush straight to my groin.

But best of all, Jacob was there, right across the table from me—shirtless and unscratched. His perfectly sculpted arms and chest gleamed like he'd just come from a bodybuilding competition, and his eyes, which had seemed so pinched with fatigue and concern lately, were just deep and melty and oh-so-sexy. Jacob reached under the table and ran his fingers up my thigh. I don't normally go in for public displays of affection, but since we were in the world's gayest coffee house, and everyone else there seemed to have sex on the brain too, I let myself relax into Jacob's caress.

Something buzzed against my thigh and I did a double-take at Jacob. A vibrator? In public? My cock stiffened and I slouched lower. I was shocked that he'd do something so dirty where anyone could see, but it turned me on nonetheless.

The vibrator pulsed against my leg, and I caught my lower lip between my teeth. I'm not a big sex-toy aficionado, but damn, it was sexy. And Crash was right over there with that tongue stud…maybe Jacob wasn't as uptight as Crash had thought. Maybe he just needed to be approached the right way….

The buzzing drilled into my thigh.

"Higher," I told Jacob.

The buzz pulsed again.

I woke up to the feel of my phone going off in my pocket. My head was wooly and my tongue was, too. I looked around the room. A single reading lamp was on, and Roger's bed was rumpled. Roger was gone. My phone vibrated again.

I flipped it open. Lisa. "Hello?" I said, and the word came out a little slurred.

"Vic? Oh my God, Vic, where are you?"

I looked around at the trout wallpaper. "In the fishing room."

"You sound funny—are you okay?"

I found the idea of her asking me a yes or no question pretty amusing. "I dunno," I said. "Am I?"

"You're on drugs? Yes. Okay, what kind? Wait, never mind, it doesn't matter. Are you alone? Yes."

"If you say so."

"You're not safe. You need to get out of there."

I looked up at a bad oil painting of a couple of guys casting their lines from an old, scenic bridge and wondered if it was going to fall off the wall and decapitate me. "Why?"

"I don't know," she said. "Ask me some questions so I can figure it out."

"You warned me about Crash." I stared down at the tent of my hard-on pressing up against my jeans. "What was I in danger of there—a killer orgasm?"

Lisa sighed. "I have no idea what you're talking about, Victor, and you're all messed up. What's Crash? Some kind of drug?"

"Maybe," I said, sitting up. My head spun a little and I paused to enjoy the feeling. "Or maybe he's a young blond man."

"No."

"Yes he is."

"No. He's not the one."

The clipped, hushed tone of her voice was a buzzkill, but it got me to thinking. I knew another blond man who was younger than me. "Is it Roger?"

"Yes!"

"It can't be. Roger's helping me get to California so I can talk to you."

"No he isn't. Victor, listen to me. Wherever you are, just get up and go. Is he nearby? Yes."

PsyTrain had taught Lisa how to ask her own questions. Useful, but something she probably could've figured out without flying across the damn country and going incommunicado. I stood up and the room dipped a little, but I had pretty good sea legs from years of chemical experimentation. I went to the door and turned the handle. Locked. I took a look at the lock. It was shiny and new. And very sturdy. "I'm locked in. Lemme find my gun."

My shoulder holster was draped over a desk chair beneath my jean jacket. It was empty. "Did Roger take my gun?"

"Yes."

I closed my eyes and wished the room would stop spinning. "Was that a muscle relaxant he gave me?"

"Yes."

"Was it as mild as he said it was?"

"No."

There was some background noise on Lisa's end. I heard her cover the phone and say, "Not now, this is really important. Who? Oh my God, really?" She got back on the phone with me. "Vic, Jacob's here."

I was busy staring at my empty holster. "Where, in California? How'd he get there? Are you shitting me?"

She'd stopped listening to me, though. "Yeah, I'm on the phone with him right now. I don't think he knows where he is."

"Vic." Jacob had taken Lisa's phone away from her. "Something's going on. We're going to get to the bottom of it."

A key turned in the lock, and I decided there wasn't any more time for me to play twenty questions. "Someone's coming, gotta go." I flipped off my phone, stuck it in my pocket and fell back into bed, feigning sleep. I forced myself to take slow, even breaths, and I even let my eyes flicker back and forth a little bit under my lids.

The door to the fishing room opened. "Vic?" Roger called softly. "Are you awake?"

I moved my eyes around under my closed lids and said nothing. The orderlies at Camp Hell usually fell for the fake R.E.M. routine. And after a long, horrible pause, it seemed like Roger did, too.

I heard him move quietly around the room, stopping for a moment at the television armoire, and then at my jean jacket. Fabric rustled, and then the floorboards creaked softly as he approached the bed. I wished I could see through my eyelids. I wondered if some psychics actually could; heck, I've heard of weirder talents. Why not see-through eyelids?

I probably would've flinched when he put his hand on me if not for the muscle relaxant. The pill had delayed my reaction time long enough to give me some kind of doped-up control over myself. I wondered if I was still sporting wood from my dirty dream, if he was gonna cop a feel while I was out cold. It didn't seem like a Roger kind of thing to do, but when it was all said and done, how well did I know Roger, anyway?

He made a little "tch" noise in his throat, whatever that meant, his hand slipped into my pocket, and he took my phone. Damn. I felt like a wuss for not trying to fight him off, springing into action and taking him by surprise, but he had both his gun and mine, and I was doped-up and slow.

He stayed there in the room and eventually I must've drifted off again, thanks to the pills. I have no idea how long it was before the sound of a key in the lock woke me. I lay still with my eyes shut and listened.

"How long has he been out?" Though it was a whisper, the female voice seemed vaguely familiar.

"Most of the night."

Fabric rustled and something was set down and unzipped. "We could probably wake him up," whispered the woman. "Or we can wait until it's light out. We don't want to blow it after we've gotten this far."

Roger sighed and moved to his own bed. It creaked gently as he settled on it. "We've waited this long. What's another couple of hours?"

I personally wished they'd just wake me up and get on with whatever they had in mind. Since they thought I was asleep, I had to just lay there and wonder what the fuck was going on. I had no idea if I normally shifted and rolled around in my sleep, and if so, how much. So I had to be perfectly still for what seemed like forever to the sound of quiet footsteps, the gentle rustle of paper and the occasional sigh.

Eventually I couldn't take the not knowing anymore and I rolled onto my side and opened my eyes. Roger was there, propped in his bed, watching me intently. "Hey, Vic," he said. "How're you feeling?"

Like I could kill someone, except someone had taken my gun. "I dunno," I lied. "Okay."

"Detective Bayne?" said the female voice, and I turned and found Dr. Chance standing at the foot of my bed. She wasn't wearing the hippie-chick ensemble she'd had on at the clinic—instead she wore a black knit suit, casual but smart, cut to just cover something at her waist that looked suspiciously like a gun belt. I wondered if maybe she was a Fed.

"Dr. Chance?" I did my best to sound bewildered. I was actually a little surprised to see her, but I tried to make it look like I hadn't realized anyone was there besides me and Roger.

"That's right," she said. "Do you mind if I take your vitals?"

I sat up. "Why? Am I sick?"

She pulled a stethoscope and blood pressure cuff out of a bag. She handled them confidently enough that I assumed she actually was a doctor—but what if she wasn't? If only I'd been born with the *si-no* instead of a direct line to the afterlife, I'd know.

"Just checking to make sure you haven't had an adverse reaction to the new meds."

"No, they're fine," I said as she velcroed the cuff onto my biceps. "But they don't work anywhere near as well as the Auracel."

She nodded and stuck a digital thermometer in my mouth, pumped up the cuff so tightly it hurt, then let some air out in a slow hiss. "That's to be expected. They function differently than your old medication."

She shone a penlight into each of my eyes. "Everything's normal," she told me, and I swallowed back a laugh. "Now, listen. You might feel a little lightheaded, but what I have to tell you is very important: we've got access to some new medication that will alter your ability to communicate with the dead. If you work with us, I think we can get your hypersensitivity under control."

That part of the plan sounded fine, until she opened a small case that contained a dozen pre-filled syringes. My heart pounded. It's not a fear of needles or anything. It's just more Camp Hell baggage. "What's that?"

"The latest in anti-psyactives." She swabbed the crook of my arm with an antiseptic wipe, flicked the syringe a couple of times, then looked at me over the rim of her glasses. "You do want to get your visions under control, don't you?"

"I think half an Auracel would do the trick. Maybe we could adjust my dose...."

Roger stood behind her with his hand resting on his holstered gun. He didn't look like his normal cheerful self, and I doubted he was going to offer to go get me some Starbucks.

"Detective," said Chance. "This is the cutting edge of current Psy research. You're lucky to be a part of it."

Oh God. Cutting edge. Just like Camp Hell, back in the day. My breathing went shallow and rapid and I tensed up to spring.

"Hold him," Chance said, her voice bland.

Roger was airborne in less than a second. His forearm snapped my jaw shut and wedged under my chin; his hard, muscled body pinned mine; his upper thigh drove into my groin, and he forced my arm out to the side with its white, vulnerable, undersurface extended. I struggled to move—knee-jerk reaction, I guess, since I'd still be drugged and locked in a room even if I managed to throw Roger. Not that my stunted flailing even budged him.

"Just a pinprick," Chance said. There was a sting on my inner elbow and then warmth spread through my arm.

My panic died away immediately and I went limp. A rush of well-being stole over me and I had to admit that Chance's new miracle drug wasn't half bad.

"That's better," said Chance, and Roger climbed off me. "To get a baseline, I'm going to need to ask you some questions."

She started firing them off, grilling me about the type of contact I had with the dead, the frequency and intensity, and my ability to pull information from them that they might not want to part with.

I answered her as best I could, but the overwhelming feeling of good cheer coursing through my veins was far more interesting to me than Chance. Would I get access to this wonderdrug if I helped them test it out? Would it eventually be available in some kind of syrup or pill so I didn't have to poke holes in my arm?

"Let's move on to your level of control," she said. "If you tell a spirit to do something, does it generally comply?"

"I dunno. No, not really. They're kinda stupid, can't usually tell you much other than the way they died." My headrush ebbed a little, and it occurred to me that I felt an awful lot like I did when I was celebrating with a fresh batch of Seconal.

Chance looked at her watch. "How's the medication? Shall we try a supporting dose?"

I don't think it was actually a question. I wasn't sure how much time had gone by, but not long, maybe ten minutes since Roger had bodyslammed me. He held me again—just my arm this time—and she shot a little more juice into me. There was the warmth, and the wonderful, wonderful high.

"Try to recall a time when you successfully encouraged a dead subject to talk about something other than its own passing."

"A guy in a coffee shop…I used him as a witness." I laughed. "Don't tell anyone, it's off the record."

"And so you would say that you might possess the ability to command dead subjects, maybe with more training?"

I pressed the back of my head into the headboard and rode the wave of contentment that had taken hold of me. It felt so much like Seconal that it made me wonder if it was laced with barbiturates. Yeah, that made sense. Barbiturates were a drug group that I could understand.

"Detective?"

"Depends on the dead."

"How so?"

"I think this guy wanted to talk to me because he just liked to talk. Probably was the sort of guy who never shut up when he was alive."

A word popped into my head: Amytal. Seconal's close cousin. Also known as truth serum. Not that it actually makes anyone tell the truth; confessions taken with the aid of Amytal aren't admissible in court. But it keeps the subject in happy, la-la, everybody's-my-friend land. I'd have to concede that I was currently visiting that very spot.

"Detective Bayne?"

"Huh?"

"Your assessment of the amount of personality retained by the deceased?"

I thought about it. "I've always thought that they're more like the living when they're fresh."

Chance nodded. "It might have to do with the degradation of their signal over time."

"Signal?"

There was a rap on the door. Roger left his post at my bedside and opened it. The guy with the crew cut who'd let us in the night before stuck his head inside. "There's a deputy here," he said quietly. "I'll try not to let him upstairs, but there's only so much I can do. If I tell him to go get a search warrant, he'll get suspicious."

"I'll handle it," said Roger.

"He thinks I've got a honeymooning couple here. He wanted to see both of you."

Chance looked at me. "How're you doing on that medication, Detective?"

"Fine," I said. My voice sounded a little distant.

She pulled out another syringe and shot it into me without even bothering to ask Roger to hold me down. I closed my eyes and enjoyed the headrush.

"He'll be sedated for at least fifteen minutes. Longer, if he falls asleep," she said. "Let's go." They left the room and locked the door behind them.

I sat up. Did they really think I was out for the count? I felt loose-limbed and high, sure. But my years of self-medicating with Seconal must've built up some kind of tolerance. And here I'd thought the quality of the pills had been going down.

14

The jarring sound of an old-fashioned phone ringing startled me out of my dazed inertia. I stared at the gigantic plastic behemoth on the table between the beds. It rang again. I picked it up and held it to my ear. It might be Chance calling from downstairs, after all, acting like everything between us was hunky-dory and she was really concerned about my well being.

"Vic?"

Except if it was Chance, she was doing a pretty damn good impression of Jacob.

"How did you get this number?" I whispered, worried that Chance and Roger had heard it ring and were making tracks back to the room. Frankly, I was shocked that they'd take my cell and leave a working phone just sitting there beside me. But since I was in a hotel, maybe outgoing calls were blocked. Incoming calls were apparently free game.

"Lisa narrowed it down. You're in Missouri, twenty miles away from a town of any size. The sheriff sent someone over, but I really couldn't give him much to go on."

"Crap." I steadied myself against the headboard and tried to remain upright. "I'm locked in a room and they've got my cell phone and my gun. What do I do?"

"I'm putting you on speakerphone," said Jacob. "Okay. Ask us something Lisa can work with."

I racked my brain for a question other than, "What can I do?" Yes or no, I told myself. "The door's locked," I said. "Is there anything in here I can open it with?"

"No."

"Can I get out through the window?"

"No."

I pushed the curtain aside. A decorative metal grating covered the outside of the window. In the country, on the second floor? Why?

"If I make lots of noise, will the deputy hear me?"

"No."

"They didn't pick this place out at random," I said, "Did they?"

"No."

"Who else is there besides Roger?" Jacob asked.

"The guy who let us in—it seems like he's in on it. And Dr. Chance," I said, "if that's even her name. If she even is a doctor."

"He's in on it," said Lisa. "And Chance is a doctor."

"Think," Jacob said. "Is there anything you can use as a weapon?"

"Against two armed people?" I tried to keep an edge of hysteria out of my voice. "Should I just keep going along with them?"

Lisa huffed in frustration. "Too complicated. I can't tell."

"There must be something I can do," I said.

"Yes."

"Jesus fucking Christ, what?"

"You're not helping," she said. "Yes or no questions."

A bark of a laugh worked its way through. "Is it bigger than a breadbox?"

"Yes."

I looked all around the room. "The desk?"

"No."

"One of the beds?"

"No."

"The TV?"

"Yes," Lisa said cautiously. "Yes and no. Look at it and tell me what…."

I heard a key turning in the lock and cut her off. "They're back," I said, and hung up the phone. I threw myself into bed and tried to look medicated.

The door swung open and Crewcut Guy peeked his head in to check on me. I lay there with my eyelids nearly shut and didn't move. He stared at me for a while, then closed and locked the door again.

I stared at the rotary dial for a long moment and then my stomach sank. I'd planned on doing a star-69 to get Lisa back on the phone, but there was no star. I picked up the handset. There was no dial tone, either. My theory about the outgoing calls must have been on the mark.

I looked back at the big wooden bureau that housed the TV. That had to be it—though what "it" was, exactly, I hadn't figured out. I opened the door and looked at the set. Nothing unusual there. I tried the drawers. Empty. There was maybe an inch of clearance between the bureau and the wall. I peeked behind it and saw a mess of cables.

It seemed like a lot of cables for a TV hookup. Maybe they had satellite. That would explain the off-season basketball game. I searched for the remote but came up empty-handed. That didn't make any sense. I could see Roger taking my gun and my cell phone. But the remote?

I swung around and started pulling and pushing at the TV set, hoping to find something, anything I could use, before Roger and Chance got back.

Something clicked on the front of the television set as I yanked on it, and the big tube tilted forward into my hands. I had no idea what the inside of a television was supposed to look like, but I suspected that the panel of hidden knobs and LCD readouts weren't standard-issue. A slim DVD player was duct-taped to the inside. I figured that probably explained the basketball game.

I could just take a handful of wires and yank them out—but what would that possibly accomplish? I wished Lisa would call me back and tell me what to do. Unplug the thing? Smash it? Change the settings?

I forced myself to think. If Roger and Chance wanted me dead, I'd be dead. They needed me alive, presumably for my talent. I saw myself hooked up to a gurney, electrodes wired to my head and a bunch of IVs feeding into my arm, and my vision started to tunnel. Camp Hell all over again.

Damn it. It wasn't the time to be crying over Camp Hell, not now.

Okay. So there was a machine and it was doing something electrical. It was on. I could turn it up or down.

I turned some dials up. The numbers on the LCDs increased, but nothing happened, at least that I could tell. I turned them down.

A big black guy in a turn-of-the-century butler's uniform appeared beside me. He reached for me and I backed away.

A thin girl with Mary Pickford hair in a floor-length nightgown appeared to my right. She reached toward me too.

"Don't touch me," I snapped, but it didn't look like she heard. I began to back off from both of them but decided I should probably peek over my shoulder first to make sure I wasn't headed for anything creepier.

Dr. Morganstern stood behind me. "Holy shit," I cried. How did he get to Missouri? Had he ever really been in Japan? "You're in on it too?"

He pointed at the TV guts. "Turn the second dial up a little," he said. "You'll filter out the older ones."

The little girl was trying to grab my arm, but the farther I got from her, the farther I'd be from the TV. The room was small enough that she'd grab me eventually, and if not her, the black guy would. I grabbed the second knob and turned it the opposite way, and she seemed to dissolve. The butler grew very faint.

"Not so much," said a faraway voice. I turned around and Dr. Morganstern was almost as transparent as the butler.

"You're dead?"

He pointed at the console, and I turned the knob down just a little. Morganstern grew more substantial. But so did the butler, who got his hand around my wrist.

I felt resistance, and then a little give as his hand slipped inside my forearm. "Holy fucking God," I yelped, and pulled my arm away. "Don't you dare get in me."

"Try the other dials," said Morganstern.

"Which one?" I demanded, wondering if wrapping myself in tin foil would help, since supposedly everything was made of particles and electrons. Not that I had any tin foil.

I twisted another knob and the butler got really solid. I imagined a white bubble around him—my very lame method of shielding, on par with hopscotch and pixy stix. The ghost seemed puzzled by it for a fraction of a second, but it was enough for me to spin down the second knob before he used me for a human condom. He grew faint.

I turned back to Morganstern. He was solid enough. "My God," I said. "You stuck around just to help me?"

"Not exactly." He looked somewhat abashed. "I'm following Roger Burke. But that's all I can seem to do with him. Follow."

I shook my head, trying to wrap my head around the idea that someone I knew—and knew pretty well—had died. "Isn't there some kind of light you're supposed to go toward?"

"You were wrong, back there in the car. Sometimes people do have one more message, one more task to complete, before they can move on."

"But why…?"

"Put it back together." Morganstern pointed at the TV. "They're coming."

"Shit." I snapped the TV up and closed the bureau, then flopped down on the bed. If Chance took my pulse again, I'd be fucked. My heart was pounding double-time.

"Detective," Chance said as she came through the door, Roger hot on her heels. "How are those meds doing?"

"Fine," I said. "I'm fine. I think I'm good for now."

"They want you to go along with them," said Morganstern, "but they're terrified that you won't. They were just going to pay you off at first, but Roger got a look at that bank balance you never touch and decided that money wasn't a viable incentive."

Roger'd been stealing my mail. Great, just great. I did my best to relax and look out-of-it. If I could pull off a decent fake stupor, I'd have plenty of time to be pissed off later, once I gave them the slip.

Chance pulled up a chair. There was no discussion of moving me, so I figured they'd gotten rid of the deputy easily enough. "Let's talk about the increase in spirit activity you've been experiencing."

"Okay."

"It's those pills she gave you," said Morganstern. "They're psyactives, and they're opening your power up so that it runs both ways. You've been shining like a beacon to the dead." He pointed a ghostly finger at Roger. "This one's been slipping them into your coffee until Chance found an opportunity to just give you the pills and trick you into taking them. And they fed you that line about your liver so you wouldn't counteract the drug with your Auracel."

My liver was okay? The Hallelujah Chorus started to play in my head.

"We'd like to do some tests with you," said Chance, talking at the same time as Morganstern. "See if it's possible for you to command the spirits once they're in visual range."

"They want to get you to use spirits to blackmail people," said Morganstern. "They'll tell you it's to fine-tune that new drug, or that electronic technology. But once you're part of their inner circle, they'll want more funding. Lots of it."

"I hate tests," I groaned.

The lock tumbled and the guy with the crewcut came back into the room. "That deputy's back, and now he's got three more with him. We should abort."

Chance looked hard at me. "Out of the question." She brushed my hair back from my forehead in an eerily tender fashion.

"Go along with her," said Morganstern, "or Burke will murder you. Like he did me."

Oh. So that was why he was following Roger. Morganstern had never struck me as a particularly vengeful man, but then again, I only knew him as my doctor. Not the dead husband of a widowed woman, or the dead father who wouldn't walk his daughter down the aisle. Dead people are pretty big on grudges.

Chance's hand lingered at my temple. "Detective Bayne is perfect for our project. You want to be part of this groundbreaking Psy research," she said to me, "don't you?"

Morganstern seemed to know what he was talking about, and I struggled to figure out how to play along without seeming as if aliens had landed and turned me into a pod person. I gave Chance a vacant grin, and did my best to look like an oblivious, doped-up fool. "You're the one with the meds."

The tension left the room as if I'd found the magical switch. I couldn't be bribed with money, since no amount of money ever brought me peace. But it was entirely plausible that I could be bought with drugs. Morganstern smiled and nodded; I must've been convincing.

Chance smiled, too. "I'm going to have Roger drive you to another safehouse while I talk to the deputies. I'll do everything I can to keep you comfortable, Detective. You and I have got a lot of work to do together."

Chance left with Crewcut Guy while Roger turned to gather our bags.

"Do something," said Morganstern.

I did a palms-up gesture at him. What was I supposed to do? The Amytal had started to wear off, but come on. I was no match for Roger, especially unarmed.

"Mister Bayne, you've got to get him while you're alone."

Roger shrugged his blazer on, and stuffed my jacket in a bag. He disappeared into the bathroom. "He'd kick my ass," I whispered. "What do you expect me to do?"

Morganstern looked down at the remaining syringes by the side of the bed. "Amytal. Inject it into an artery and you'll subdue him immediately."

"That's easy for you to say. Sure—I'll just find an artery. And I'll ask him real nice to hold still while I do it."

Roger came back into the main room with a damp washcloth, and started wiping our prints off all the surfaces.

"It's the only way," said Morganstern.

I gave him my best "yeah, right" look.

"If you can't do it, then let me."

I swallowed hard and slid a syringe into my pocket while Roger's back was turned. I'd relied on Morganstern in life, but I wasn't sure he was entirely trustworthy in death. What if he didn't want to leave me once he got under my skin? Would he march around inside my body forever, leaving my friends to wonder when I'd taken to wearing sweater vests?

And what if a shot of Amytal to the artery would kill Roger? Without Carolyn or Lisa to back me up, I had no way of knowing if Morganstern was using me for revenge.

Roger threw the washcloth into the bathroom, snapped up the case of syringes and drew his gun. "C'mon, Bayne. Time to go."

I stood and the room dipped—I guess I was still woozier than I'd thought. Morganstern hovered beside me, and said, "You've got to subdue him. It's the only way."

Roger got a shoulder under my armpit to help me to the door, and I fumbled between us to try and palm the syringe in my pocket. My hand brushed against his hip, and he stopped hauling me along and cringed back. "Touch me again and

I'll blow your hand off, faggot." He resumed hustling me toward the door.

It wasn't the threat that did it; it was the realization that Roger would just as soon shoot me as not, regardless of how integral I was to their precious operation. Because I was queer.

"Okay," I whispered. Roger would think I was talking to him, but it was really aimed at Morganstern. I did my best to relax.

I felt Morganstern entering, like the sickening rush of an unfamiliar drug. He came through somewhere in my core and extended himself into my extremities, arms and legs, fingers and toes. I felt numb and disconnected as Morganstern settled in. And then my body surged into action.

My hand whipped the syringe out and flicked the protective cap off with my thumb, holding it as easily as I might have held a pencil, or a gun. I stuck the needle into Roger's neck and plunged in one smooth motion. Roger raised his gun and started to pull the trigger—and then collapsed with his double-action semi-automatic just another small squeeze from putting a hole in my forehead.

I made to reach for Roger's gun but I couldn't move. "Get the gun," I tried to say, and I guess Morganstern understood. I picked up the semi-automatic and felt myself jerked toward the door before I could even see if Roger was still breathing. My body jogged to the end of the hall and down a back staircase I hadn't known about, heading unerringly toward a way out.

Morganstern stopped me at the back door, twisted the knob a few times, and then tried harder.

"It's locked," I thought. "The more you rattle it, the worse you're making things."

The room lurched and I was myself again, with a semi-transparent Morganstern standing beside me. "Can't you kick the door in?" he demanded. "Or shoot the lock out?"

"You watch too many cop shows," I told him, noting that my mouth worked again. I raised a hand, and that worked, too. I pulled the curtains aside on the back hall window. It was barred.

I would have to shoot the lock out, after all—though I doubted it would be as neat or efficient as they make it out to be in the movies. I tore down a curtain and wrapped my arm and hand to give it some kind of protection from the spray of wood and metal I was about to cause, took aim at the lock at the best angle I could figure, and squeezed.

The gun popped and there was a clatter of metal. There were also shouts and running footsteps. "Drop the gun and put your hands above your head," someone shouted.

I didn't think it was Crewcut Guy, but I didn't know for sure. I spun around and found a pair of men in sheriff's khakis pounding down the hallway toward me, weapons drawn. I started to put my gun up, but then I hesitated. What if Chance had an inside man there, too? They'd infiltrated my precinct and my clinic—why not the sheriff's department where they'd planted the safe house?

"Drop the gun," the deputy barked, as the hall behind him filled with more bodies.

Someone farther back in the mob that'd crowded into the building called out, "That's all right—that's my partner."

Maurice pushed his way to the front and my hand fell to my side, heavy. The deputies stood down. Maurice smiled and held a hand out to me. "C'mon, Victor," he said. "Let's get out of here."

15

The Lawrence County Sheriff's Department seemed like a decent enough group of guys. I'm not sure if any of them were psychic. If so, it was probably a low-level talent who'd never been certified, but was sensitive enough to notice that something just wasn't right about the B&B, or the guy with the crewcut, or maybe Jennifer Chance as the blushing bride. Crewcut Guy would've taken me down at the rear stairway if a couple of deputies hadn't already had him trussed up in the back of their SUV.

Even though these fine, corn-fed deputies had just saved my ass, I let Maurice handle the problem of getting me alone in the vicinity of Roger Burke to get a statement from Morganstern. Statements from dead people aren't considered hard evidence, but they go a long way in turning up the paydirt.

Maurice had this way of telling people what to do without being bossy, and then making them feel good for doing it. He managed to explain that I was a level five medium without creeping them out, and got them to agree to let me talk to Morganstern while Maurice gave his own statement.

The initial rush of Amytal had worn off, but I still felt woozy and off my game. I sat in a storage closet that abutted the holding cell where they'd dumped Roger Burke, and I used a mini cassette recorder that Maurice kept in his glove box for those times when I was too wrecked to write. Good thing he hadn't cleaned out his glovebox since he'd retired.

"They've been planning this for almost a year," Morganstern said. "Once they got the technology to this point, they targeted some mediums and put together these safe houses."

Hearsay. Morganstern had only been dead about ten days and didn't know about their planning process firsthand. But still, I repeated his statement into the recorder. It might turn out to be useful later.

"Why'd they take me across state lines?" I asked him. "Won't that bring in the Feds?" Something inside me withered a little at the prospect of dealing with the Feds again, like I hadn't seen enough of them after the incubus serial killer. I wondered if I'd need to get an apartment in Missouri so that I could finish all the damn paperwork.

"It's six of one, half-dozen of the other," said Morganstern. "Ideally, they could just recruit you and then nobody would come after them. But if things went sour, either the Feds would figure them out or the Chicago Police Department would. They figured the locals had more to lose by your disappearing and could move a heck of a lot faster, so they took you out of local jurisdiction. There were safehouses in Wisconsin, Indiana and Iowa, too. They were just looking for a way to lure you into one."

I wondered if I would've noticed Roger driving me north to Wisconsin on our trip to California and blanched. Probably not. I'd be too busy looking for ghosts. And then I wondered if every safehouse had one of those nifty GhosTVs. I conveniently paraphrased Morganstern's last statement to say, "They had several safehouses in adjoining states," without mentioning specifics. I wanted one of those TVs.

—∿∿—

I'd scored some cold medicine on the way to the Sheriff's Department. It was a sloppy way to counteract whatever traces of psyactives were left in my system, but it was the best I could do without a prescription and a pharmacy in a major metropolitan area. The ghosts weren't reaching for me anymore and trying to slip inside. But I would've given my left nut for an Auracel.

My statement to Sheriff Wilkes was kind of a blur. Since the only thing I needed to keep to myself was the location of the other three safehouses, I let everything else just spill out. I got the impression—not that my people-skills are anything to write home about—that Wilkes found the whole thing pretty farfetched, but that he was doing his best to be professional and cover all the bases.

Wilkes was an older guy, maybe sixty-five, pushing seventy, with a thick head of steel-gray hair and serious bulldog jowls. He looked like he'd never cracked a smile in his life. He asked me a few preliminaries and then just let me get my story out, disjointed and patchy as it was. I told him about Roger. I told him about Chance. I told him about the B&B and Crewcut Guy and the Amytal and the TV. Wilkes didn't make me repeat anything—you know, the way you do to imply that someone's bullshitting—so my whole schpiel took maybe an hour. I probably could have gone on a little longer, but my tongue was sandy, my concentration was for shit, and I just wanted to go back home.

Wilkes wrote on his notepad for a long stretch where I did my best to focus on his pencil holder, and then he cleared his throat. "And where is Dr. Morganstern now?"

"He's gone."

"For good? Or is he going to haunt the broom closet?"

I narrowed my eyes. I suspected Wilkes was mocking me now that he had his statement in place, but maybe not. Maybe he was just curious. He was so deadpan, it was difficult to tell. Crash would probably know. Empathy and all that. Crash also would've probably spit on Wilkes by now and then called him a pig.

"I think Morganstern's work is done and he's moving on."

"Mm hm. Suppose Officer Burke cuts some kind of deal with the Feds and gets himself a break? What then? Can the doctor come back?"

I had no idea what Wilkes was getting at. "I guess it's a possibility."

"So what's to keep people in the Great Beyond if there's a revolving door that'll just let them come and go however they please?"

If Wilkes and I were friends batting ideas back and forth over coffee, I wouldn't have minded the question. But we weren't friends. And I was fairly sure he was mocking me now. Jackass.

I sighed and reminded myself that people make fun of things they don't understand. Maybe Wilkes really did think he'd have Morganstern moaning and rattling chains right down the hall, and he was saving face by acting like a tough guy. I glanced up at the ceiling in the corner of the room that I'd avoided looking at throughout our interview. A taut rope that came from nowhere swayed gently, with a hanged body twitching in its noose. The ghost's feet danced just over the corners of Wilkes' desk, one in a worn-down cowboy boot, the other in a holey gray sock.

"I dunno." I cut my eyes away from the bloated rigor of the ghost's face. "I guess that they're good and dead, they stay that way." I started humming to myself to drown out the noise of the creaking rope while Wilkes finished dotting his i's and crossing his t's.

———

Maurice let me finish my cold medicine and doze, off and on, all the way back to Chicago. We'd been at the sheriff's department practically another whole day, and thankfully the Feds agreed to meet with us on our home turf. I considered us lucky to be able to get back home. If the Feds wanted to pull rank, they could easily have forced us to stay in the boonies. But Maurice and I were credible enough, at least to people who didn't really know us, and I imagined their agents would rather get a nice hotel room on Michigan Avenue than stay at some truck stop off Route 66.

My phone died around the fiftieth time I called Jacob just to say hello. I missed him something fierce, and I needed to look into his eyes while he reassured me that he hadn't left me. But it was probably just as well that my cell phone crapped out. I was starting to sound like a babbling idiot.

I was sleeping pretty well, given the cockeyed angle of my neck, when Maurice rested his hand on my shoulder. "Victor. We're here."

Early morning sunlight slanted through the gaps in the apartment buildings. It was my street, but it looked strange somehow. Not quite real. Jackie the Prostitute was nowhere to be seen, but maybe I couldn't count on getting a visual on her anymore, not without the spiked doses of Starbucks. And my sinuses were so bone-dry I was pretty sure the cold medicine was still in effect, too.

Maurice looped his arm through mine, once he hauled me out of the car. I batted at him since I could walk by myself—probably—but he ignored it. I decided it was easier to just lean on him and let him deal with the rusty courtyard gate.

"You're gonna stay with me, right?" I asked as Maurice helped me up the three flights of stairs to my apartment. They seemed narrower and dingier than I'd noticed before.

"I got you home, didn't I?"

He took the keys out of my jacket pocket and tried them, one after another, in my lock. He was squinting at them and trying to figure out which one to try next when the lock tumbled and my front door opened in. Jacob had flown to California and back, and somehow managed to make it home before me. He grabbed me, and pulled me to him. "Thank you," he said to Maurice.

Jacob. I hugged him, hard. My street, my building, nothing seemed exactly like I'd remembered it. Except for Jacob. Jacob felt real.

"You still want me to stay with you?" Maurice said. Even though my face was pressed into Jacob's chest and I couldn't see Maurice, I could tell he was smiling. "I'm gonna head on home and catch up on a little shuteye."

My apartment looked familiar, small and trashy and white, as usual. I made the rounds anyway, peeking in cabinets and drawers and checking the TV to make sure I didn't have any unwanted visitors. Jacob leaned on the doorjamb between the kitchen and living room while I scrutinized all the static channels between the real channels by jabbing compulsively at the remote. "Don't you think you'd better just come to bed?"

I looked at him. "How can you say that? Hugo Cooper's floating around here somewhere, just waiting for us both to go to sleep so he can get inside me and take another stab at you."

Jacob crossed his arms and looked massive. "I'm not going to let some dead murderer control where I can and can't sleep."

"Jacob...."

He crossed the room and pressed his finger to my lips. "He was only able to use you while you were on those psyactives. Take your Auracel and he won't bother us. Lisa said so."

I pushed past Jacob and went to my medicine cabinet. There were two Auracels left. Combined with the cold medicine I'd taken, one should get me through the night. I could go into The Clinic the next day and talk somebody there into giving me a refill. I doubted they'd have any objection since the new doctor they'd hired had fucking kidnapped me.

I tried not to dwell on the thought of having to start with another new doctor after all these years. And not let Jacob see me all bleary-eyed at the idea that I'd never again see Morganstern in a new and even more atrocious sweater vest.

I swallowed one Auracel and washed it down with a palmful of tap water. Jacob had resumed his man mountain pose behind me in the bathroom doorway. "How can you be so calm?" I asked him. "I had the Criss Cross Killer inside me."

"Evidently he'd been following me, since I was his arresting officer." Jacob shrugged. "I'm sure he would've loved to get inside me if he could, but I guess being a Stiff has its advantages. I had a shaman at PsyTrain smudge me before I left. He says it'll help. That, and time."

"They've got shamans at PsyTrain?" I said lamely. Jacob wedged himself past me and turned the shower on. The pattering of water on porcelain was soothing and familiar, and the tiny bathroom soon filled with steam.

Jacob stripped, and though I could pick out the X I'd carved into his chest, it wasn't as distinct as it might've been if it weren't for his chest hair. I let him pull my T-shirt over my head and unzip my jeans. I toed off my sneakers and stepped out of my clothes, and Jacob guided me into the shower.

He squeezed a shot of musk body wash into his palm and ran it down my chest. I leaned into the feel of his hands, so strong and sure, so safe. I thought he'd been leaving me, and all the while he was getting himself over to PsyTrain and talking his way in to see Lisa. I probably should've just trusted him. Maybe I did. Maybe it was me that I couldn't trust.

Jacob's hand slipped between my thighs, wet and slick, while the water sprayed against the back of my head and lulled me into my familiar Auracel daze. I wondered if I was ever totally present for Jacob, or if he always had to search for the real me between the cracks of all the drugs I took.

"It's okay," he said, with that non-psychic empathy of his, and he slid his palm around enough to make a lather.

I sighed and propped my shoulder against the shower wall.

His hands moved over my hips and met again on my ass, kneading me, teasing me with a soapy finger. I pressed my forehead into his shoulder and tried to stop worrying. My cock had already been convinced that everything was hunky-dory. It was poking Jacob in the thigh, stiff and ready.

Jacob turned his head so that his lips grazed my ear. "You don't have to channel anyone unless you want to," he said, low and close.

I shuddered and slipped a hand around his waist, and pressed myself against him tighter. I was just fine with never having someone else's ghost inside me again. Ever.

"You should take some time off. A big block of time. Rest. Take a vacation." His index finger slid into me while he talked, and his voice was gentle and hypnotic. I gasped and bit on his shoulder, working gently with my teeth as that finger of his moved in and out.

"You like playing with my ass," I whispered. Too porno for my taste, but I was going somewhere with it.

"Mm hm," he murmured, and his finger sank in deeper. His big cock was hard now, too, brushing against my stomach.

I smeared some of the body wash off my chest and grabbed him by the cock with a soap-slick hand. He gasped and his head fell back, eyes closed, lips parted. I gave him a few good strokes, then turned myself around and ground my backside against him. "Take it, then."

He ran his hands down my back, sliding his hot, wet cock experimentally along my ass crack.

"Come on," I prompted. Just me, Jacob, and some body wash. Because all the talk about not having any condoms around had only been an excuse. We get blood tests quarterly on the force; all the cops do, even the elite ones like us. I'd just been a little leery about letting him in. Figuratively and literally.

Another squirt of body wash ran down my back, and Jacob's hands followed. He smoothed the slickness over my skin. His palms glided over my spine and ribs, working up a lather. He pushed his soapy fingers into my ass again, and he sucked his breath in hard as he did it.

I got my feet planted and tried not to hurry him. I thought he'd probably wanted to just throw me down and fuck me for so long that he needed to savor the moment now. It felt amazing to be wanted like that. I wiped a trace of soap from my chest and grabbed my own cock, stroking it slowly.

Something pressed against my ass that was definitely not a finger. I let my breath out and rocked back, hungry for the moment that its girth would fill me up. Jacob murmured a stream of encouragement, "Oh God, oh yeah..." that turned into a more primal, wordless sound as he pushed in. A shallow thrust, and another, and then he pressed in—deep.

I let my breath out as he clasped me against him with his cock buried to the root. It hurt, and it was awesome. Eventually I'd adjust to having a boyfriend who was hung like that, but for now it was practically like getting my cherry popped all over again.

A whimpery noise escaped me, and Jacob's slick hands raked over my chest. He found a nipple and tweaked it hard. He pulled out and pushed in again, and my cock felt deliciously, painfully stiff. I had to stop stroking it and just hold myself up as Jacob started to move, my ass just barely stretching around him.

"Uhnn, God," I finally said. My forehead mashed against the shower wall as his thrusts turned into a steady pounding, and his fingertips left stinging trails behind as he struggled to grip me but couldn't quite do it because of the slipperiness of the soap. Jacob made an inarticulate noise in reply and finally got one arm around my waist, while his other hand groped my balls and cock.

I pressed my palms flat against the shower wall and pushed back, slamming onto his cock as hard as the slippery, sloppy shower would allow. The sound of his wet balls slapping against my ass rang loud in the hard-walled enclosure, and I could hear it even over the steady hiss and patter of the water. His arm was so tight around my middle I could hardly breathe, and his hand pulled my cock in time with every hard, deep thrust.

It got so intense that I stopped caring if we'd fall. I gave up trying to hold onto anything and stopped pushing back at Jacob. I let him take over and hold us both up. He fucked me so hard he'd started lifting me off the floor of the tub, and the pulse in my cock thrummed in time with the rhythm of his thrusts.

My come shot out in a brief arc that was battered away in the spray of the shower. I moaned out loud, and water filled my eyes and mouth as my head lolled back. There was a moment that seemed to extend as Jacob held me there, both of my feet off the shower floor, as my ass throbbed, and another spurt of mine shot its way into the stream.

Jacob grunted and slammed me onto him again, and once more, and then the sensation of heat welled inside my ass, and everything turned slick.

His giant cock was still inside me. He eased me back down and pushed into me a few more times. His strokes were slick with come, just a few more gentle thrusts before he softened. He let go of my waist and ran his hands down my back again, muttering things to himself that were pretty much lost to the sound of the shower. Mostly my name.

He pressed his chest to my back and I sagged into the shower wall. His lips slid on the back of my neck, wet kisses, and he cupped his hand protectively over my spent cock.

———

Jacob was still asleep when I woke up again, mid-morning the next day. He had this way of lying diagonally on the bed so that when I got up and looked back at him, I wondered how the hell I'd even fit in there. I crept from the bedroom and eased the door shut behind me, hoping to buy him a little more well-earned sleep.

Channel 8 was its usual non-self. I watched it carefully at first, sneaking small glances to see if there were any faces there, any grasping hands. But there weren't; it was just dirty gray snow. The single Auracel I'd taken had worn off. It was such a small dose it hadn't even left me with its characteristic behind-the-eye hangover. My tongue felt a little wooly from the cold medicine, but aside from that, I was clear.

I stared at my set and thought about the television in the hotel room. Most of the actual television components had probably been gutted, since it didn't even really function as a TV. Maybe it was all just a prop, a screen and a DVD player slapped onto the front to camouflage a big hunk of equipment that generated heat and a little electronic hum. Or maybe parts of it were actually once a TV, in another life.

If I could get my hands on one of those, I could stop getting stressed out about Jackie the Hooker, the baby in the basement, and the hovering, greedy spirit of the Criss Cross Killer. I could figure out what those dials and knobs meant and totally fine-tune it. I could blow off my appointments at The Clinic and not need to worry about running out of Auracel. If the device was portable, I could take it to crime scenes and amp up the spirits that were faint, or reluctant, or just plain old.

Who was I kidding? It was unlikely I'd use it for work; I just wanted to come home to a little peace.

Crash was the only person I could think of to help me figure out what that souped-up television was so that I could get one for myself. My heart didn't palpitate at the mere thought of him anymore, and I was glad. It didn't seem like Jacob would decide I was a little too uptight for his taste and go back to someone who knew a few more tricks in bed, not after all we'd been through. And I was faithful, too, if only in my waking life. If Jacob was gonna go out for that metaphorical pack of smokes, I suspected he would have done it by now.

The hardwood floor creaked. I looked up and Jacob was standing in the bedroom doorway, arms crossed over his chest, watching me watch Channel 8. I raised my eyebrows and waited for him to say something, but he just gave me a slow, wolfish smile.

I wondered if the invitation to move in together was still on the table. Not that I was ready to give it any serious consideration just yet, but it was comforting to know that Jacob would take things to the next level, if I was game. I'd need to have my own room—white, of course. But then he could get his dining room table back.

I bet Jacob owned a piece of shelving that'd be just right for one of those kick-ass GhosTVs.

CPSIA information can be obtained at www.ICGtesting.com
Printed in the USA
BVOW08s1442031013

332741BV00001B/55/P